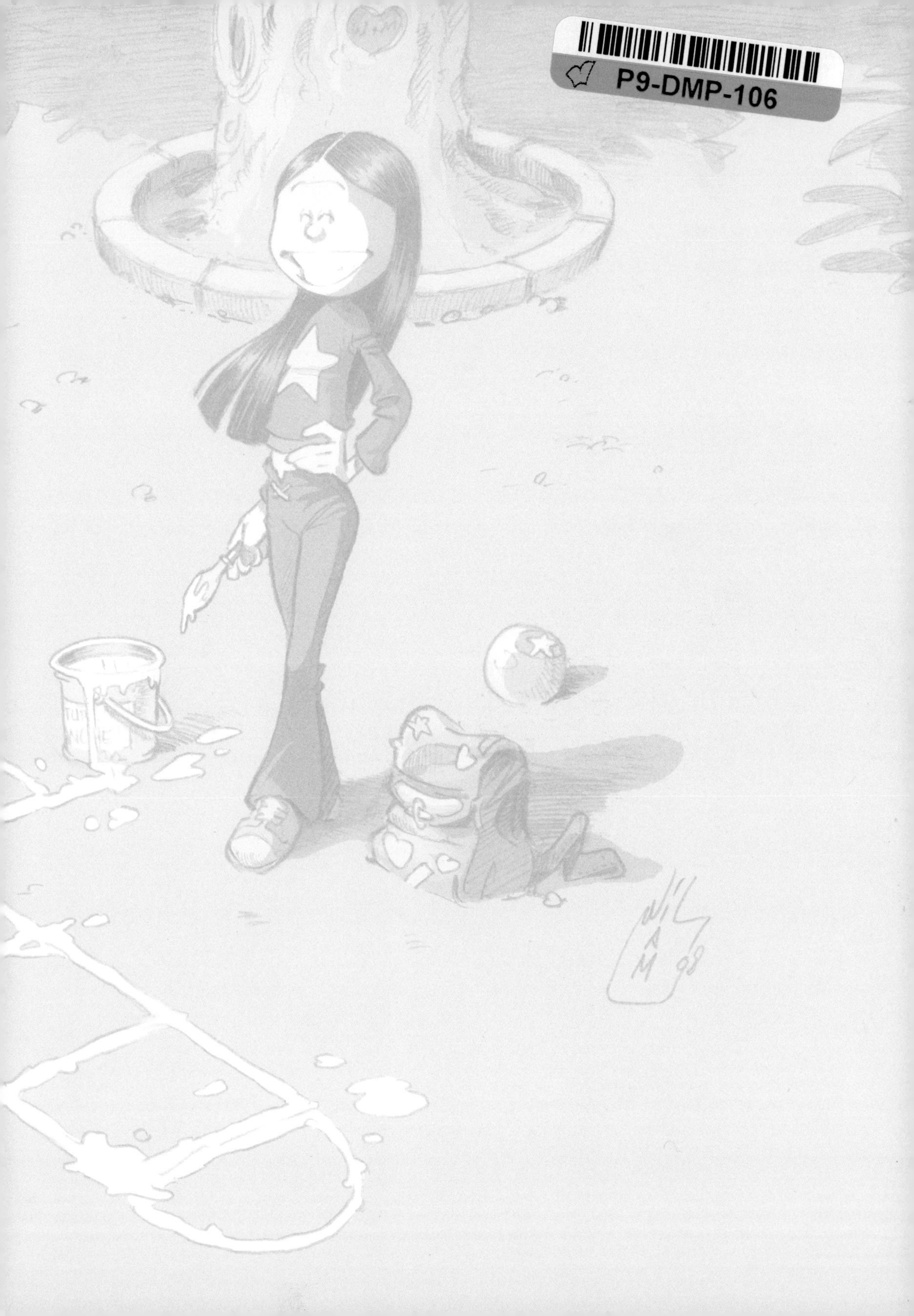

The Sisters

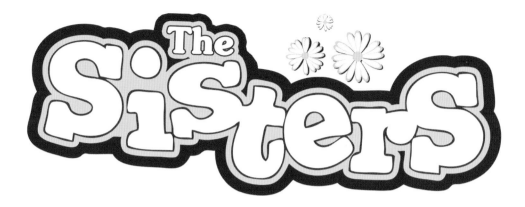

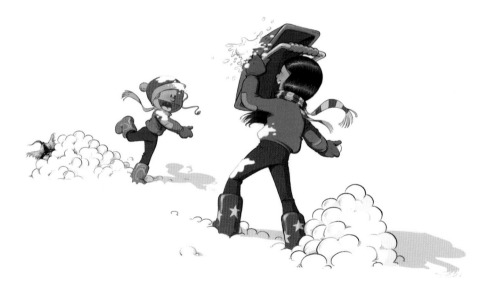

PAPERCUTZ

MORE GREAT GRAPHIC NOVEL SERIES AVAILABLE FROM PAPERCUTZ

THE SMURFS #21

MINNIE & DAISY #1

DISNEY FAIRIES #18

THE GARFIELD SHOW #6

BARBIE #1

TROLLS #1

GERONIMO STILTON #17

THEA STILTON #6

FUZZY BASEBALL

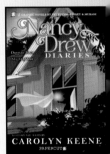

NANCY DREW DIARIES #7

THE LUNCH WITCH #1

SCARLETT

ANNE OF GREEN BAGELS #1

THE RED SHOES

THE SISTERS #1

The Sisters

2: "Doing It Our Way"

Art and colors
William

Story
Cazenove & William

PAPERCUTZ
New York

THE SISTERS #2 "Doing it Our Way"
Les Sisters [The Sisters] by Cazenove and William
© 2009 Bamboo Édition
Sisters, characters and related indicia are copyright,
trademark and exclusive license of Bamboo Édition.
English translation and all other editorial material
© 2016 by Papercutz.
All rights reserved.

Story by Christophe Cazenove and William Maury
Art and color by William
Cover by William
Translation by Anne & Owen Smith
Lettering by Wilson Ramos Jr.
Special thanks to JayJay Jackson

Papercutz books may be purchased for business or promotional use.
For information on bulk purchases please contact Macmilan
Corporate and Premium Sales Department at
(800) 221-7945 x5442

Production – Dawn Guzzo
Editorial Intern – Emelyne Tan
Editor – Jeff Whitman
Jim Salicrup
Editor-in-Chief

PB ISBN: 978-1-62991-595-1
HC ISBN: 978-1-62991-594-4

Printed in China
November 2016 by O.G. Printing Productions, LTD.
Units 2 & 3, 5/F, Lemmi Centre
50 Hoi Yuen Road
Kwon Tong, Kowloon

Distributed by Macmillan
First Papercutz Printing

To my brothers: Alex, Franck,
David, and Christopher.
To Christophe, who continues to
astonish me.
To Olivier, for his faith in me,
and for being available.

Thank you, Anelor, for your
research. You guided me through
hell!

Thank you, Marine, "Maureen,"
for not going all out on the
originals with your glitter
markers, and thank you for
your help, Wendy, for putting
the last pages in color.

—William

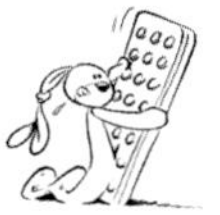

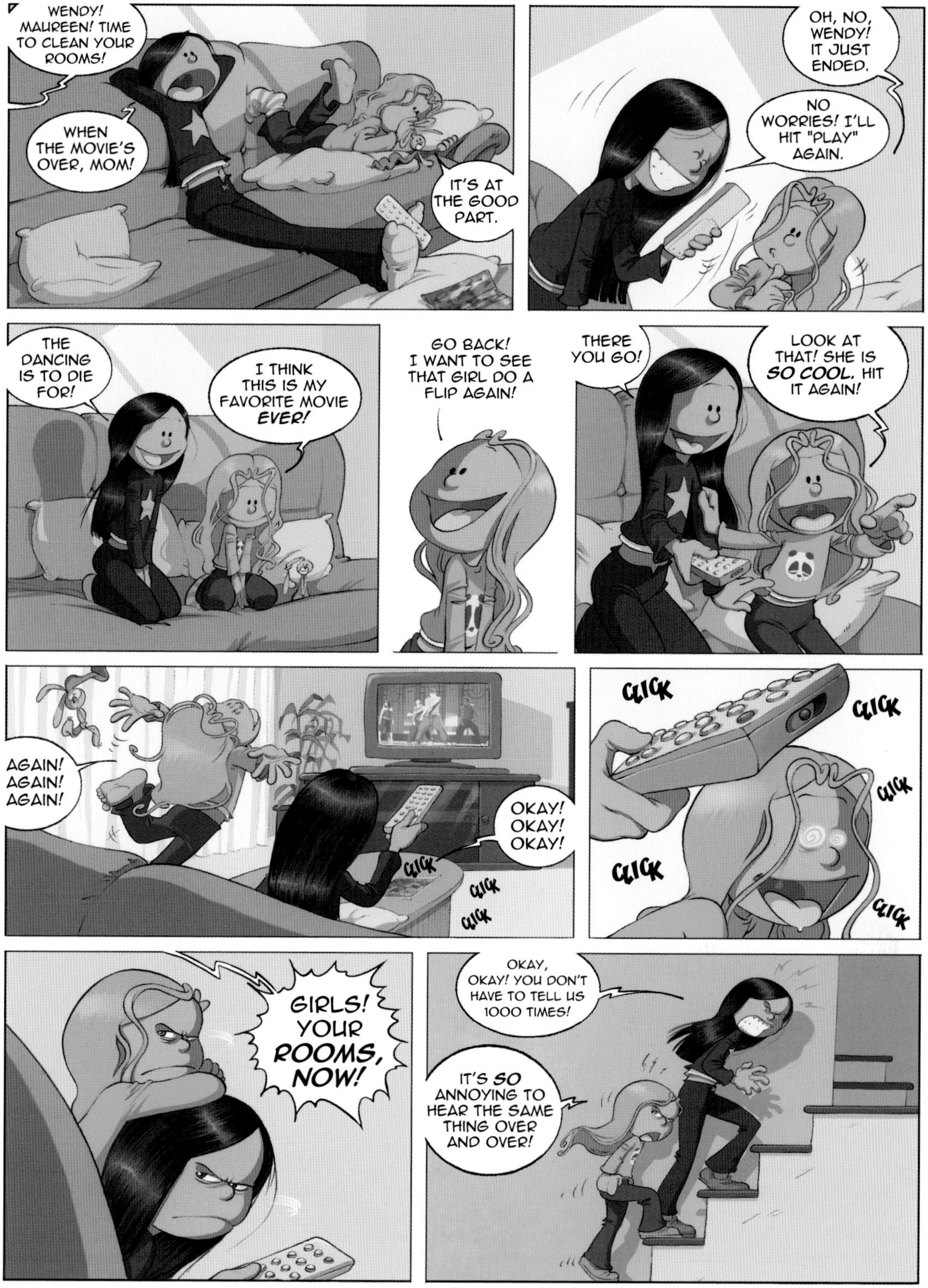
WENDY! MAUREEN! TIME TO CLEAN YOUR ROOMS!
WHEN THE MOVIE'S OVER, MOM!
IT'S AT THE GOOD PART.
OH, NO, WENDY! IT JUST ENDED.
NO WORRIES! I'LL HIT "PLAY" AGAIN.
THE DANCING IS TO DIE FOR!
I THINK THIS IS MY FAVORITE MOVIE EVER!
GO BACK! I WANT TO SEE THAT GIRL DO A FLIP AGAIN!
THERE YOU GO!
LOOK AT THAT! SHE IS SO COOL. HIT IT AGAIN!
AGAIN! AGAIN! AGAIN!
OKAY! OKAY! OKAY!
CLICK
CLICK
CLICK
CLICK
CLICK
CLICK
CLICK
CLICK
GIRLS! YOUR ROOMS, NOW!
OKAY, OKAY! YOU DON'T HAVE TO TELL US 1000 TIMES!
IT'S SO ANNOYING TO HEAR THE SAME THING OVER AND OVER!
CAZENOVE & WILLIAM

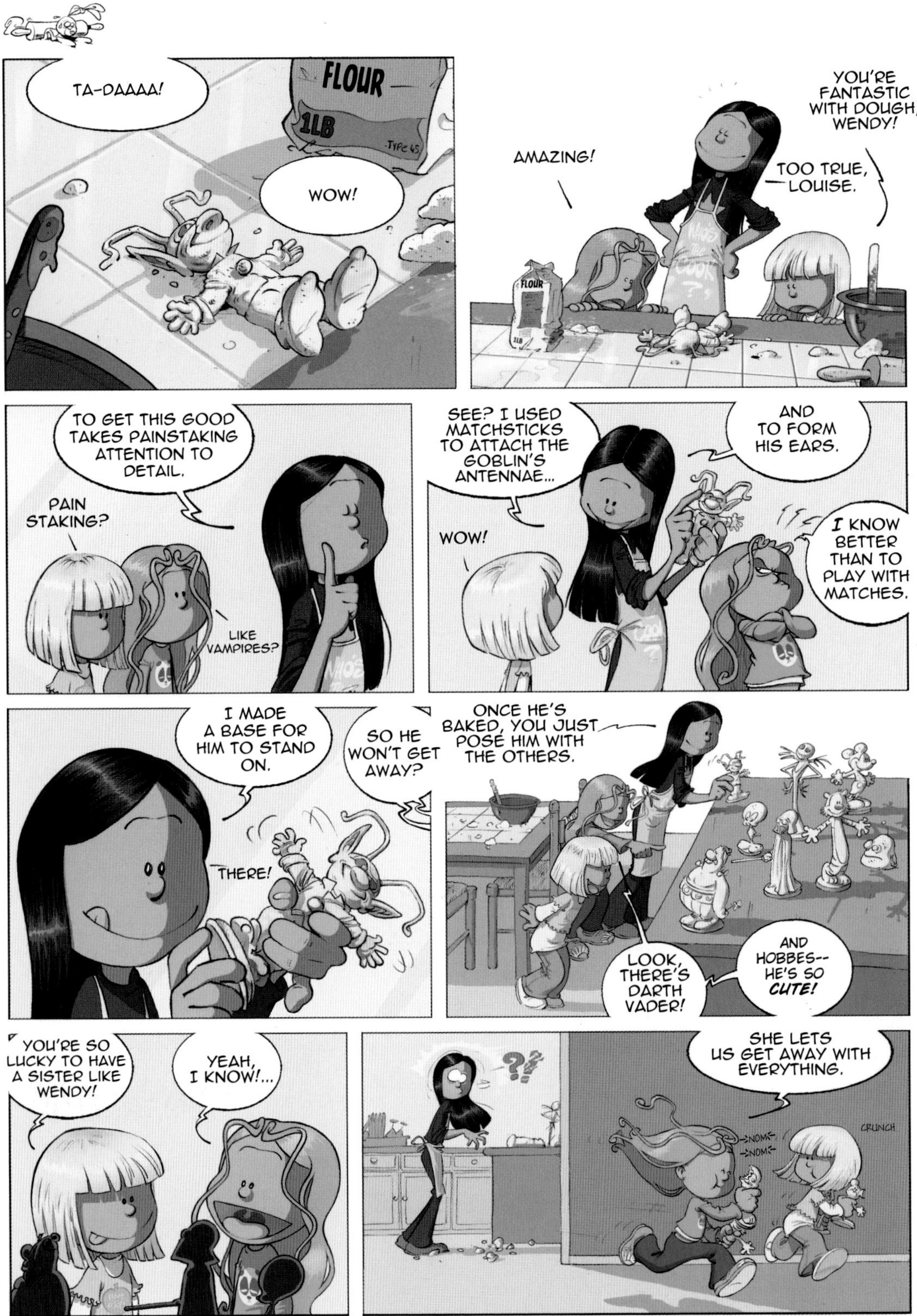
TA-DAAAA!
WOW!
AMAZING!
YOU'RE FANTASTIC WITH DOUGH, WENDY!
TOO TRUE, LOUISE.
TO GET THIS GOOD TAKES PAINSTAKING ATTENTION TO DETAIL.
PAIN STAKING?
LIKE VAMPIRES?
SEE? I USED MATCHSTICKS TO ATTACH THE GOBLIN'S ANTENNAE...
AND TO FORM HIS EARS.
WOW!
I KNOW BETTER THAN TO PLAY WITH MATCHES.
I MADE A BASE FOR HIM TO STAND ON.
SO HE WON'T GET AWAY?
THERE!
ONCE HE'S BAKED, YOU JUST POSE HIM WITH THE OTHERS.
LOOK, THERE'S DARTH VADER!
AND HOBBES-- HE'S SO CUTE!
YOU'RE SO LUCKY TO HAVE A SISTER LIKE WENDY!
YEAH, I KNOW!...
SHE LETS US GET AWAY WITH EVERYTHING.
NOM
NOM
CRUNCH

CAZENOVE & WILLIAM

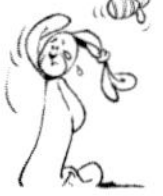

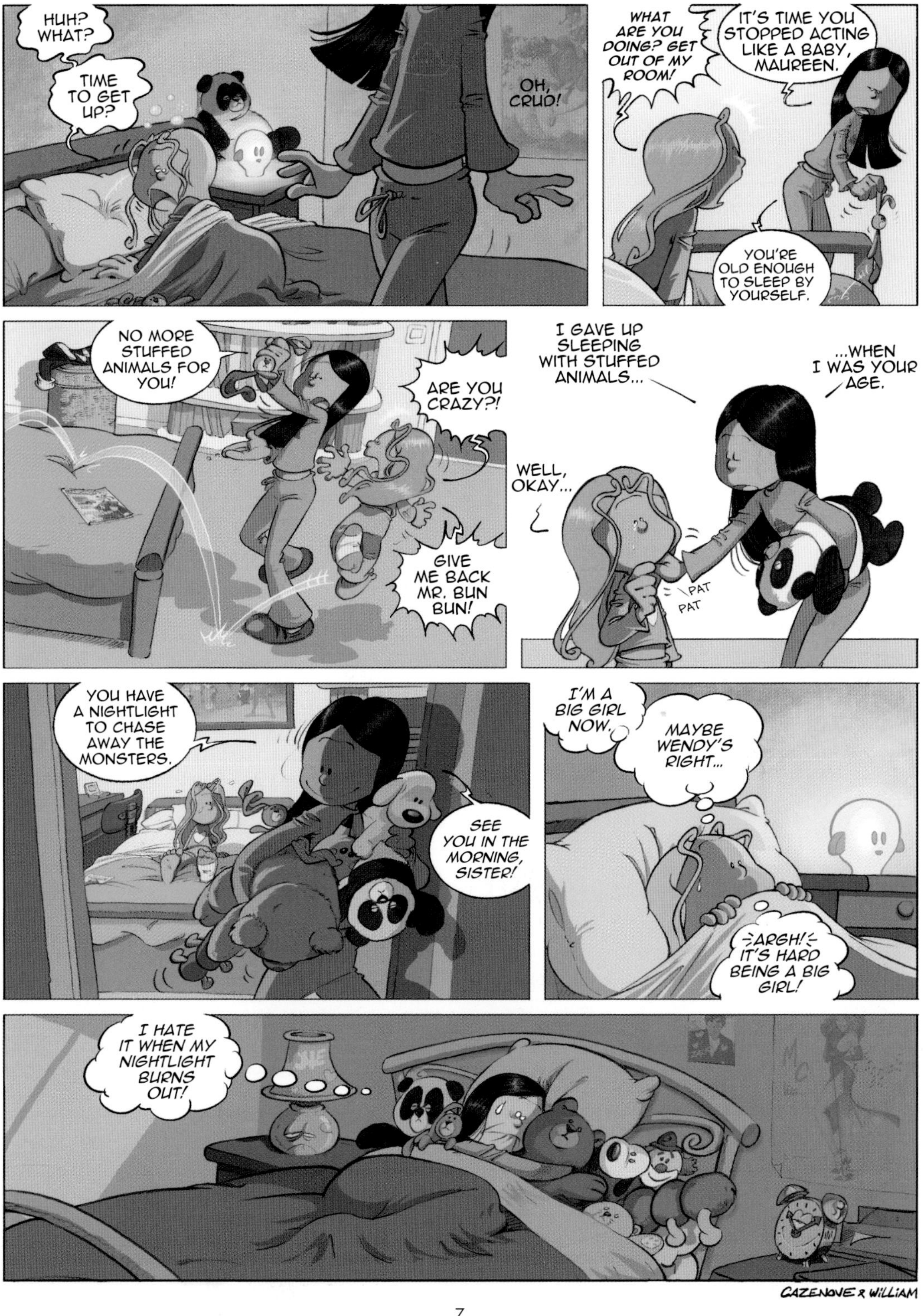
HUH? WHAT?
TIME TO GET UP?
OH, CRUD!
WHAT ARE YOU DOING? GET OUT OF MY ROOM!
IT'S TIME YOU STOPPED ACTING LIKE A BABY, MAUREEN.
YOU'RE OLD ENOUGH TO SLEEP BY YOURSELF.
NO MORE STUFFED ANIMALS FOR YOU!
ARE YOU CRAZY?!
GIVE ME BACK MR. BUN BUN!
I GAVE UP SLEEPING WITH STUFFED ANIMALS...
...WHEN I WAS YOUR AGE.
WELL, OKAY...
PAT
PAT
YOU HAVE A NIGHTLIGHT TO CHASE AWAY THE MONSTERS.
SEE YOU IN THE MORNING, SISTER!
I'M A BIG GIRL NOW.
MAYBE WENDY'S RIGHT...
ARGH! IT'S HARD BEING A BIG GIRL!
I HATE IT WHEN MY NIGHTLIGHT BURNS OUT!

CAZENOVE & WILLIAM

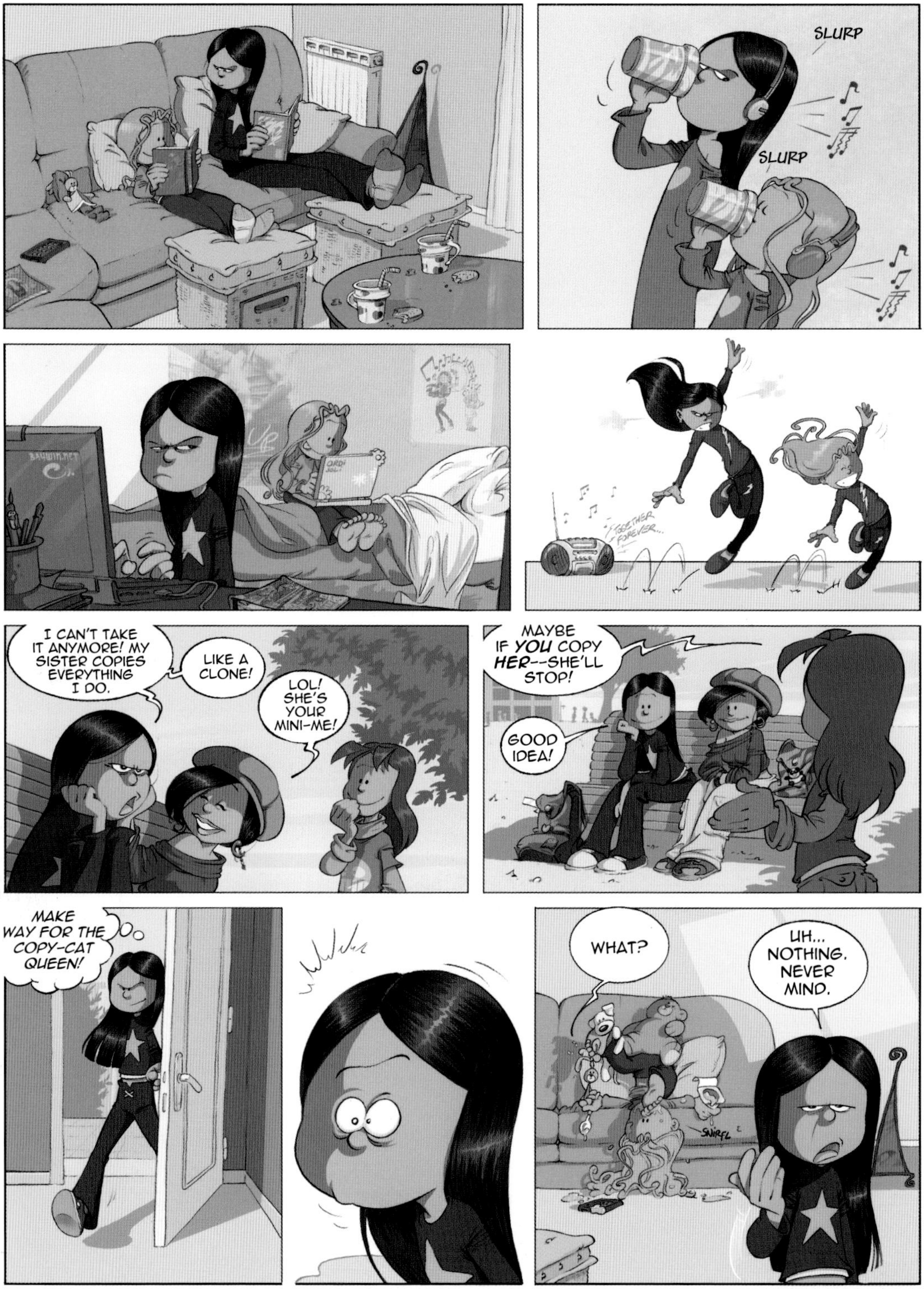
SLURP
SLURP
TOGETHER FOREVER...
I CAN'T TAKE IT ANYMORE! MY SISTER COPIES EVERYTHING I DO.
LIKE A CLONE!
LOL! SHE'S YOUR MINI-ME!
MAYBE IF YOU COPY HER--SHE'LL STOP!
GOOD IDEA!
MAKE WAY FOR THE COPY-CAT QUEEN!
WHAT?
SNIRFL
UH... NOTHING. NEVER MIND.

CAZENOVE & WILLIAM

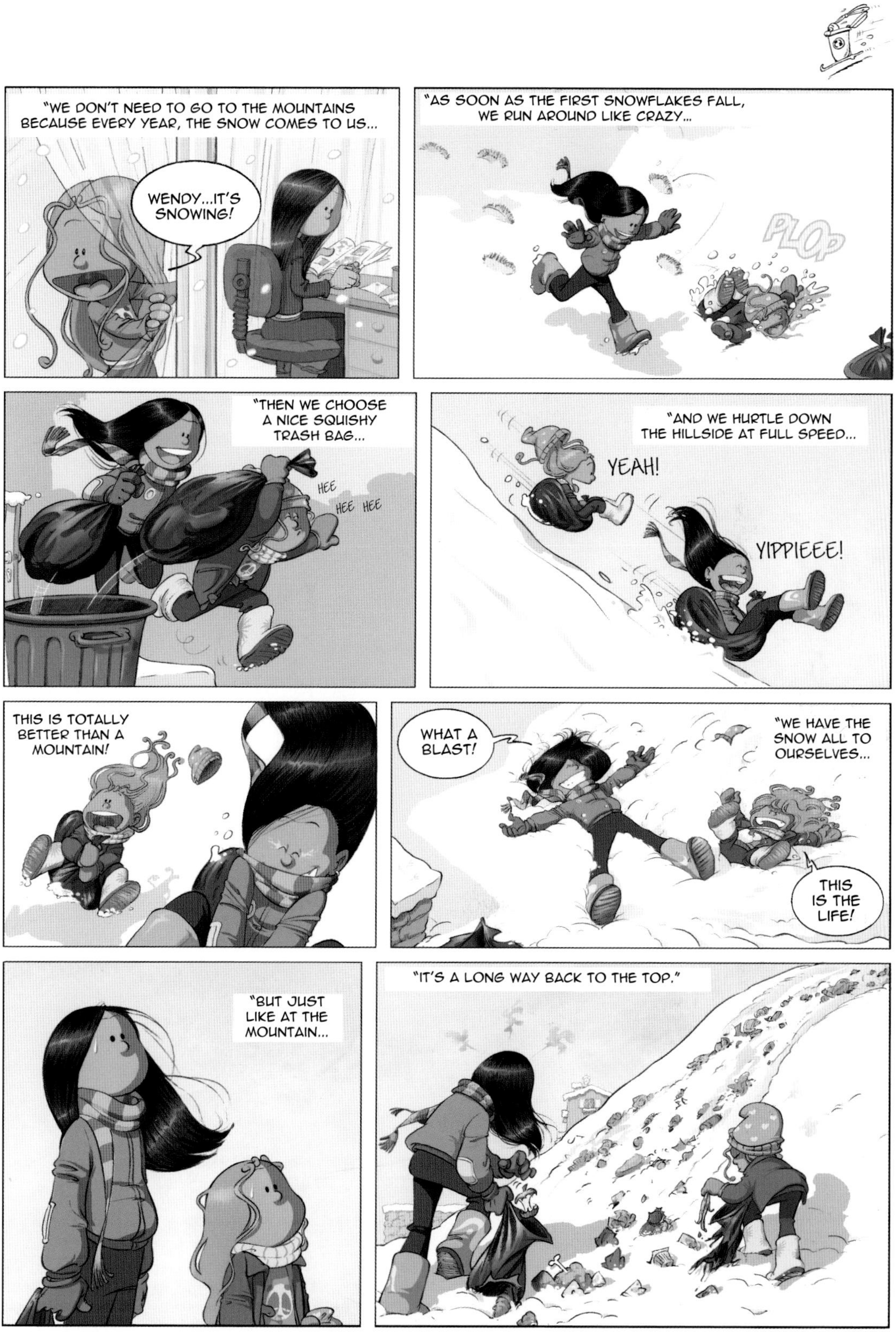
"WE DON'T NEED TO GO TO THE MOUNTAINS BECAUSE EVERY YEAR, THE SNOW COMES TO US...
WENDY...IT'S SNOWING!
"AS SOON AS THE FIRST SNOWFLAKES FALL, WE RUN AROUND LIKE CRAZY...
PLOP
"THEN WE CHOOSE A NICE SQUISHY TRASH BAG...
HEE
HEE HEE
"AND WE HURTLE DOWN THE HILLSIDE AT FULL SPEED...
YEAH!
YIPPIEEE!
THIS IS TOTALLY BETTER THAN A MOUNTAIN!
WHAT A BLAST!
"WE HAVE THE SNOW ALL TO OURSELVES...
THIS IS THE LIFE!
"BUT JUST LIKE AT THE MOUNTAIN...
"IT'S A LONG WAY BACK TO THE TOP."
CAZENOVE & WILLIAM

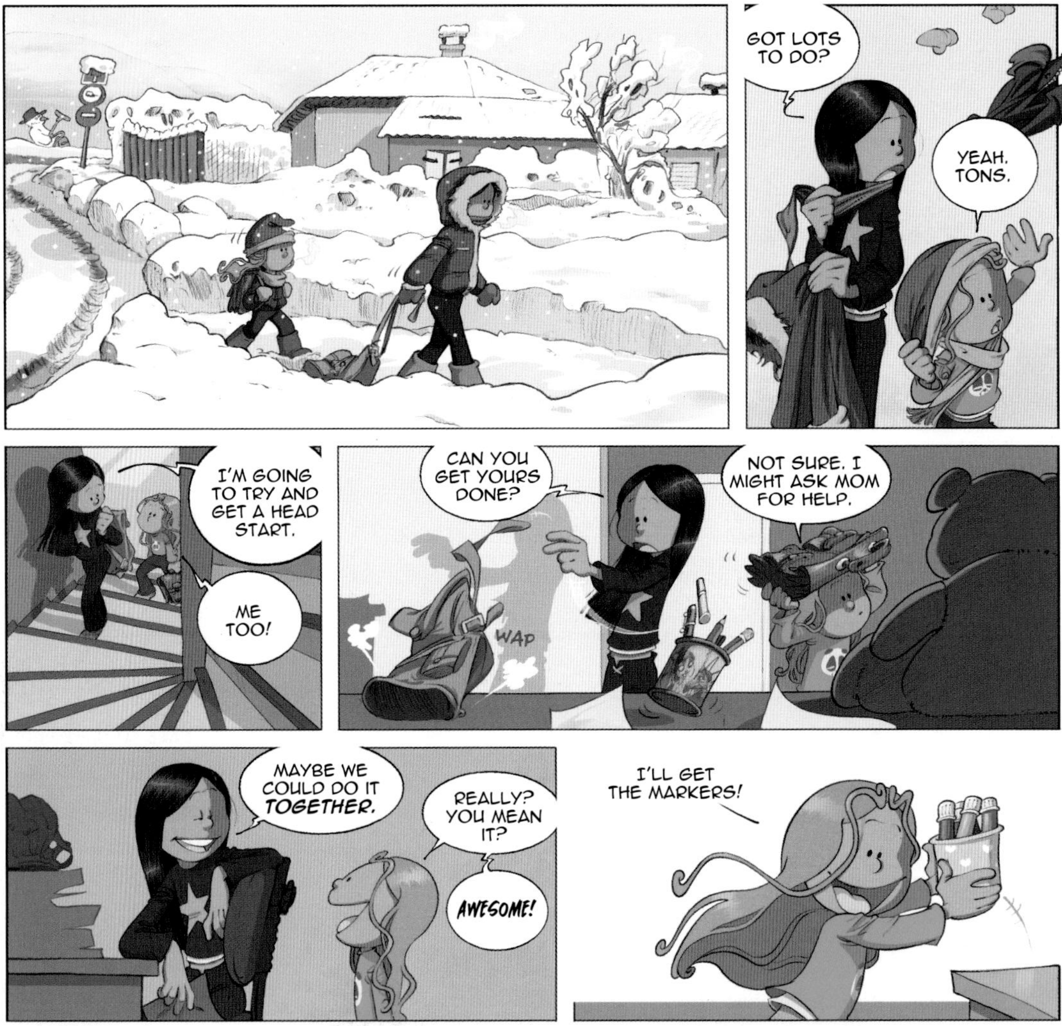
GOT LOTS TO DO?
YEAH. TONS.
I'M GOING TO TRY AND GET A HEAD START.
ME TOO!
CAN YOU GET YOURS DONE?
WAP
NOT SURE. I MIGHT ASK MOM FOR HELP.
MAYBE WE COULD DO IT TOGETHER.
REALLY? YOU MEAN IT?
AWESOME!
I'LL GET THE MARKERS!
WE NEED TO GET GOING ON THESE CHRISTMAS WISH LISTS!
RIGHT! THERE'S NO TIME LIKE THE PRESENT!
SUPER CHRISTMAS
NOEL

CAZENOVE & WILLIAM

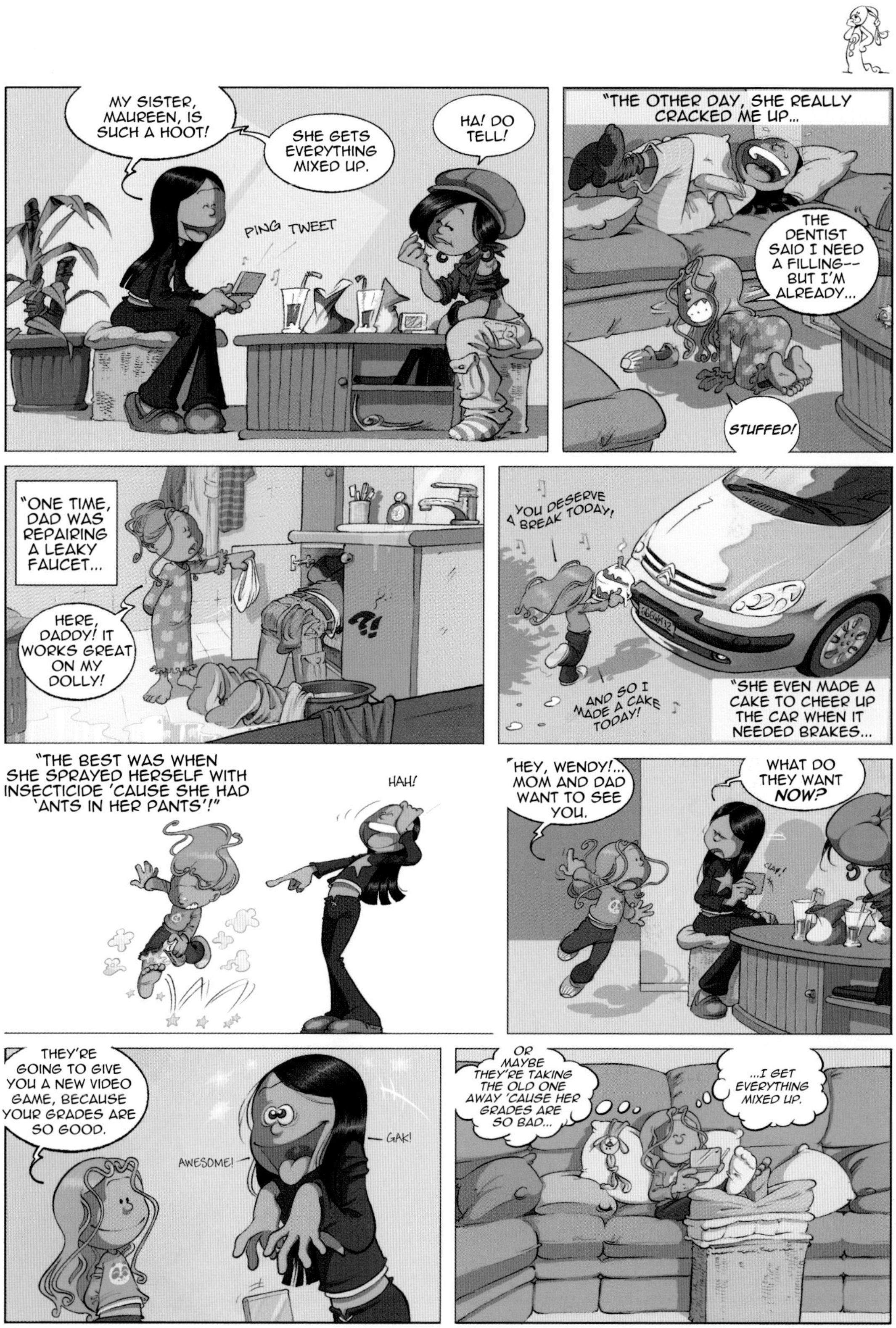
MY SISTER, MAUREEN, IS SUCH A HOOT!
SHE GETS EVERYTHING MIXED UP.
HA! DO TELL!
PING TWEET
"THE OTHER DAY, SHE REALLY CRACKED ME UP...
THE DENTIST SAID I NEED A FILLING-- BUT I'M ALREADY...
STUFFED!
"ONE TIME, DAD WAS REPAIRING A LEAKY FAUCET...
HERE, DADDY! IT WORKS GREAT ON MY DOLLY!
?!
YOU DESERVE A BREAK TODAY!
AND SO I MADE A CAKE TODAY!
"SHE EVEN MADE A CAKE TO CHEER UP THE CAR WHEN IT NEEDED BRAKES...
"THE BEST WAS WHEN SHE SPRAYED HERSELF WITH INSECTICIDE 'CAUSE SHE HAD 'ANTS IN HER PANTS'!"
HAH!
HEY, WENDY!... MOM AND DAD WANT TO SEE YOU.
WHAT DO THEY WANT NOW?
THEY'RE GOING TO GIVE YOU A NEW VIDEO GAME, BECAUSE YOUR GRADES ARE SO GOOD.
AWESOME!
GAK!
OR MAYBE THEY'RE TAKING THE OLD ONE AWAY 'CAUSE HER GRADES ARE SO BAD...
...I GET EVERYTHING MIXED UP.
CAZENOVE & WILLIAM

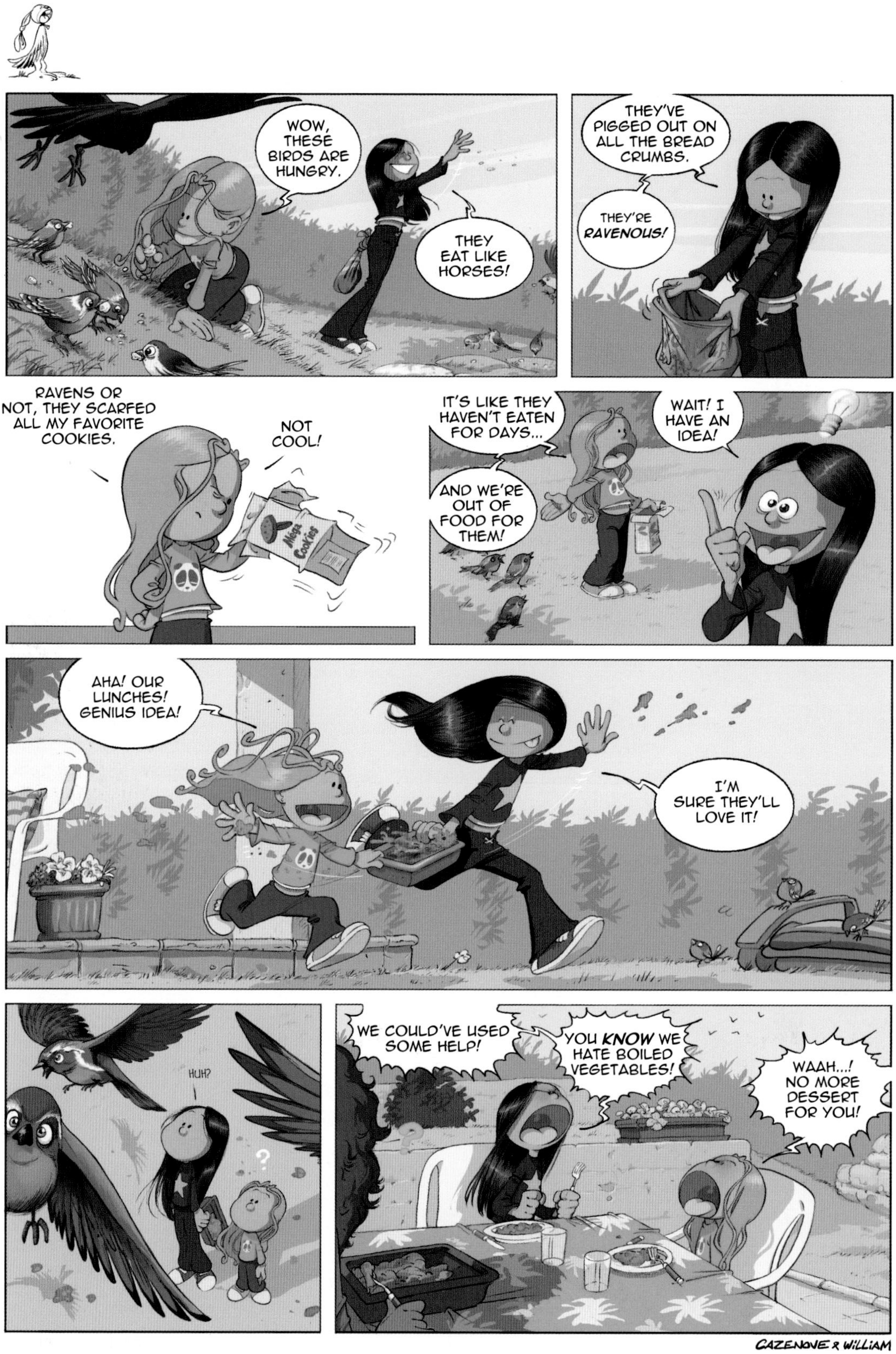
WOW, THESE BIRDS ARE HUNGRY.
THEY EAT LIKE HORSES!
THEY'VE PIGGED OUT ON ALL THE BREAD CRUMBS.
THEY'RE *RAVENOUS!*
RAVENS OR NOT, THEY SCARFED ALL MY FAVORITE COOKIES.
NOT COOL!
Mega Cookies
IT'S LIKE THEY HAVEN'T EATEN FOR DAYS...
AND WE'RE OUT OF FOOD FOR THEM!
WAIT! I HAVE AN IDEA!
AHA! OUR LUNCHES! GENIUS IDEA!
I'M SURE THEY'LL LOVE IT!
HUH?
?
WE COULD'VE USED SOME HELP!
YOU **KNOW** WE HATE BOILED VEGETABLES!
WAAH...! NO MORE DESSERT FOR YOU!
CAZENOVE & WILLIAM

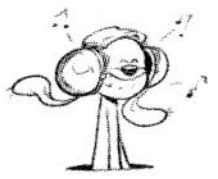

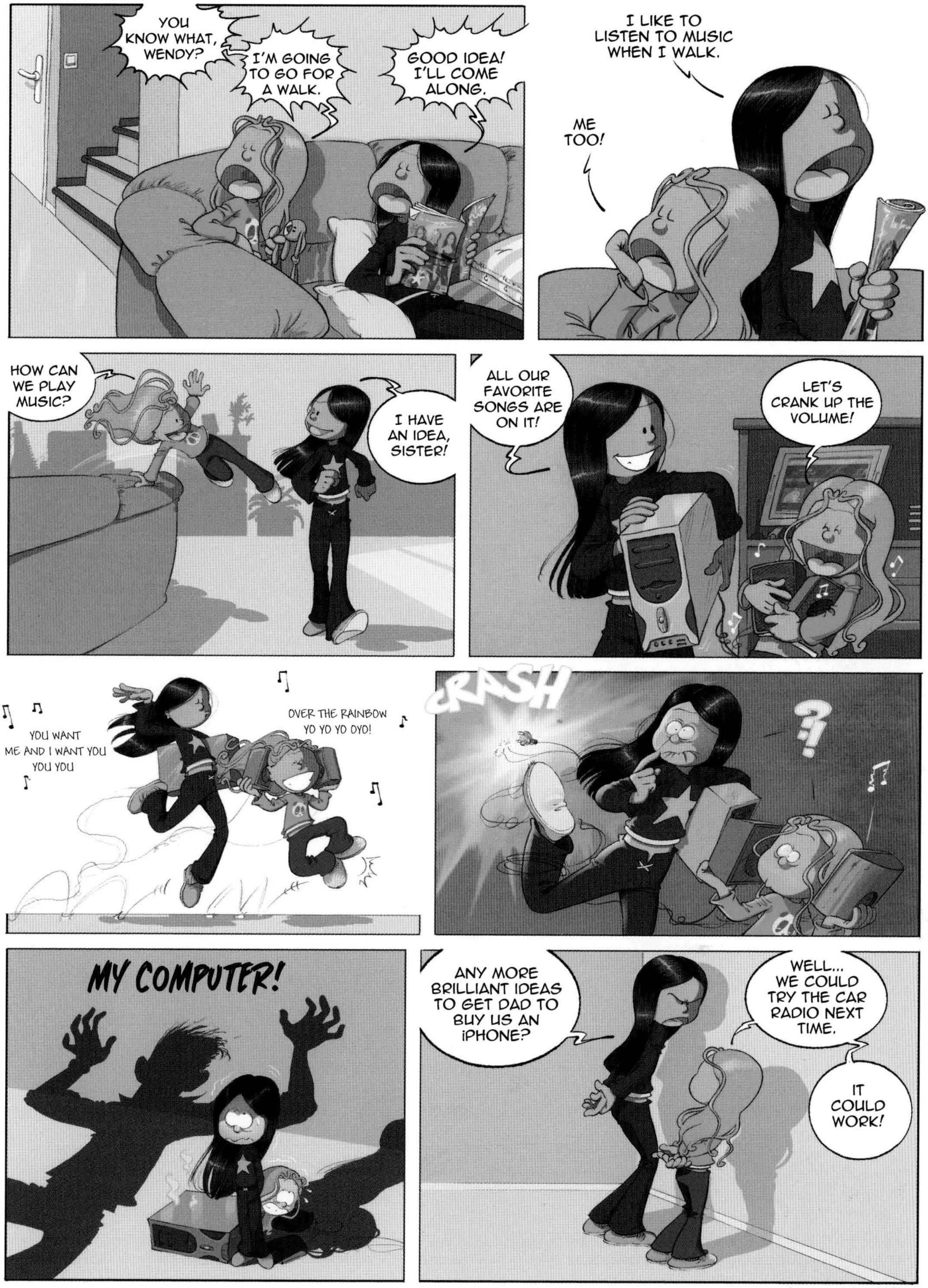
YOU KNOW WHAT, WENDY?
I'M GOING TO GO FOR A WALK.
GOOD IDEA! I'LL COME ALONG.
I LIKE TO LISTEN TO MUSIC WHEN I WALK.
ME TOO!
HOW CAN WE PLAY MUSIC?
I HAVE AN IDEA, SISTER!
ALL OUR FAVORITE SONGS ARE ON IT!
LET'S CRANK UP THE VOLUME!
YOU WANT ME AND I WANT YOU YOU YOU
OVER THE RAINBOW YO YO YO OYO!
CRASH
?!
MY COMPUTER!
ANY MORE BRILLIANT IDEAS TO GET DAD TO BUY US AN iPHONE?
WELL... WE COULD TRY THE CAR RADIO NEXT TIME.
IT COULD WORK!

CAZENOVE & WILLIAM

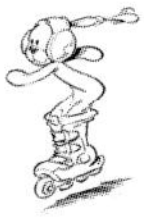

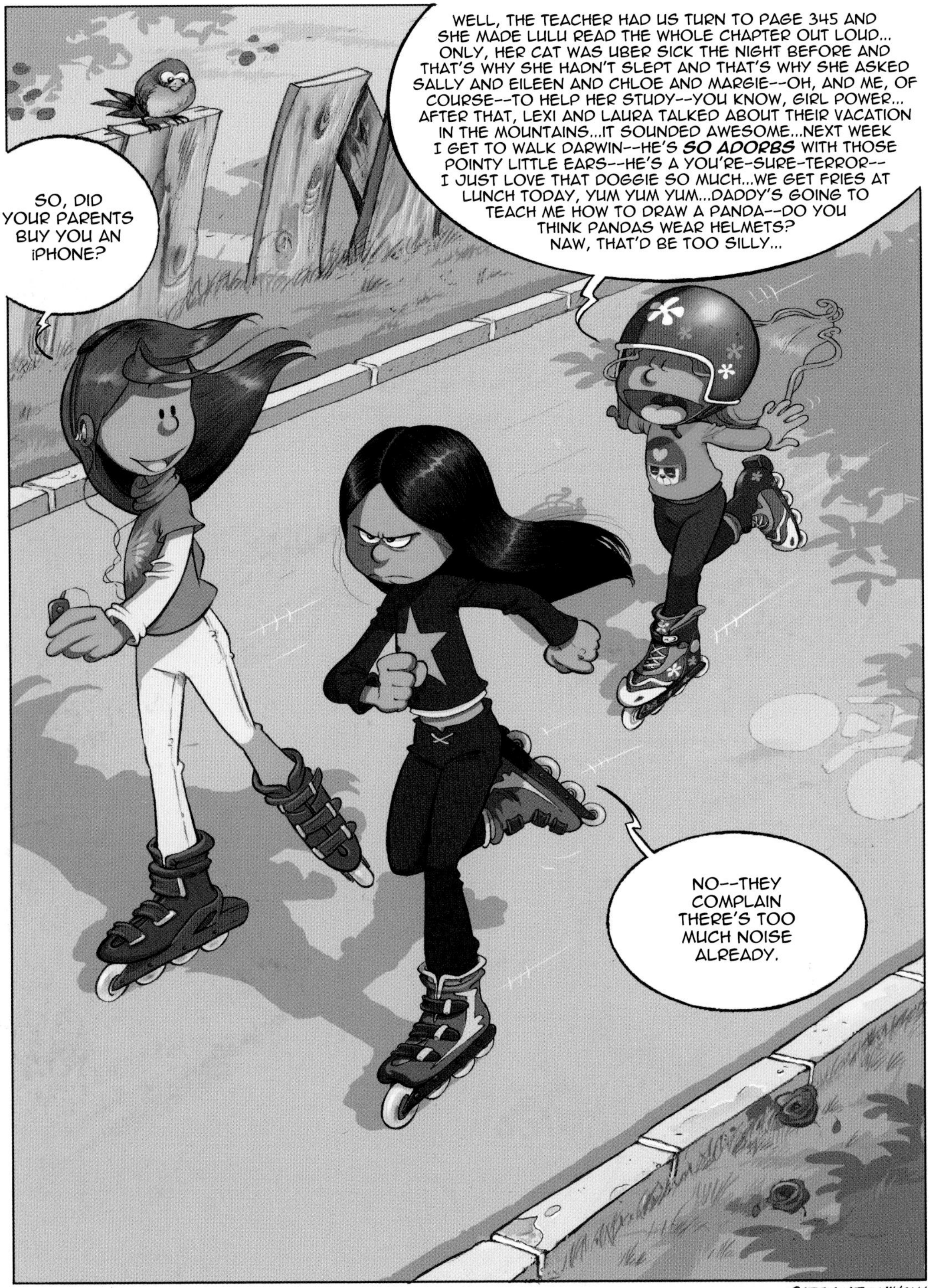
WELL, THE TEACHER HAD US TURN TO PAGE 345 AND SHE MADE LULU READ THE WHOLE CHAPTER OUT LOUD... ONLY, HER CAT WAS UBER SICK THE NIGHT BEFORE AND THAT'S WHY SHE HADN'T SLEPT AND THAT'S WHY SHE ASKED SALLY AND EILEEN AND CHLOE AND MARGIE--OH, AND ME, OF COURSE--TO HELP HER STUDY--YOU KNOW, GIRL POWER... AFTER THAT, LEXI AND LAURA TALKED ABOUT THEIR VACATION IN THE MOUNTAINS...IT SOUNDED AWESOME...NEXT WEEK I GET TO WALK DARWIN--HE'S ***SO ADORBS*** WITH THOSE POINTY LITTLE EARS--HE'S A YOU'RE-SURE-TERROR--I JUST LOVE THAT DOGGIE SO MUCH...WE GET FRIES AT LUNCH TODAY, YUM YUM YUM...DADDY'S GOING TO TEACH ME HOW TO DRAW A PANDA--DO YOU THINK PANDAS WEAR HELMETS? NAW, THAT'D BE TOO SILLY...
SO, DID YOUR PARENTS BUY YOU AN iPHONE?
NO--THEY COMPLAIN THERE'S TOO MUCH NOISE ALREADY.

CAZENOVE & WILLIAM

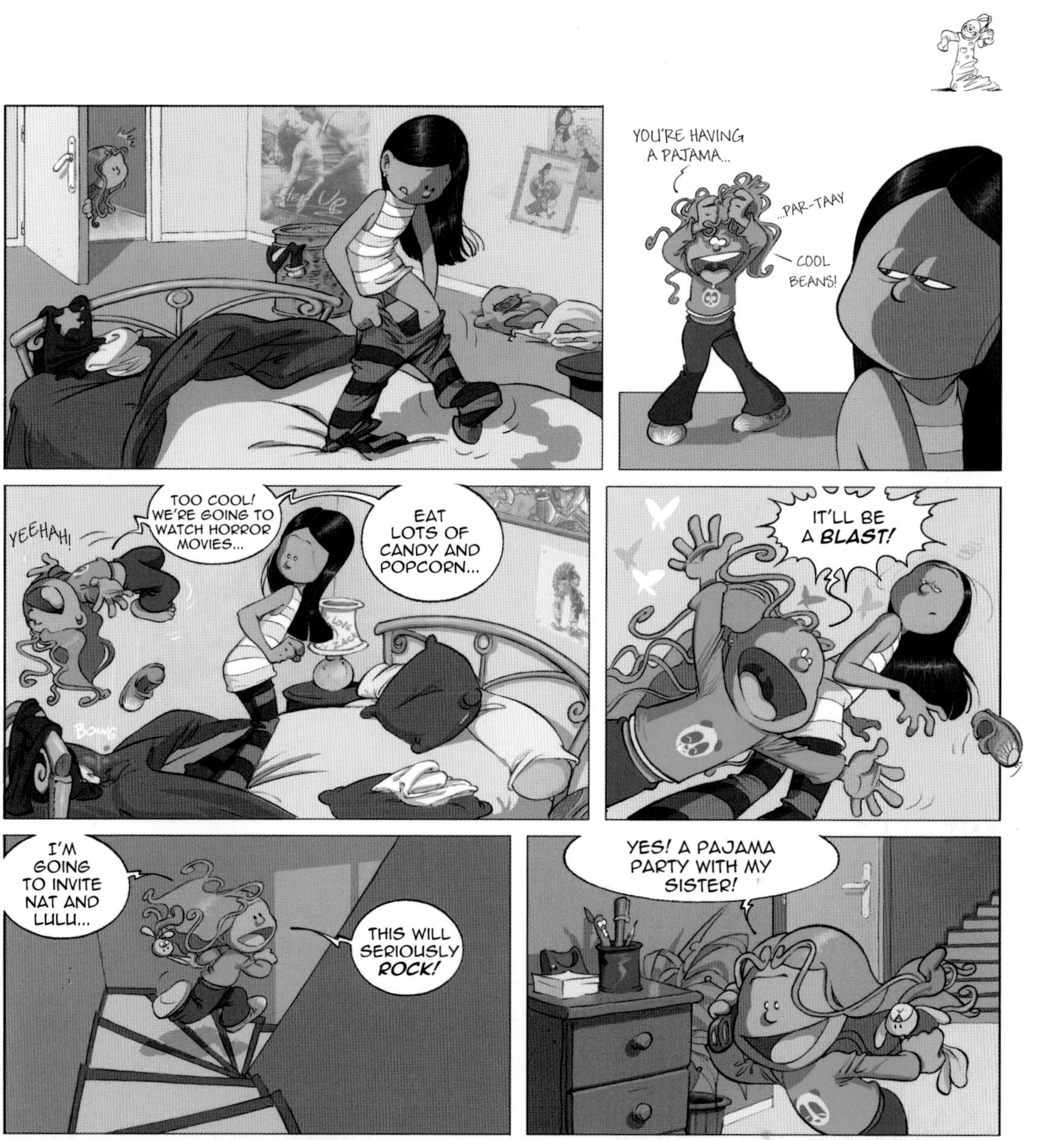
YOU'RE HAVING A PAJAMA...
...PAR-TAAY
COOL BEANS!
YEEHAH!
TOO COOL! WE'RE GOING TO WATCH HORROR MOVIES...
EAT LOTS OF CANDY AND POPCORN...
BOING
IT'LL BE A **BLAST!**
I'M GOING TO INVITE NAT AND LULU...
THIS WILL SERIOUSLY **ROCK!**
YES! A PAJAMA PARTY WITH MY SISTER!
A-HEM!
UM... THAT'S NOT A PAJAMA PARTY.
PFF! KIDS TODAY HAVE NO FASHION SENSE!
CAZENOVE & WILLIAM

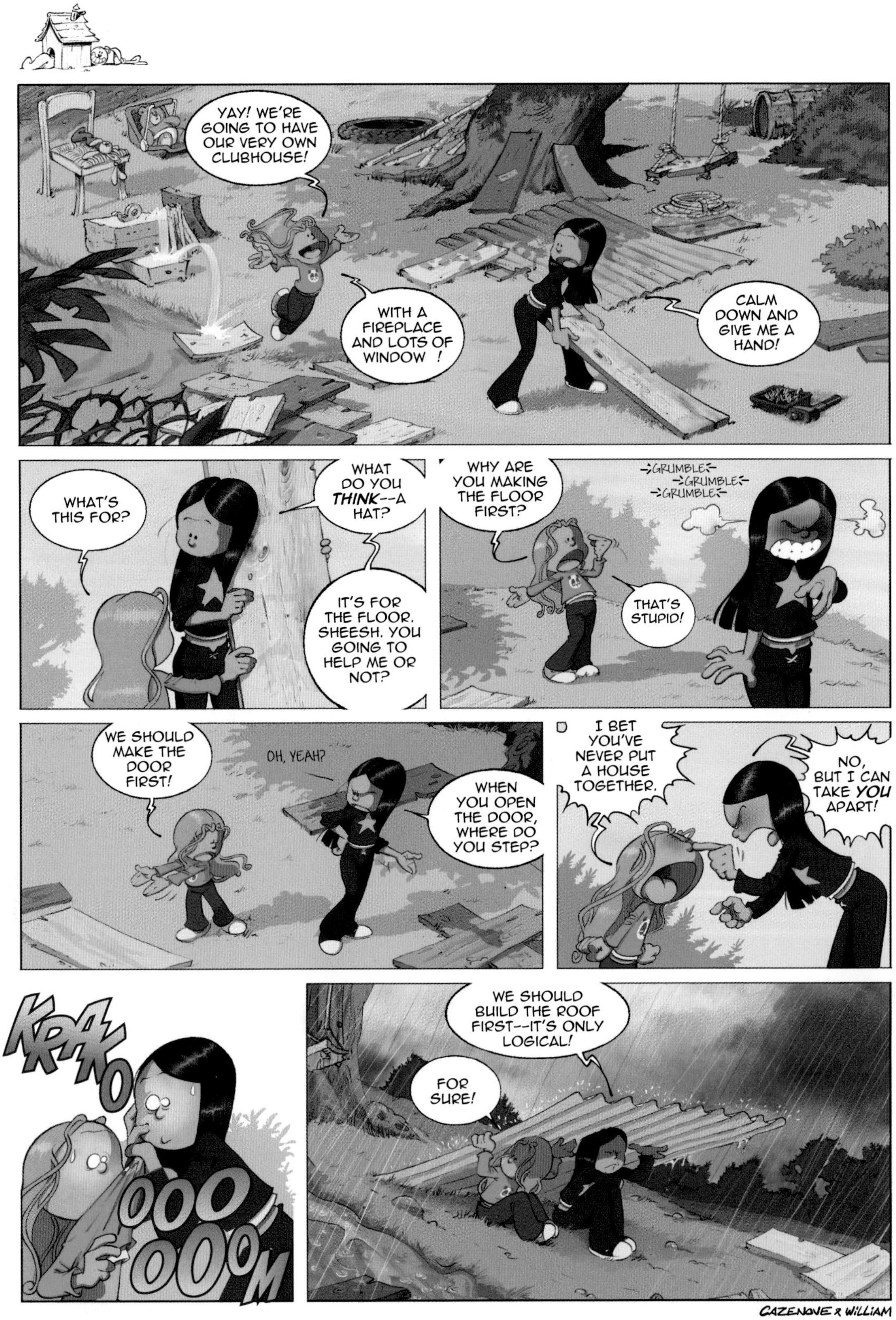

YAY! WE'RE GOING TO HAVE OUR VERY OWN CLUBHOUSE!
WITH A FIREPLACE AND LOTS OF WINDOW !
CALM DOWN AND GIVE ME A HAND!
WHAT'S THIS FOR?
WHAT DO YOU THINK--A HAT?
IT'S FOR THE FLOOR. SHEESH. YOU GOING TO HELP ME OR NOT?
WHY ARE YOU MAKING THE FLOOR FIRST?
GRUMBLE GRUMBLE GRUMBLE
THAT'S STUPID!
WE SHOULD MAKE THE DOOR FIRST!
OH, YEAH?
WHEN YOU OPEN THE DOOR, WHERE DO YOU STEP?
I BET YOU'VE NEVER PUT A HOUSE TOGETHER.
NO, BUT I CAN TAKE YOU APART!
KRAKOOOOOOOOM
WE SHOULD BUILD THE ROOF FIRST--IT'S ONLY LOGICAL!
FOR SURE!
CAZENOVE & WILLIAM

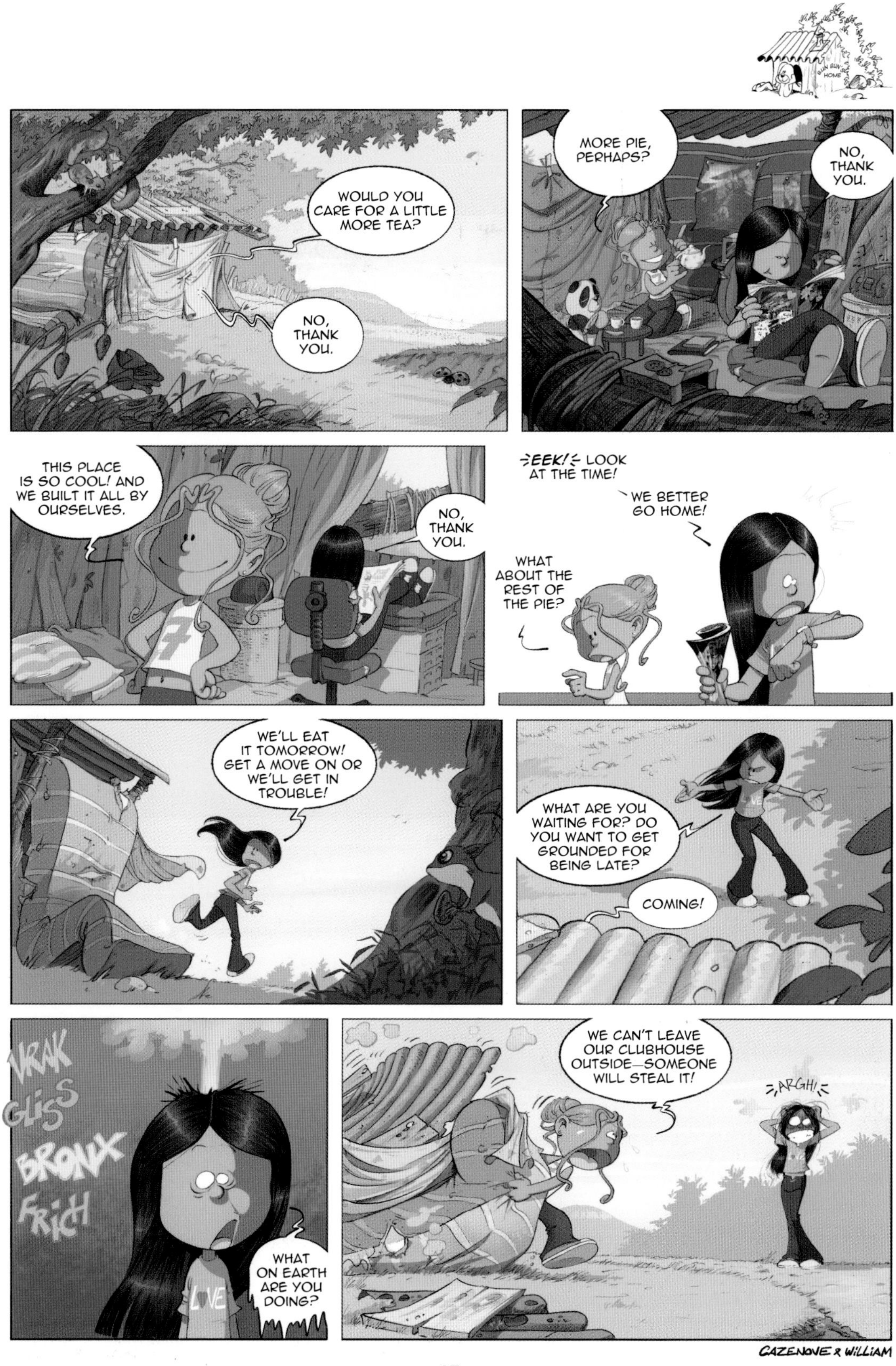
RUN RUN'S HOME
WOULD YOU CARE FOR A LITTLE MORE TEA?
NO, THANK YOU.
MORE PIE, PERHAPS?
NO, THANK YOU.
THIS PLACE IS SO COOL! AND WE BUILT IT ALL BY OURSELVES.
NO, THANK YOU.
EEK! LOOK AT THE TIME!
WE BETTER GO HOME!
WHAT ABOUT THE REST OF THE PIE?
WE'LL EAT IT TOMORROW! GET A MOVE ON OR WE'LL GET IN TROUBLE!
WHAT ARE YOU WAITING FOR? DO YOU WANT TO GET GROUNDED FOR BEING LATE?
COMING!
VRAK
GLISS
BRONX
FRICH
WHAT ON EARTH ARE YOU DOING?
WE CAN'T LEAVE OUR CLUBHOUSE OUTSIDE—SOMEONE WILL STEAL IT!
ARGH!
CAZENOVE & WILLIAM

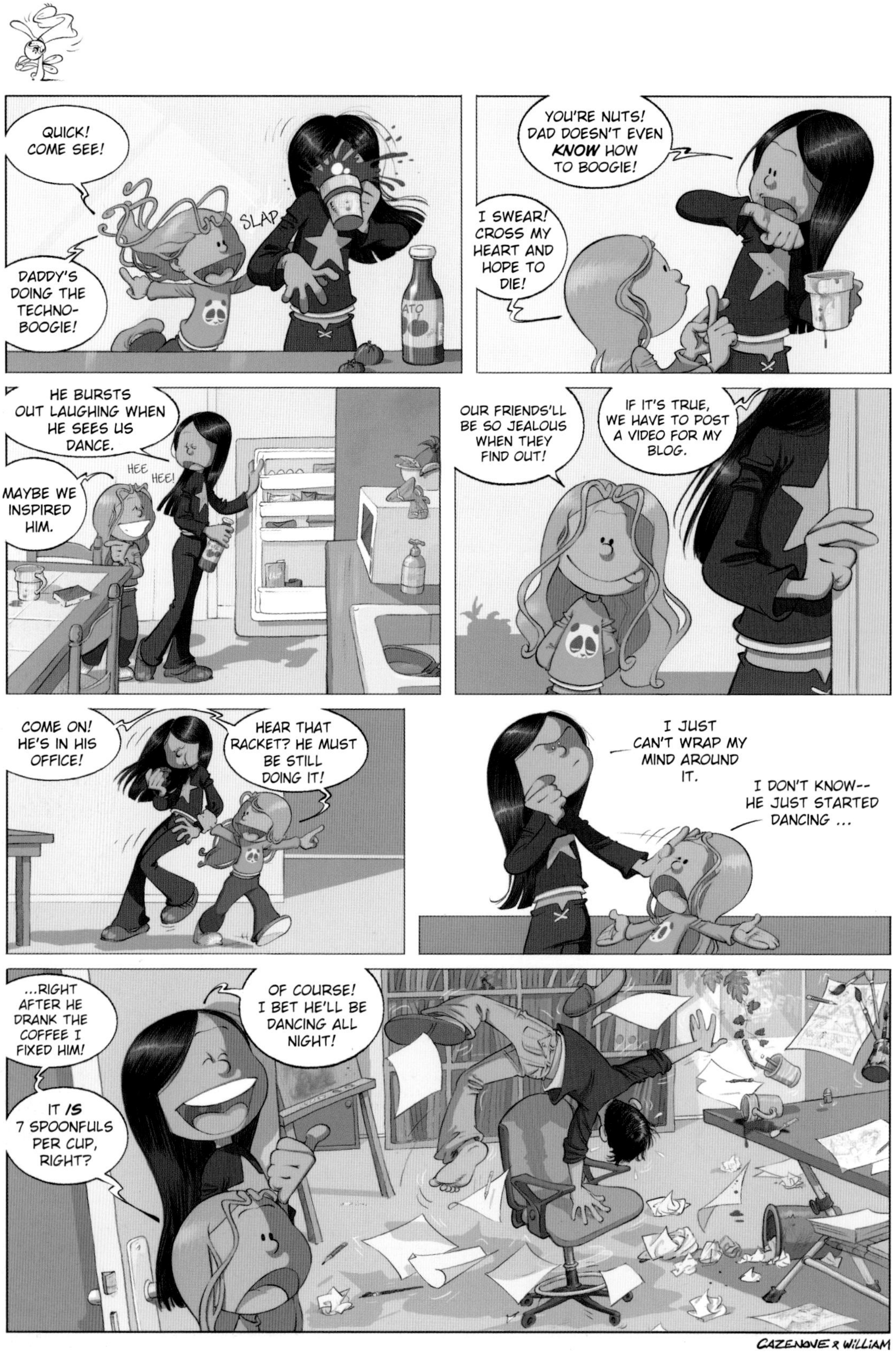
QUICK! COME SEE!
SLAP
DADDY'S DOING THE TECHNO-BOOGIE!
YOU'RE NUTS! DAD DOESN'T EVEN KNOW HOW TO BOOGIE!
I SWEAR! CROSS MY HEART AND HOPE TO DIE!
HE BURSTS OUT LAUGHING WHEN HE SEES US DANCE.
HEE HEE!
MAYBE WE INSPIRED HIM.
OUR FRIENDS'LL BE SO JEALOUS WHEN THEY FIND OUT!
IF IT'S TRUE, WE HAVE TO POST A VIDEO FOR MY BLOG.
COME ON! HE'S IN HIS OFFICE!
HEAR THAT RACKET? HE MUST BE STILL DOING IT!
I JUST CAN'T WRAP MY MIND AROUND IT.
I DON'T KNOW-- HE JUST STARTED DANCING ...
...RIGHT AFTER HE DRANK THE COFFEE I FIXED HIM!
OF COURSE! I BET HE'LL BE DANCING ALL NIGHT!
IT IS 7 SPOONFULS PER CUP, RIGHT?

CAZENOVE & WILLIAM

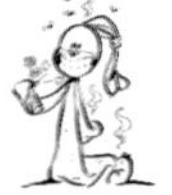

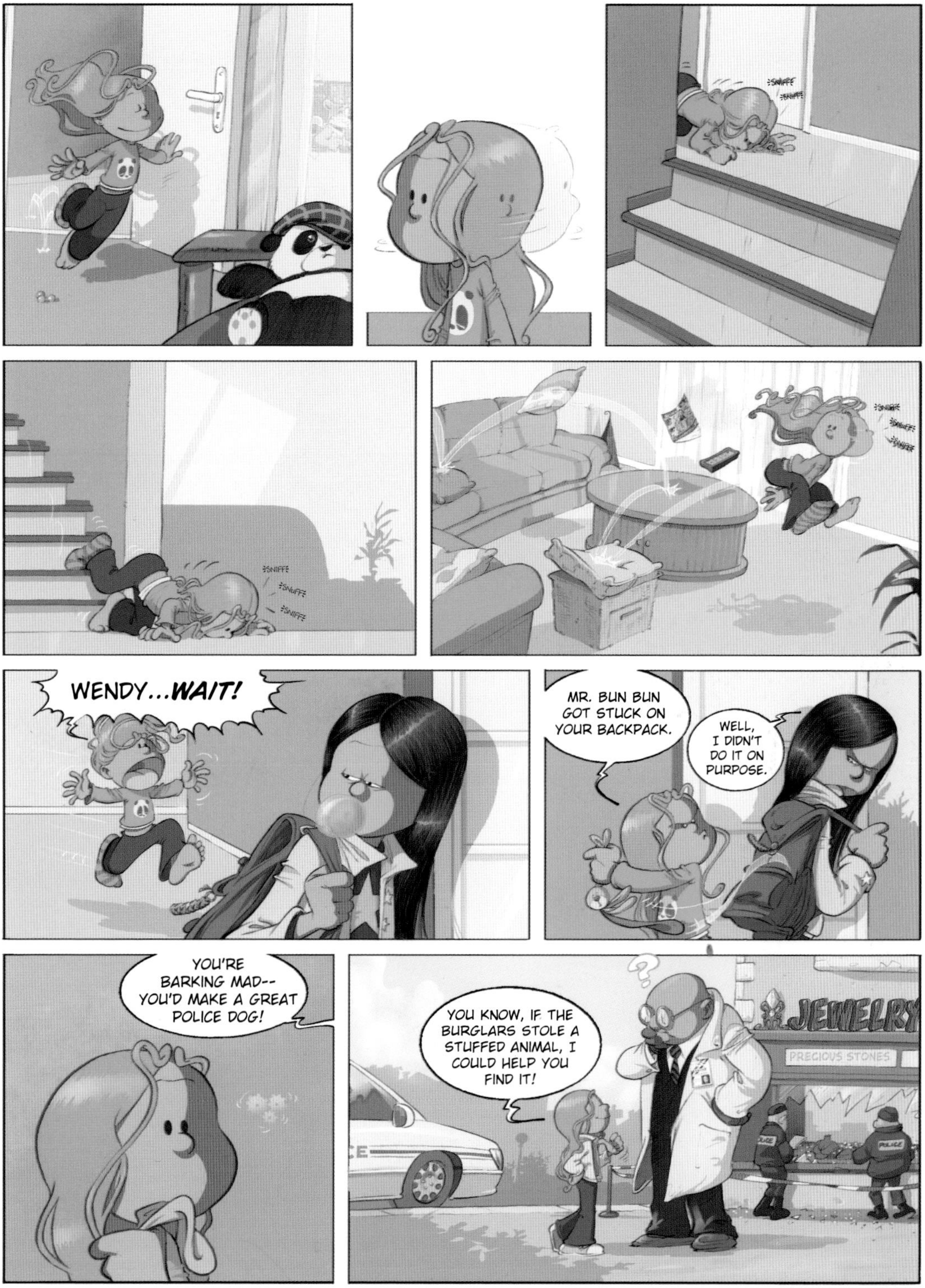
SNIFF
SNUFF
SNIFF
WENDY...WAIT!
MR. BUN BUN GOT STUCK ON YOUR BACKPACK.
WELL, I DIDN'T DO IT ON PURPOSE.
YOU'RE BARKING MAD-- YOU'D MAKE A GREAT POLICE DOG!
JEWELRY
PRECIOUS STONES
YOU KNOW, IF THE BURGLARS STOLE A STUFFED ANIMAL, I COULD HELP YOU FIND IT!
POLICE
POLICE

CAZENOVE & WILLIAM

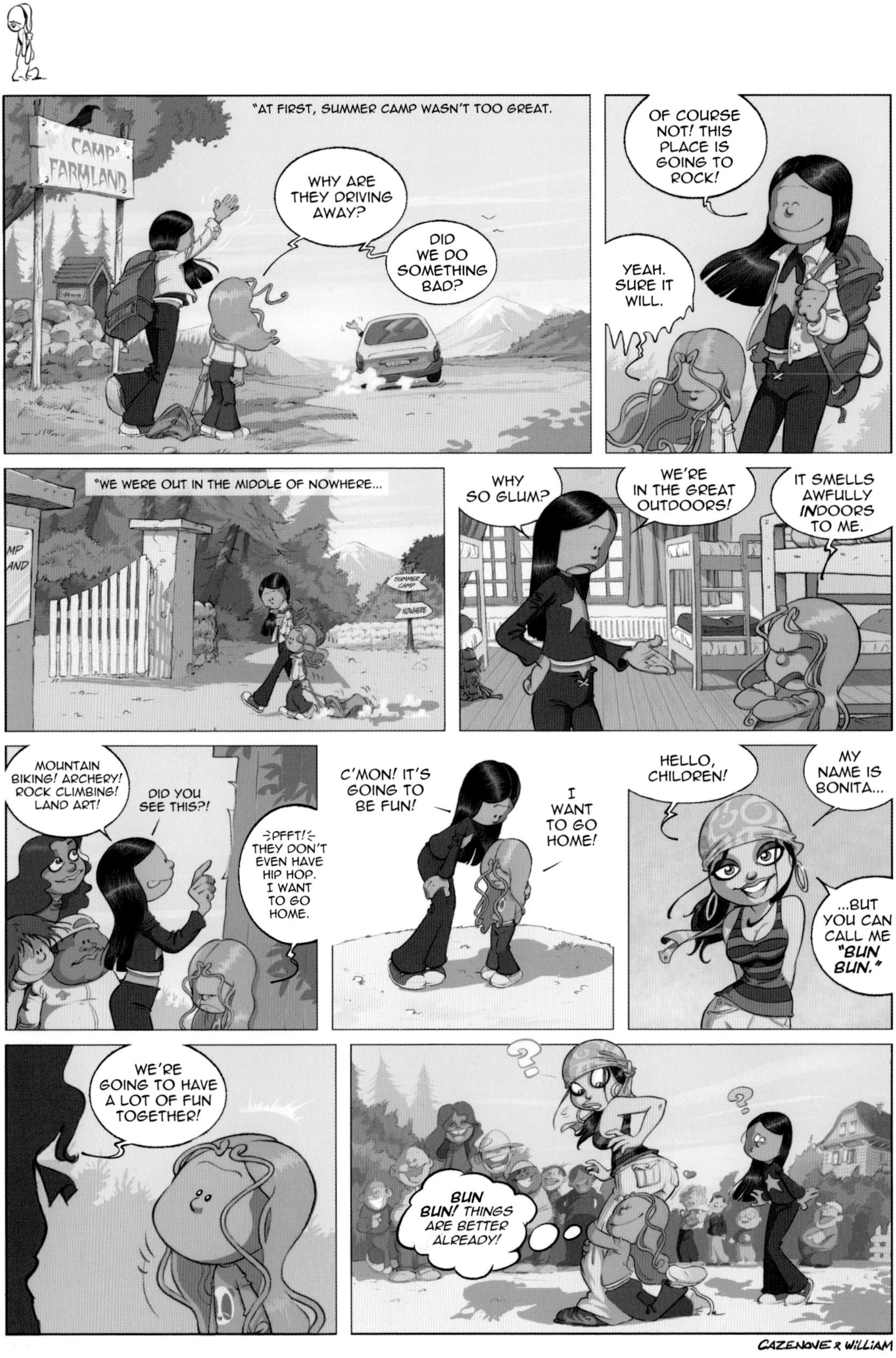
CAMP FARMLAND
"AT FIRST, SUMMER CAMP WASN'T TOO GREAT.
WHY ARE THEY DRIVING AWAY?
DID WE DO SOMETHING BAD?
OF COURSE NOT! THIS PLACE IS GOING TO ROCK!
YEAH. SURE IT WILL.
"WE WERE OUT IN THE MIDDLE OF NOWHERE...
SUMMER CAMP
NOWHERE
WHY SO GLUM?
WE'RE IN THE GREAT OUTDOORS!
IT SMELLS AWFULLY INDOORS TO ME.
MOUNTAIN BIKING! ARCHERY! ROCK CLIMBING! LAND ART!
DID YOU SEE THIS?!
PFFT! THEY DON'T EVEN HAVE HIP HOP. I WANT TO GO HOME.
C'MON! IT'S GOING TO BE FUN!
I WANT TO GO HOME!
HELLO, CHILDREN!
MY NAME IS BONITA...
...BUT YOU CAN CALL ME "BUN BUN."
WE'RE GOING TO HAVE A LOT OF FUN TOGETHER!
BUN BUN! THINGS ARE BETTER ALREADY!
CAZENOVE & WILLIAM

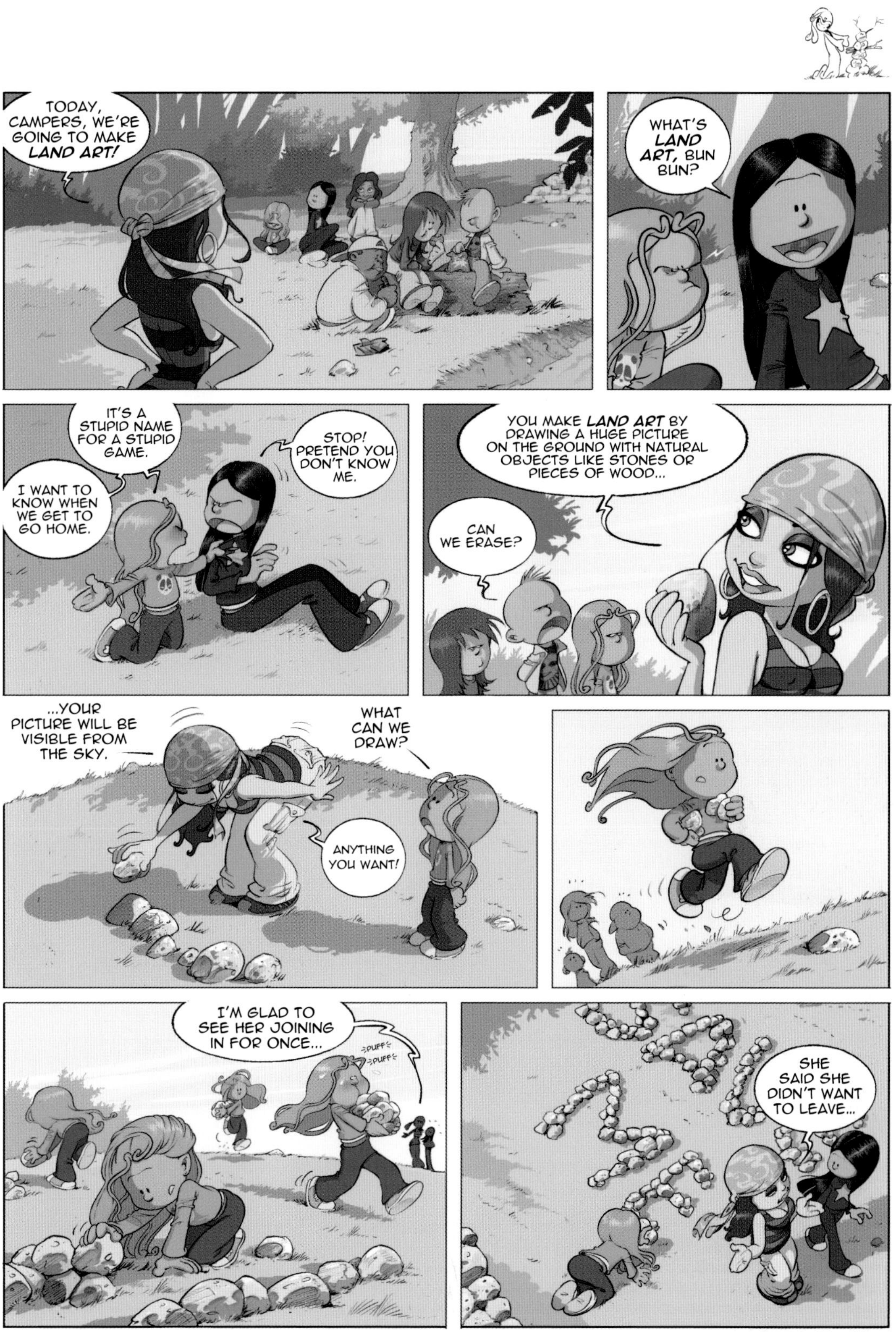
TODAY, CAMPERS, WE'RE GOING TO MAKE LAND ART!
WHAT'S LAND ART, BUN BUN?
IT'S A STUPID NAME FOR A STUPID GAME.
I WANT TO KNOW WHEN WE GET TO GO HOME.
STOP! PRETEND YOU DON'T KNOW ME.
YOU MAKE LAND ART BY DRAWING A HUGE PICTURE ON THE GROUND WITH NATURAL OBJECTS LIKE STONES OR PIECES OF WOOD...
CAN WE ERASE?
...YOUR PICTURE WILL BE VISIBLE FROM THE SKY.
WHAT CAN WE DRAW?
ANYTHING YOU WANT!
I'M GLAD TO SEE HER JOINING IN FOR ONCE...
PUFF PUFF
SHE SAID SHE DIDN'T WANT TO LEAVE...

CAZENOVE & WILLIAM

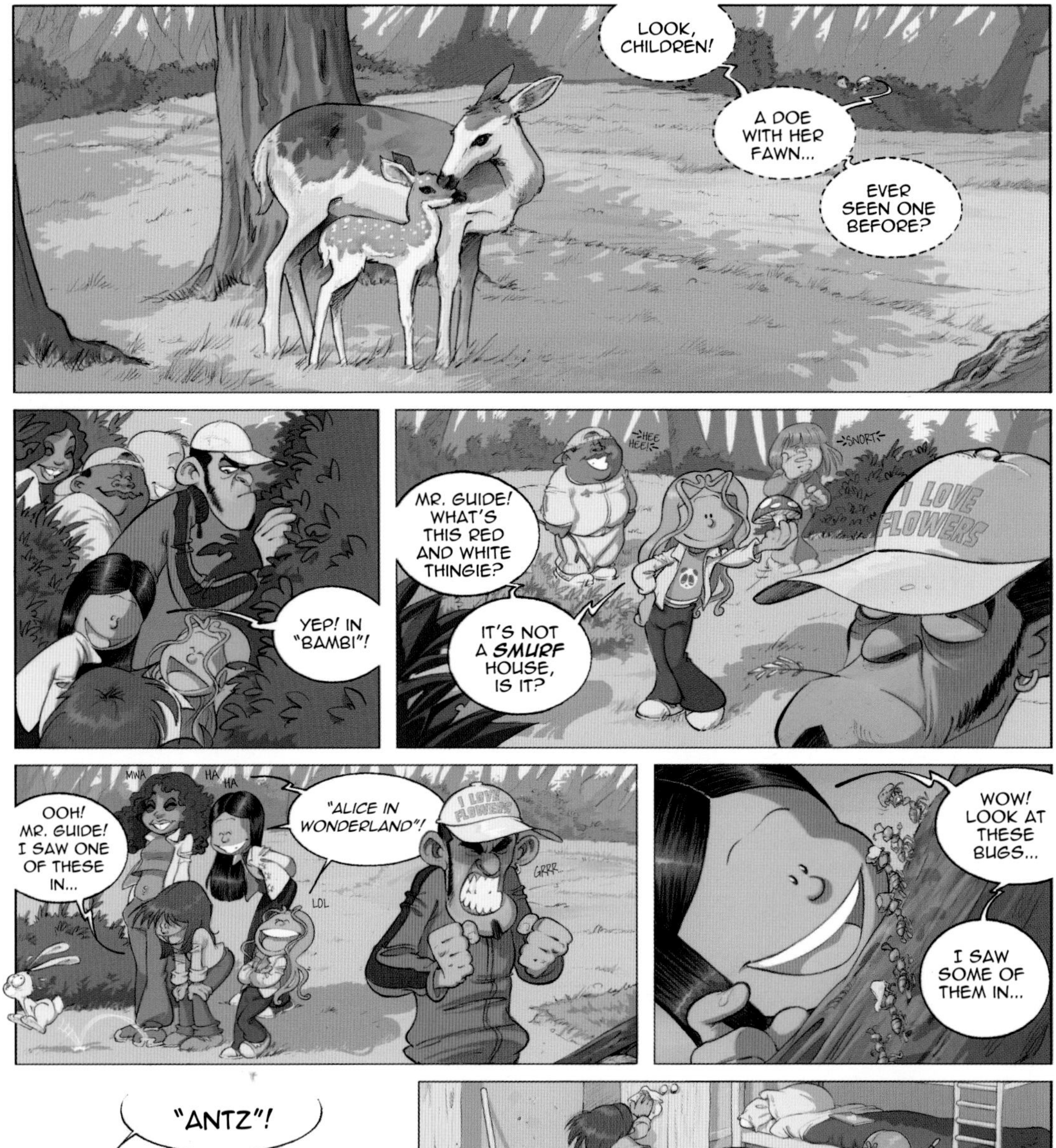
LOOK, CHILDREN!
A DOE WITH HER FAWN...
EVER SEEN ONE BEFORE?
YEP! IN "BAMBI"!
HEE HEE!
SNORT
MR. GUIDE! WHAT'S THIS RED AND WHITE THINGIE?
IT'S NOT A **SMURF** HOUSE, IS IT?
I LOVE FLOWERS
MWA HA HA
OOH! MR. GUIDE! I SAW ONE OF THESE IN...
"ALICE IN WONDERLAND"!
LOL
I LOVE FLOWERS
GRRR
WOW! LOOK AT THESE BUGS...
I SAW SOME OF THEM IN...
"ANTZ"!
GRUMBLE
GRUMBLE
JUST OUR LUCK, **HIS** FAVORITE MOVIE IS "CINDERELLA"!
SO LAME!

CAZENOVE & WILLIAM

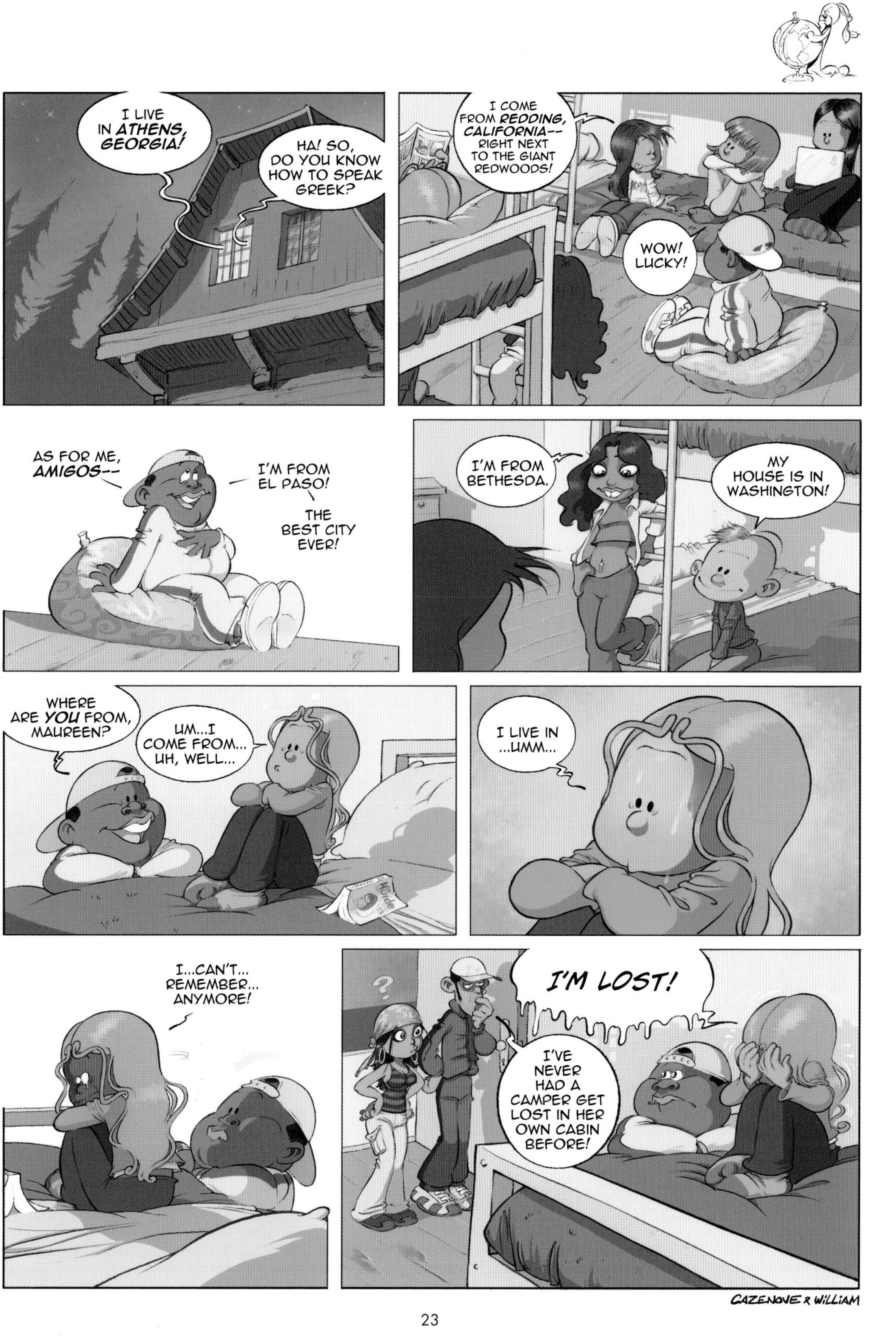
I LIVE IN ATHENS, GEORGIA!
HA! SO, DO YOU KNOW HOW TO SPEAK GREEK?
I COME FROM REDDING, CALIFORNIA-- RIGHT NEXT TO THE GIANT REDWOODS!
WOW! LUCKY!
AS FOR ME, AMIGOS--
I'M FROM EL PASO!
THE BEST CITY EVER!
I'M FROM BETHESDA.
MY HOUSE IS IN WASHINGTON!
WHERE ARE YOU FROM, MAUREEN?
UM...I COME FROM... UH, WELL...
I LIVE IN ...UMM...
I...CAN'T... REMEMBER... ANYMORE!
I'M LOST!
I'VE NEVER HAD A CAMPER GET LOST IN HER OWN CABIN BEFORE!
CAZENOVE & WILLIAM

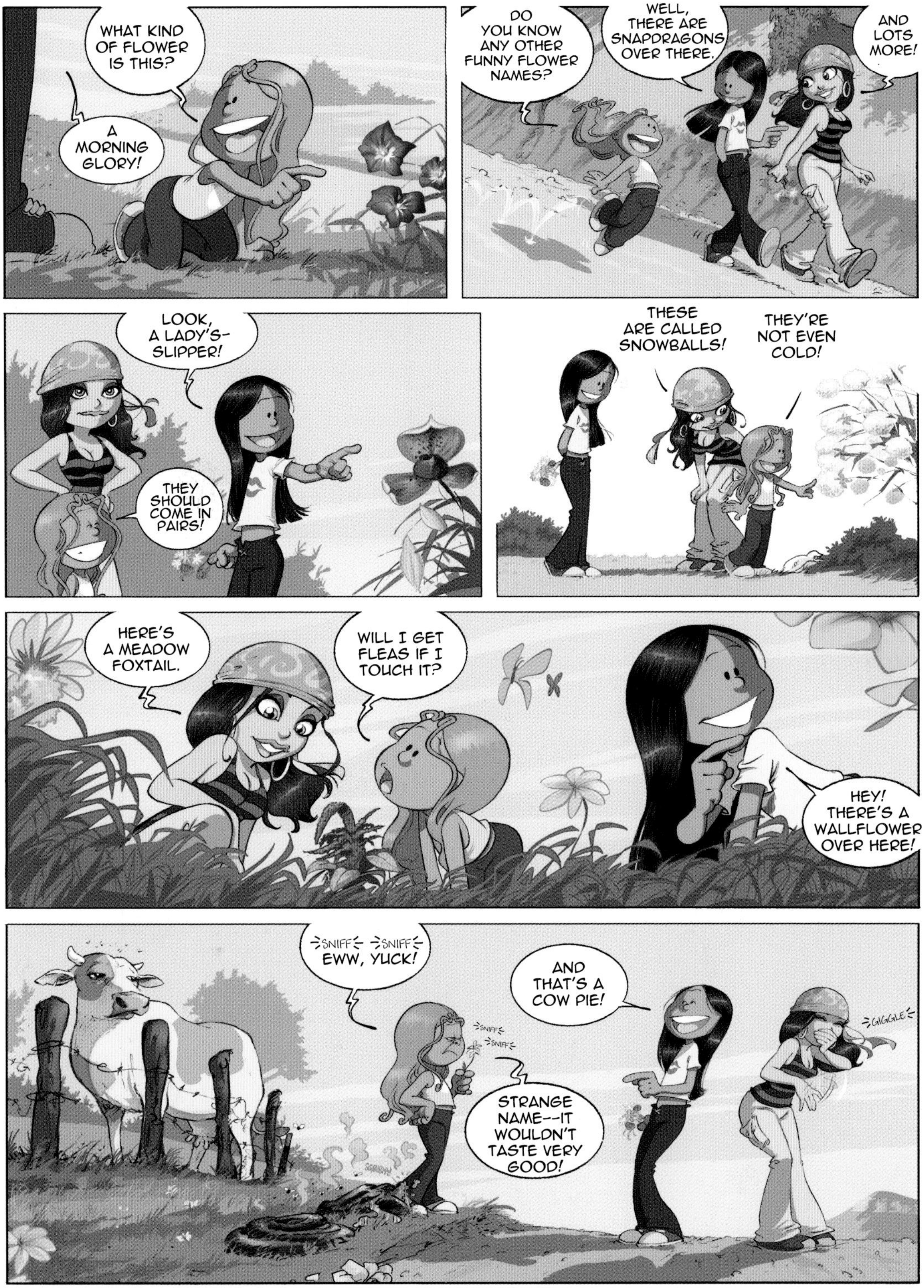
WHAT KIND OF FLOWER IS THIS?
A MORNING GLORY!
DO YOU KNOW ANY OTHER FUNNY FLOWER NAMES?
WELL, THERE ARE SNAPDRAGONS OVER THERE.
AND LOTS MORE!
LOOK, A LADY'S-SLIPPER!
THEY SHOULD COME IN PAIRS!
THESE ARE CALLED SNOWBALLS!
THEY'RE NOT EVEN COLD!
HERE'S A MEADOW FOXTAIL.
WILL I GET FLEAS IF I TOUCH IT?
HEY! THERE'S A WALLFLOWER OVER HERE!
SNIFF SNIFF EWW, YUCK!
AND THAT'S A COW PIE!
GIGGLE
STRANGE NAME--IT WOULDN'T TASTE VERY GOOD!

CAZENOVE & WILLIAM

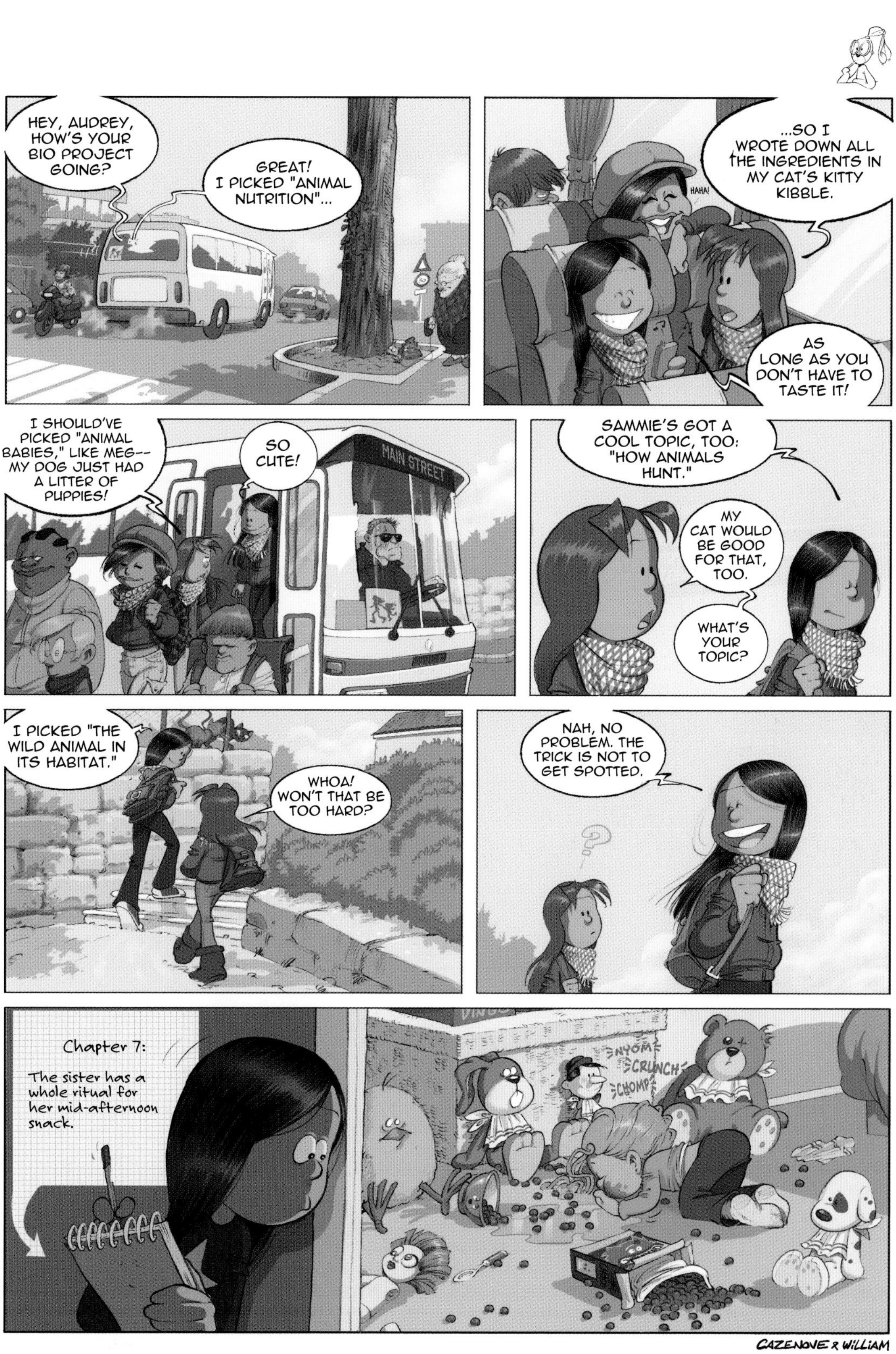
HEY, AUDREY, HOW'S YOUR BIO PROJECT GOING?
GREAT! I PICKED "ANIMAL NUTRITION"...
...SO I WROTE DOWN ALL THE INGREDIENTS IN MY CAT'S KITTY KIBBLE.
HAHA!
AS LONG AS YOU DON'T HAVE TO TASTE IT!
I SHOULD'VE PICKED "ANIMAL BABIES," LIKE MEG-- MY DOG JUST HAD A LITTER OF PUPPIES!
SO CUTE!
MAIN STREET
SAMMIE'S GOT A COOL TOPIC, TOO: "HOW ANIMALS HUNT."
MY CAT WOULD BE GOOD FOR THAT, TOO.
WHAT'S YOUR TOPIC?
I PICKED "THE WILD ANIMAL IN ITS HABITAT."
WHOA! WON'T THAT BE TOO HARD?
NAH, NO PROBLEM. THE TRICK IS NOT TO GET SPOTTED.
Chapter 7:
The sister has a whole ritual for her mid-afternoon snack.
NYOM
CRUNCH
CHOMP
CAZENOVE & WILLIAM

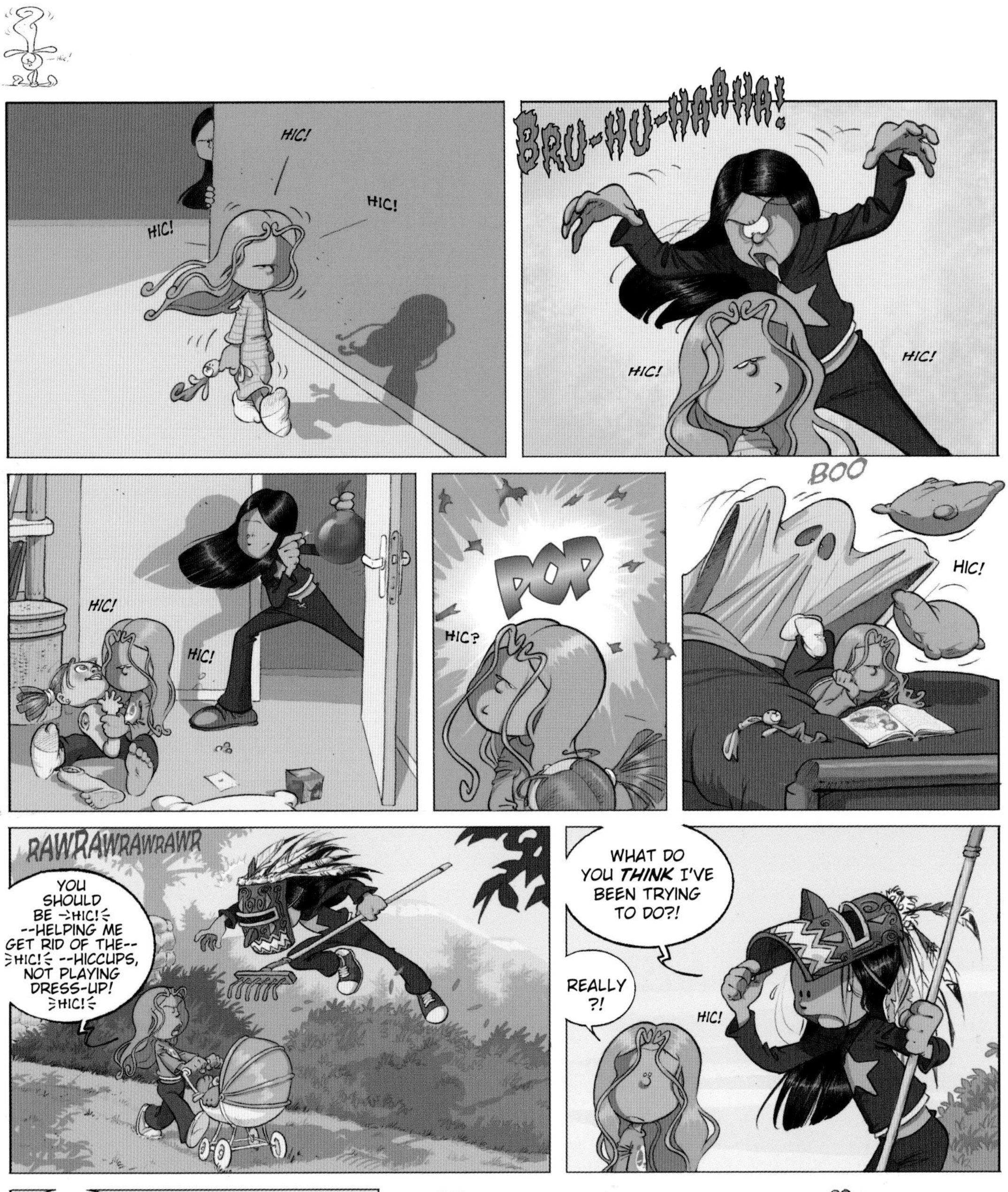
HIC!
HIC!
HIC!
BRU-HU-HAAHA!
HIC!
HIC!
HIC!
HIC!
POP
HIC?
BOO
HIC!
RAWRAWRAWRAWR
YOU SHOULD BE -HIC!- --HELPING ME GET RID OF THE-- -HIC!- --HICCUPS, NOT PLAYING DRESS-UP! -HIC!-
WHAT DO YOU THINK I'VE BEEN TRYING TO DO?!
REALLY ?!
HIC!
WAIT-- DON'T MOVE. I'LL SHOW YOU.
HIC!
SEE, IT'S NOT TOO HARD TO SCARE PEOPLE!
HIC! HIC! HIC!
NO FAIR! I DON'T HAVE THE HICCUPS!
CAZENOVE & WILLIAM

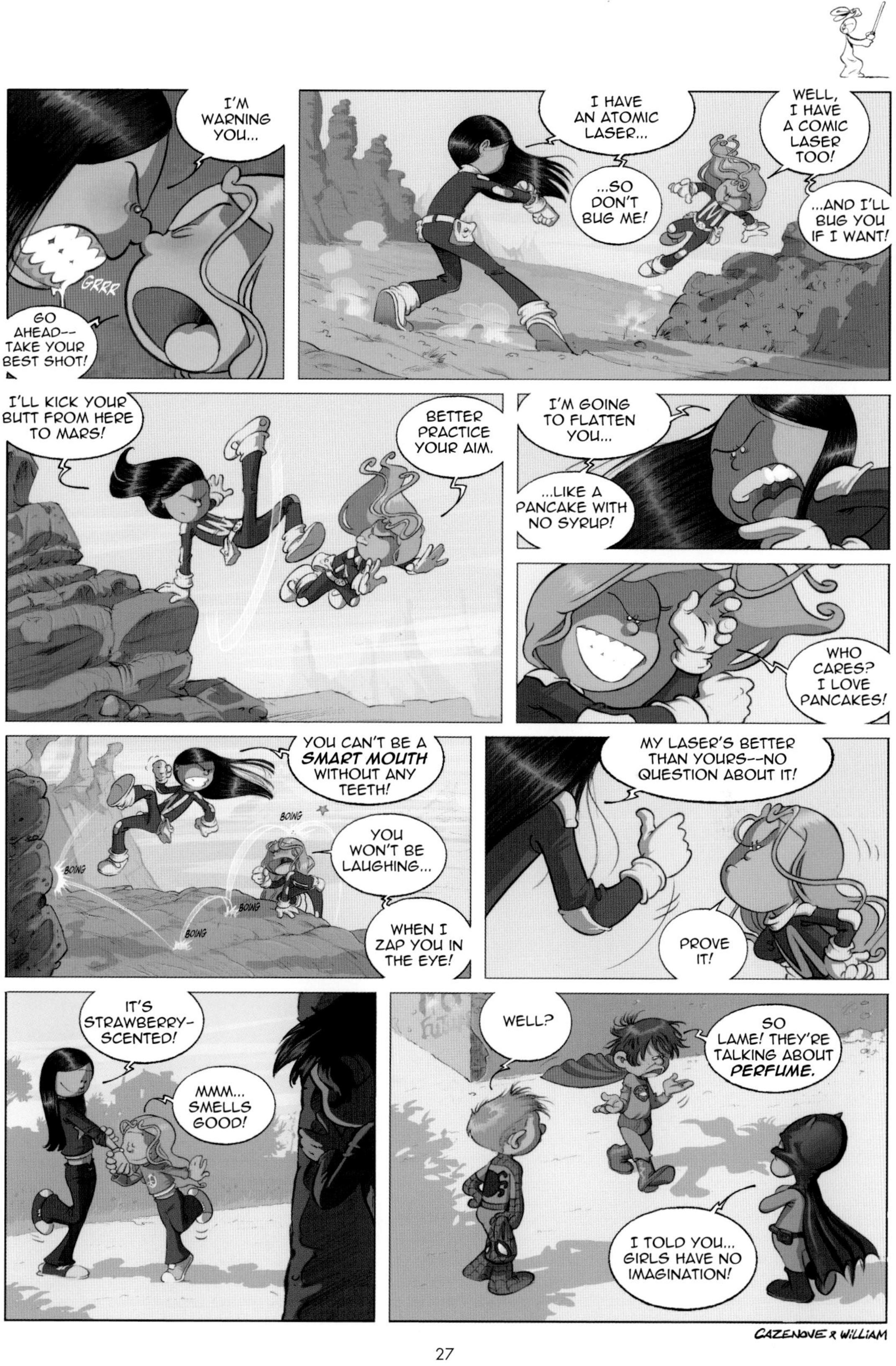
I'M WARNING YOU...
GRRR
GO AHEAD--TAKE YOUR BEST SHOT!
I HAVE AN ATOMIC LASER...
...SO DON'T BUG ME!
WELL, I HAVE A COMIC LASER TOO!
...AND I'LL BUG YOU IF I WANT!
I'LL KICK YOUR BUTT FROM HERE TO MARS!
BETTER PRACTICE YOUR AIM.
I'M GOING TO FLATTEN YOU...
...LIKE A PANCAKE WITH NO SYRUP!
WHO CARES? I LOVE PANCAKES!
YOU CAN'T BE A SMART MOUTH WITHOUT ANY TEETH!
BOING
BOING
BOING
BOING
YOU WON'T BE LAUGHING...
WHEN I ZAP YOU IN THE EYE!
MY LASER'S BETTER THAN YOURS--NO QUESTION ABOUT IT!
PROVE IT!
IT'S STRAWBERRY-SCENTED!
MMM... SMELLS GOOD!
WELL?
SO LAME! THEY'RE TALKING ABOUT PERFUME.
I TOLD YOU... GIRLS HAVE NO IMAGINATION!

CAZENOVE & WILLIAM

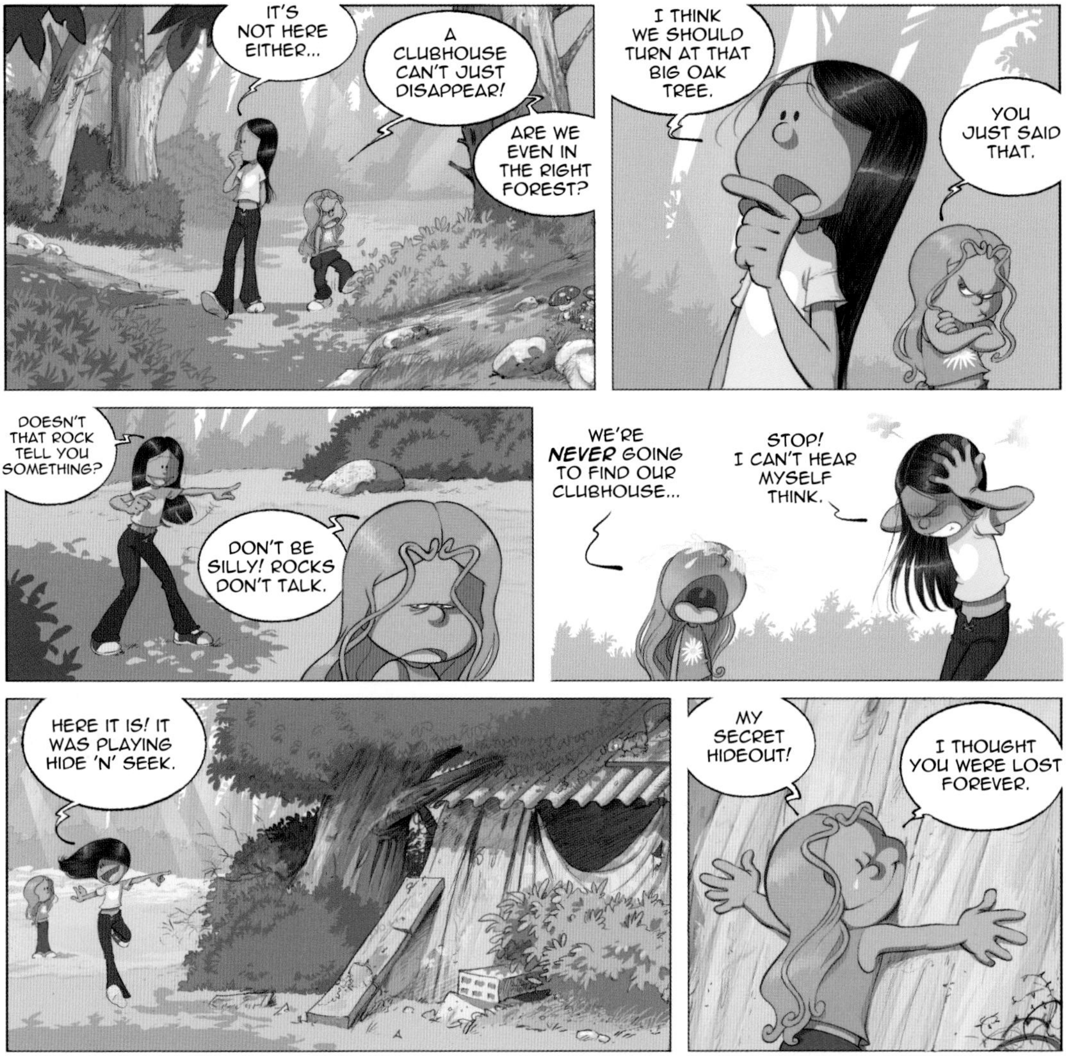
IT'S NOT HERE EITHER...
A CLUBHOUSE CAN'T JUST DISAPPEAR!
ARE WE EVEN IN THE RIGHT FOREST?
I THINK WE SHOULD TURN AT THAT BIG OAK TREE.
YOU JUST SAID THAT.
DOESN'T THAT ROCK TELL YOU SOMETHING?
DON'T BE SILLY! ROCKS DON'T TALK.
WE'RE **NEVER** GOING TO FIND OUR CLUBHOUSE...
STOP! I CAN'T HEAR MYSELF THINK.
HERE IT IS! IT WAS PLAYING HIDE 'N' SEEK.
MY SECRET HIDEOUT!
I THOUGHT YOU WERE LOST FOREVER.
THERE'S GOT TO BE AN EASIER WAY TO FIND IT.
NOW WE'LL ALWAYS KNOW THE WAY!
BAM
BAM
BAM
you're getting close
here!
this way
go left
SO MUCH FOR KEEPING IT SECRET!

CAZENOVE & WILLIAM

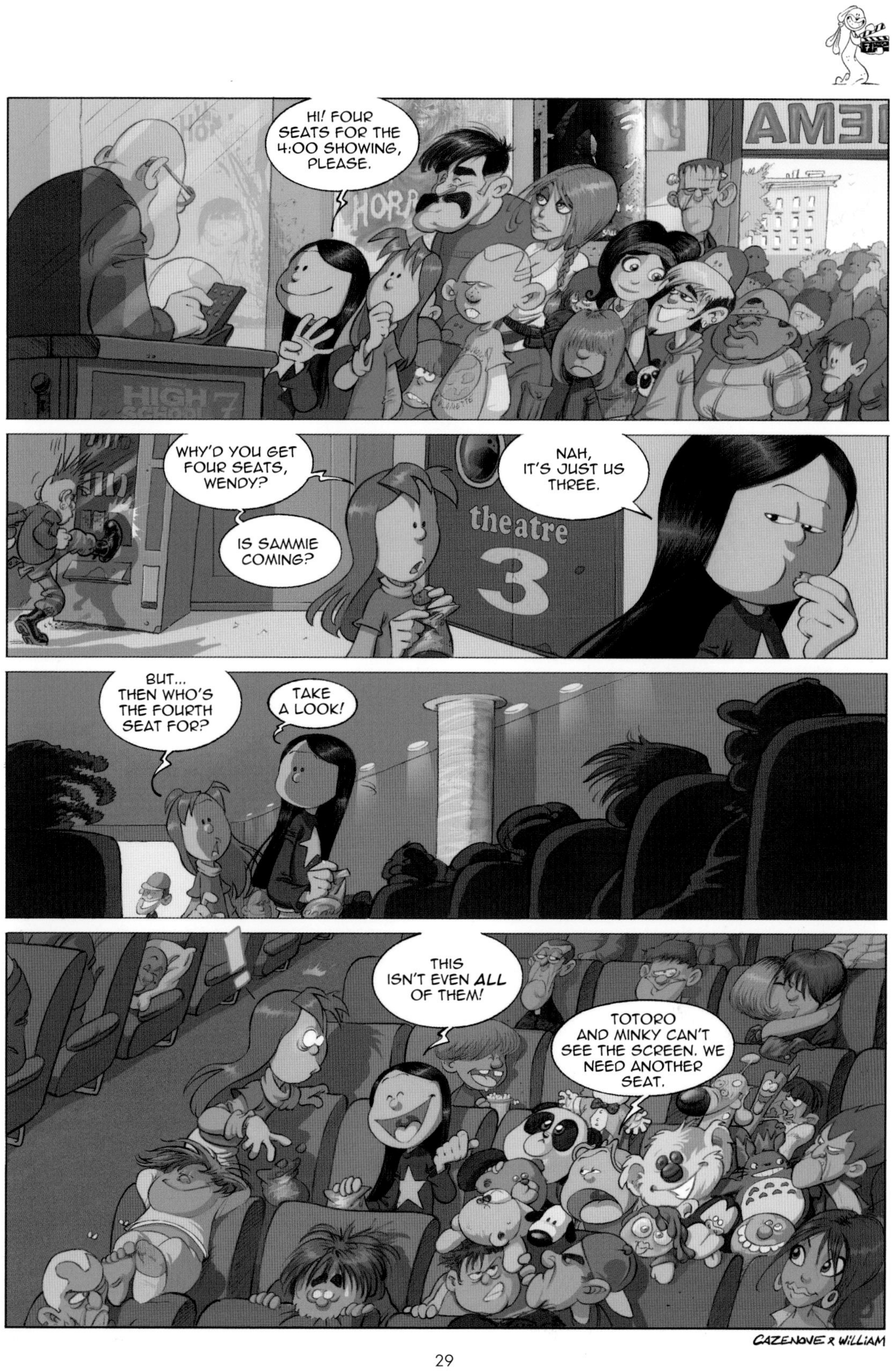
HI! FOUR SEATS FOR THE 4:00 SHOWING, PLEASE.
WHY'D YOU GET FOUR SEATS, WENDY?
IS SAMMIE COMING?
NAH, IT'S JUST US THREE.
theatre 3
BUT... THEN WHO'S THE FOURTH SEAT FOR?
TAKE A LOOK!
THIS ISN'T EVEN ***ALL*** OF THEM!
TOTORO AND MINKY CAN'T SEE THE SCREEN. WE NEED ANOTHER SEAT.

CAZENOVE & WILLIAM

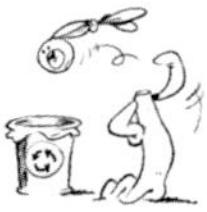

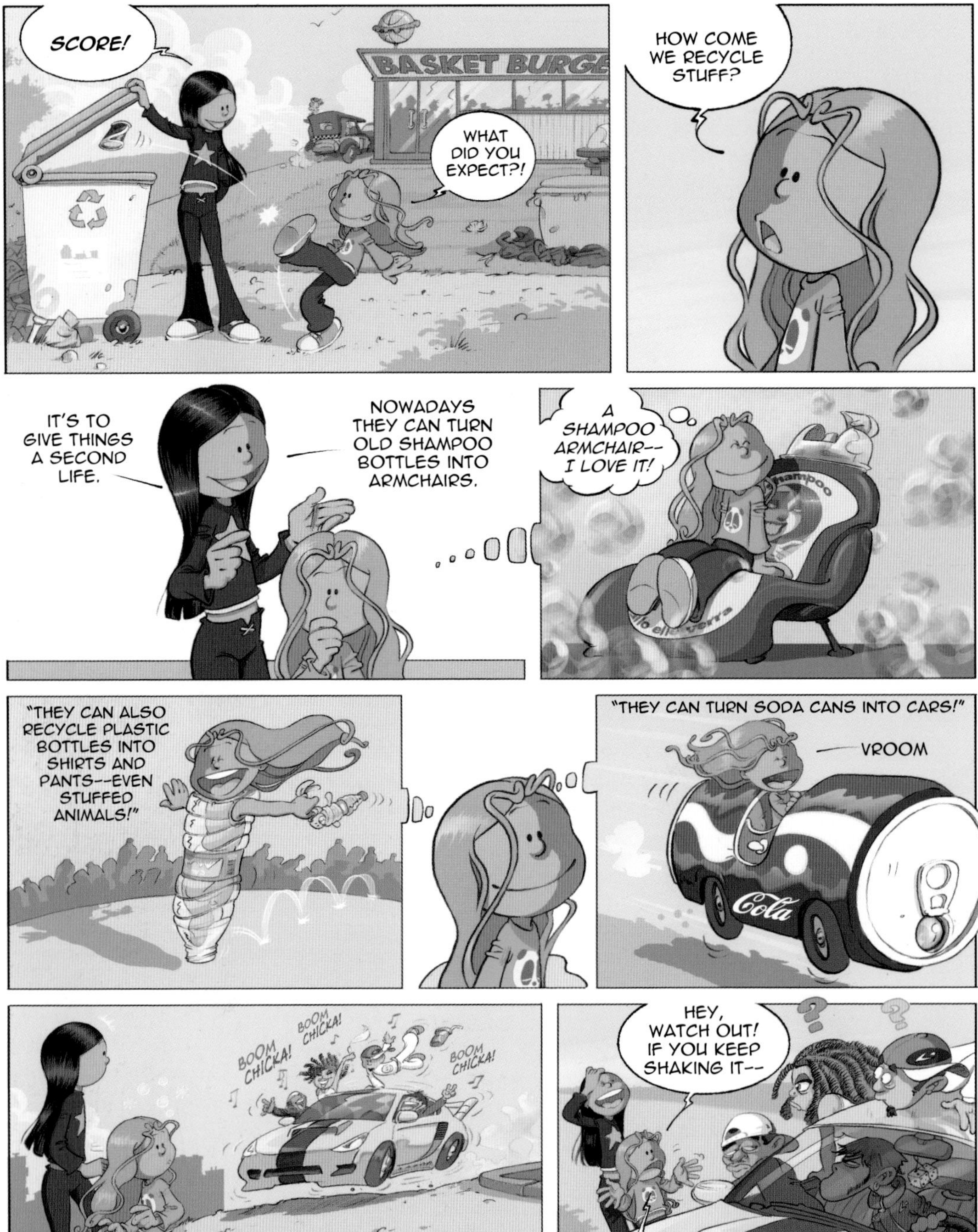
SCORE!
BASKET BURGE
WHAT DID YOU EXPECT?!
HOW COME WE RECYCLE STUFF?
IT'S TO GIVE THINGS A SECOND LIFE.
NOWADAYS THEY CAN TURN OLD SHAMPOO BOTTLES INTO ARMCHAIRS.
A SHAMPOO ARMCHAIR-- I LOVE IT!
"THEY CAN ALSO RECYCLE PLASTIC BOTTLES INTO SHIRTS AND PANTS--EVEN STUFFED ANIMALS!"
"THEY CAN TURN SODA CANS INTO CARS!"
VROOM
Cola
BOOM CHICKA!
BOOM CHICKA!
BOOM CHICKA!
HEY, WATCH OUT! IF YOU KEEP SHAKING IT--
-- IT'LL EXPLODE IN YOUR FACE!

CAZENOVE & WILLIAM

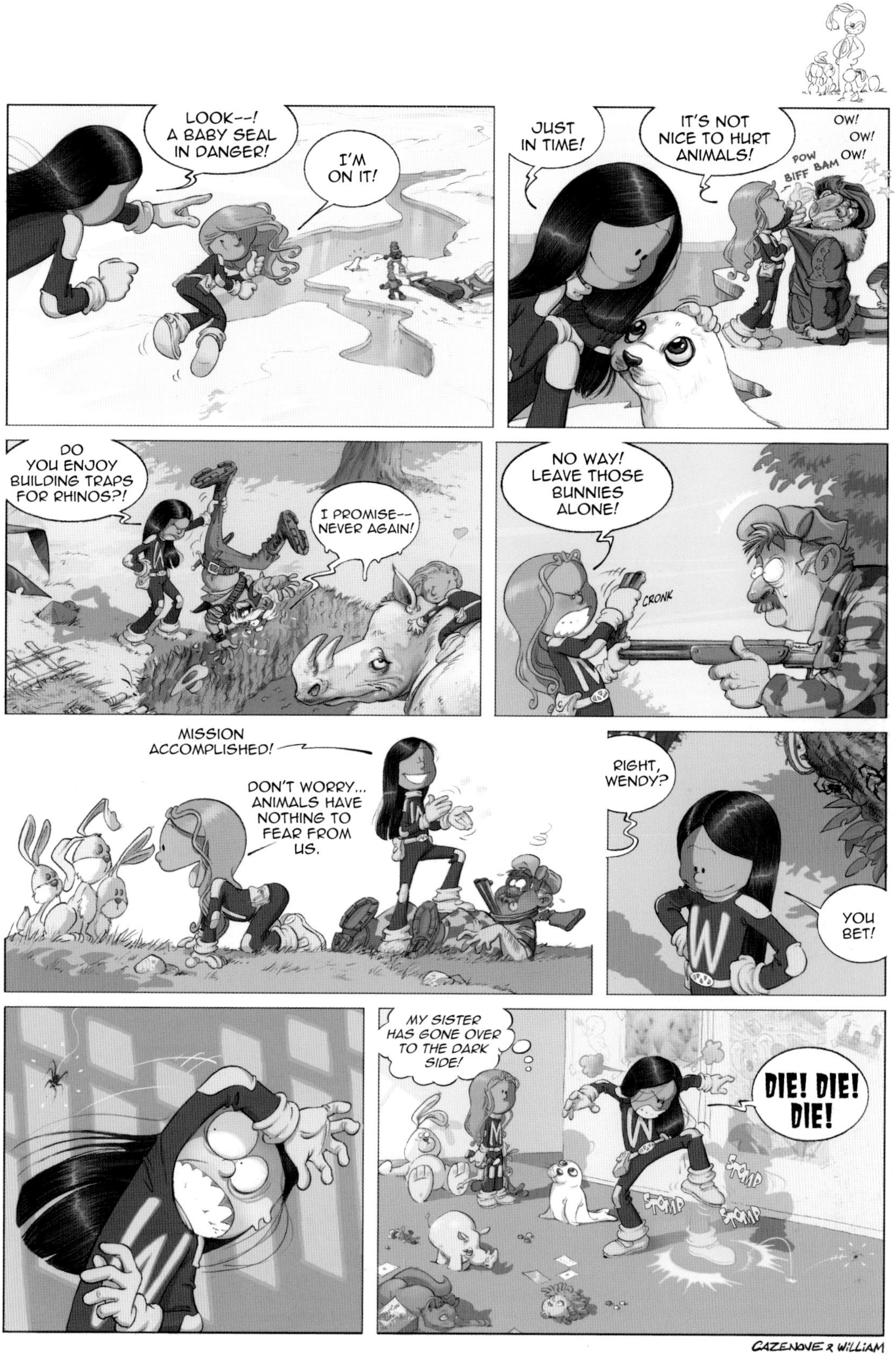
LOOK--! A BABY SEAL IN DANGER!
I'M ON IT!
JUST IN TIME!
IT'S NOT NICE TO HURT ANIMALS!
OW! OW! OW!
POW BIFF BAM
DO YOU ENJOY BUILDING TRAPS FOR RHINOS?!
I PROMISE-- NEVER AGAIN!
NO WAY! LEAVE THOSE BUNNIES ALONE!
CRONK
MISSION ACCOMPLISHED!
DON'T WORRY... ANIMALS HAVE NOTHING TO FEAR FROM US.
RIGHT, WENDY?
YOU BET!
MY SISTER HAS GONE OVER TO THE DARK SIDE!
DIE! DIE! DIE!
STOMP
STOMP
STOMP
CAZENOVE & WILLIAM

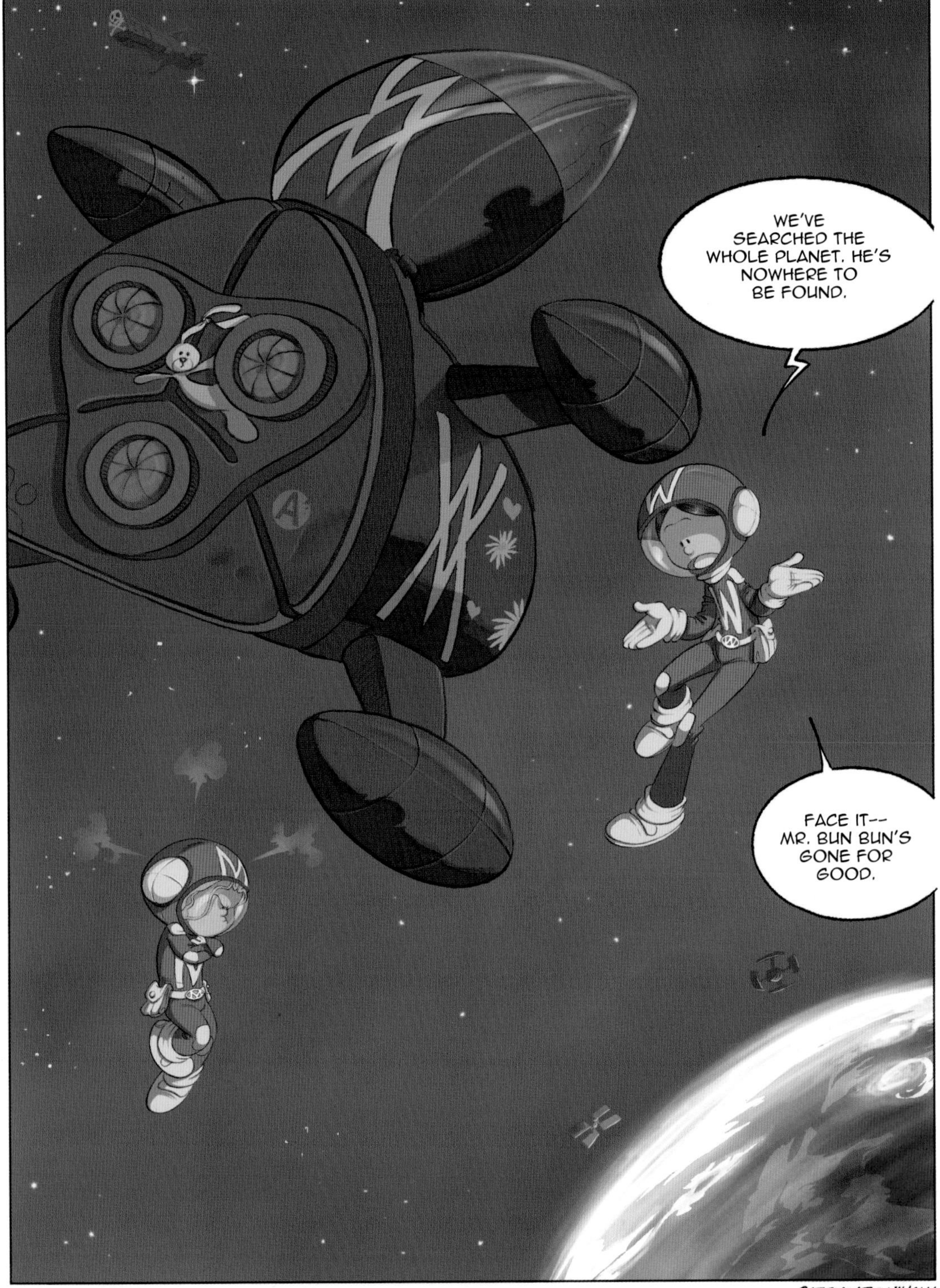
WE'VE SEARCHED THE WHOLE PLANET. HE'S NOWHERE TO BE FOUND.
FACE IT-- MR. BUN BUN'S GONE FOR GOOD.

CAZENOVE & WILLIAM

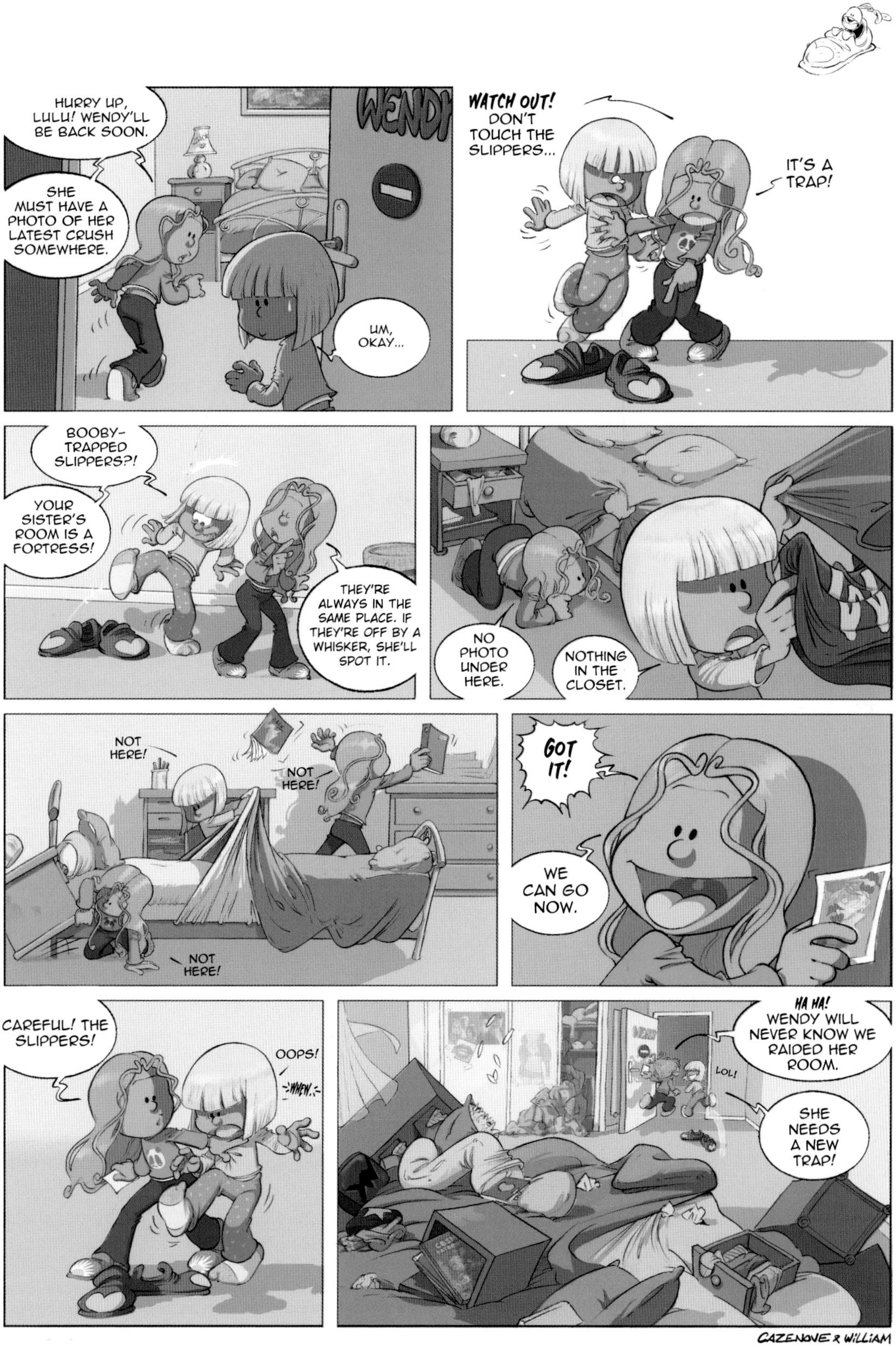
HURRY UP, LULU! WENDY'LL BE BACK SOON.
SHE MUST HAVE A PHOTO OF HER LATEST CRUSH SOMEWHERE.
UM, OKAY...
WATCH OUT! DON'T TOUCH THE SLIPPERS...
IT'S A TRAP!
BOOBY-TRAPPED SLIPPERS?!
YOUR SISTER'S ROOM IS A FORTRESS!
THEY'RE ALWAYS IN THE SAME PLACE. IF THEY'RE OFF BY A WHISKER, SHE'LL SPOT IT.
NO PHOTO UNDER HERE.
NOTHING IN THE CLOSET.
NOT HERE!
NOT HERE!
NOT HERE!
GOT IT!
WE CAN GO NOW.
CAREFUL! THE SLIPPERS!
OOPS!
WHEW.
HA HA! WENDY WILL NEVER KNOW WE RAIDED HER ROOM.
LOL!
SHE NEEDS A NEW TRAP!
CAZENOVE & WILLIAM

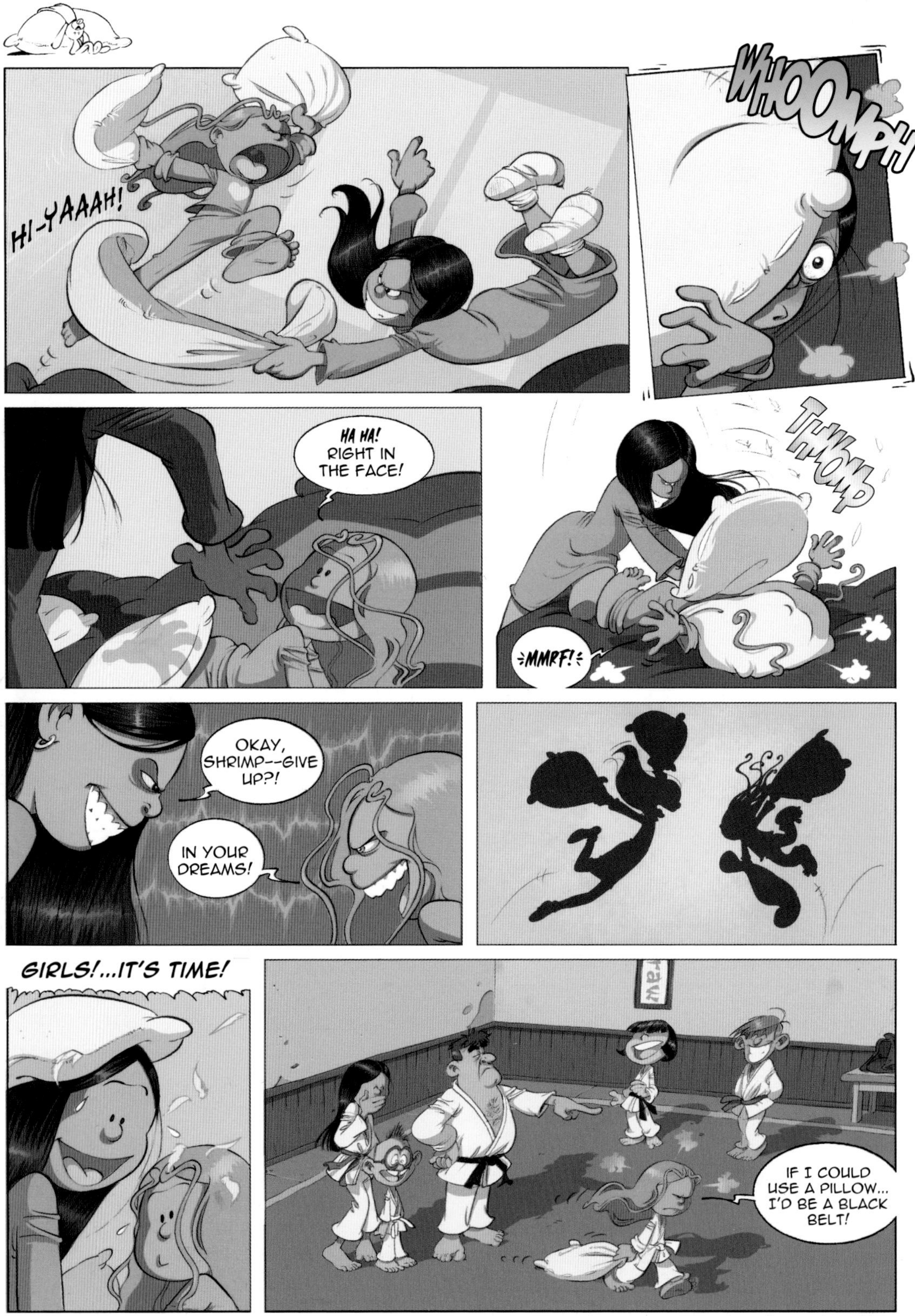
HI-YAAAH!
WHOOOMPH
HA HA! RIGHT IN THE FACE!
THWOMP
MMRF!
OKAY, SHRIMP--GIVE UP?!
IN YOUR DREAMS!
GIRLS! ...IT'S TIME!
IF I COULD USE A PILLOW... I'D BE A BLACK BELT!
CAZENOVE & WILLIAM

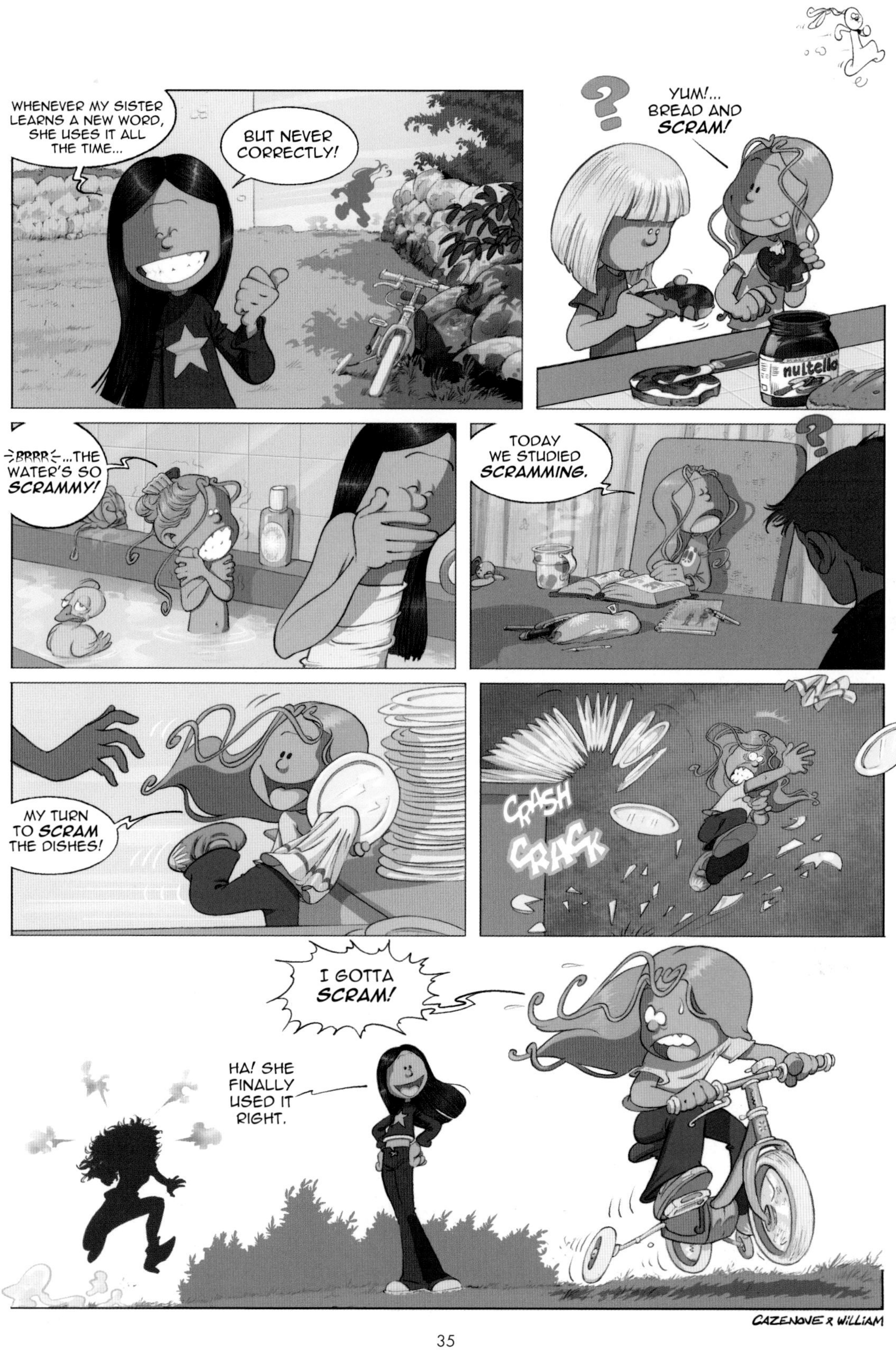

WHENEVER MY SISTER LEARNS A NEW WORD, SHE USES IT ALL THE TIME...
BUT NEVER CORRECTLY!
YUM!... BREAD AND SCRAM!
nultello
BRRR ...THE WATER'S SO SCRAMMY!
TODAY WE STUDIED SCRAMMING.
MY TURN TO SCRAM THE DISHES!
CRASH
CRACK
I GOTTA SCRAM!
HA! SHE FINALLY USED IT RIGHT.
CAZENOVE & WILLIAM

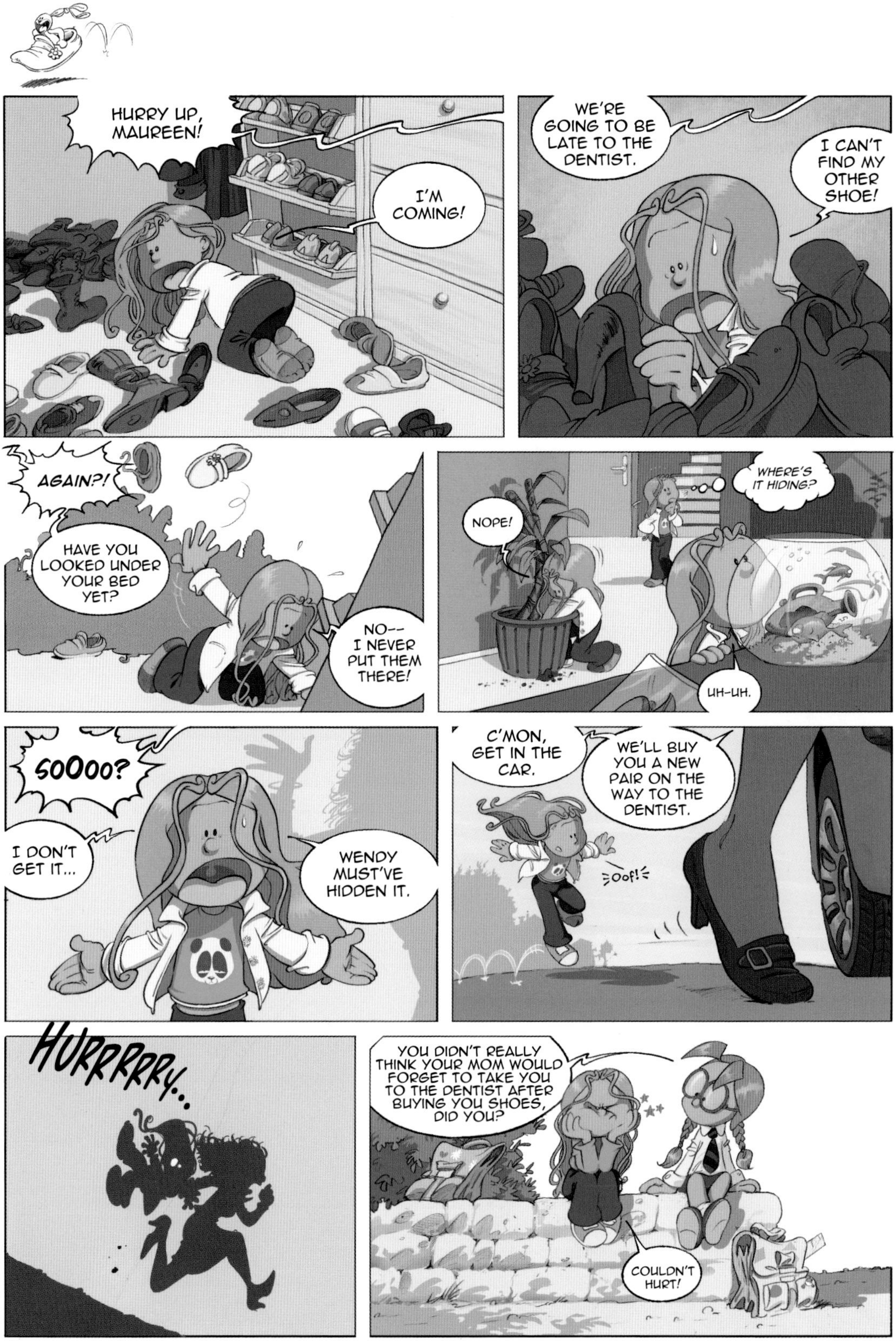
HURRY UP, MAUREEN!
I'M COMING!
WE'RE GOING TO BE LATE TO THE DENTIST.
I CAN'T FIND MY OTHER SHOE!
AGAIN?!
HAVE YOU LOOKED UNDER YOUR BED YET?
NO-- I NEVER PUT THEM THERE!
NOPE!
WHERE'S IT HIDING?
UH-UH.
SOOOO?
I DON'T GET IT...
WENDY MUST'VE HIDDEN IT.
C'MON, GET IN THE CAR.
WE'LL BUY YOU A NEW PAIR ON THE WAY TO THE DENTIST.
OOF!
HURRRRRY...
YOU DIDN'T REALLY THINK YOUR MOM WOULD FORGET TO TAKE YOU TO THE DENTIST AFTER BUYING YOU SHOES, DID YOU?
COULDN'T HURT!
CAZENOVE & WILLIAM

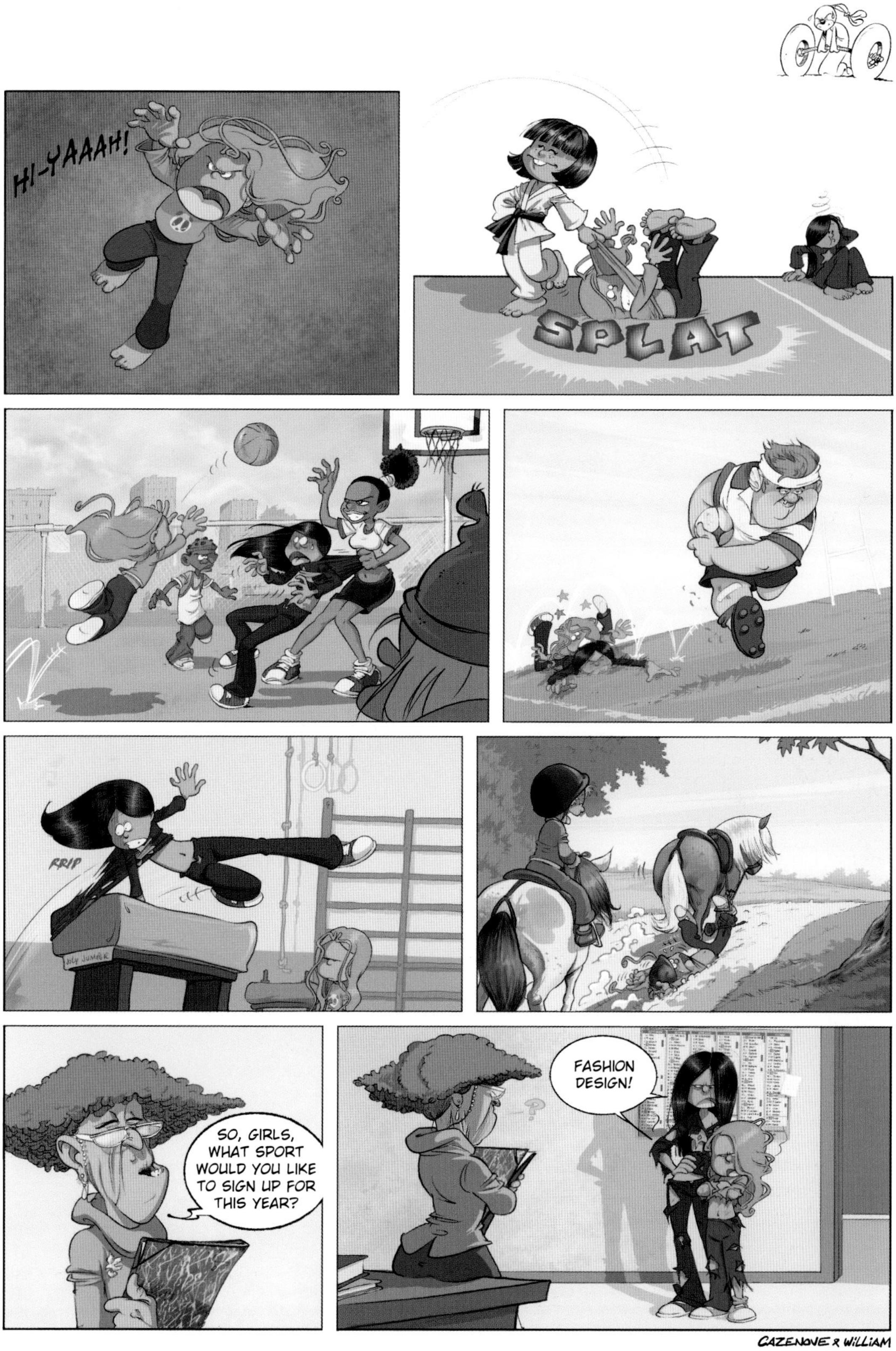
HI-YAAAH!
SPLAT
RRIP
SO, GIRLS, WHAT SPORT WOULD YOU LIKE TO SIGN UP FOR THIS YEAR?
FASHION DESIGN!
CAZENOVE & WILLIAM

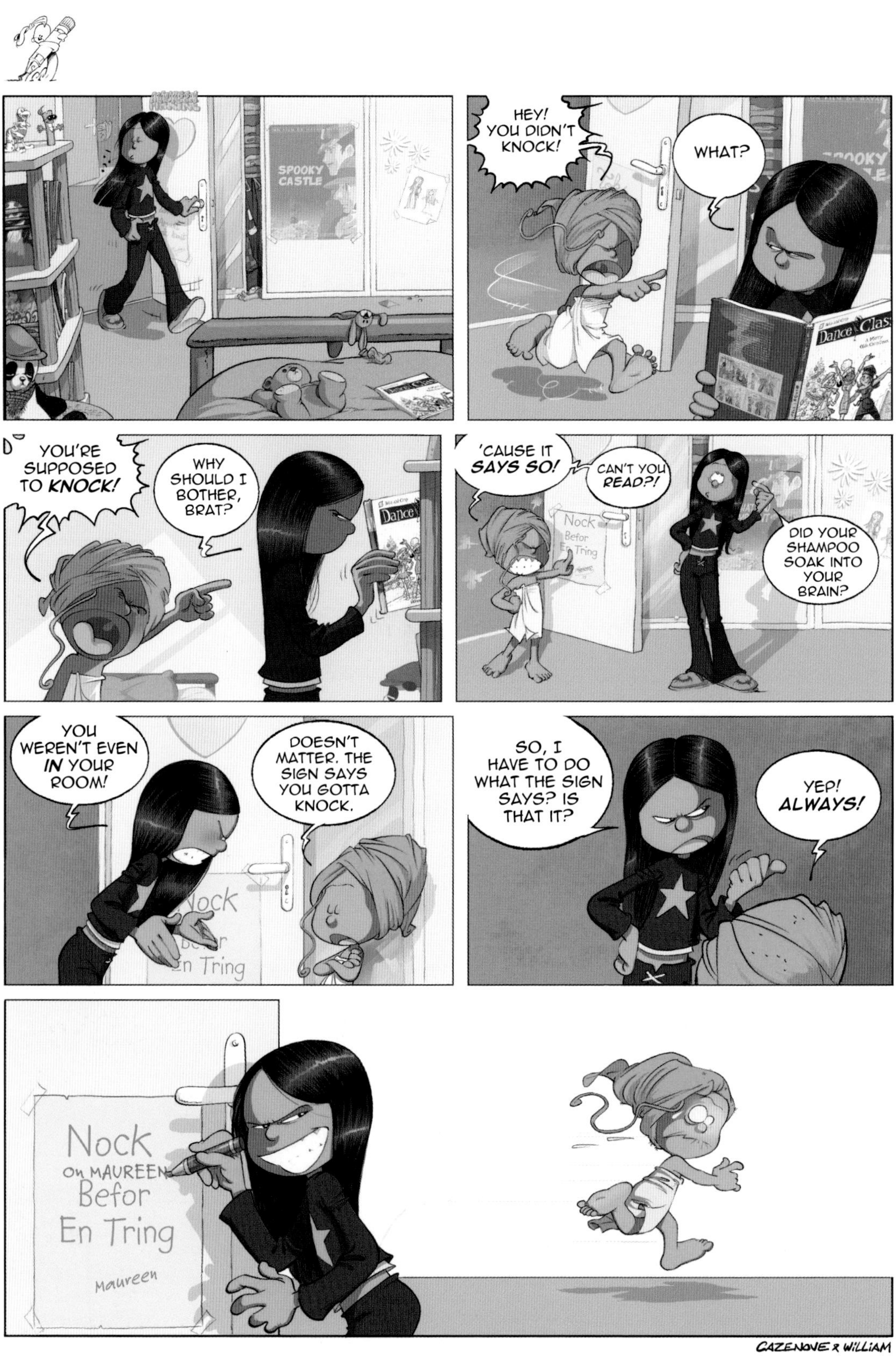

HEY! YOU DIDN'T KNOCK!
WHAT?
YOU'RE SUPPOSED TO KNOCK!
WHY SHOULD I BOTHER, BRAT?
'CAUSE IT SAYS SO!
CAN'T YOU READ?!
Nock Befor En Tring
DID YOUR SHAMPOO SOAK INTO YOUR BRAIN?
YOU WEREN'T EVEN IN YOUR ROOM!
DOESN'T MATTER. THE SIGN SAYS YOU GOTTA KNOCK.
SO, I HAVE TO DO WHAT THE SIGN SAYS? IS THAT IT?
YEP! ALWAYS!
Nock on MAUREEN Befor En Tring
Maureen

CAZENOVE & WILLIAM

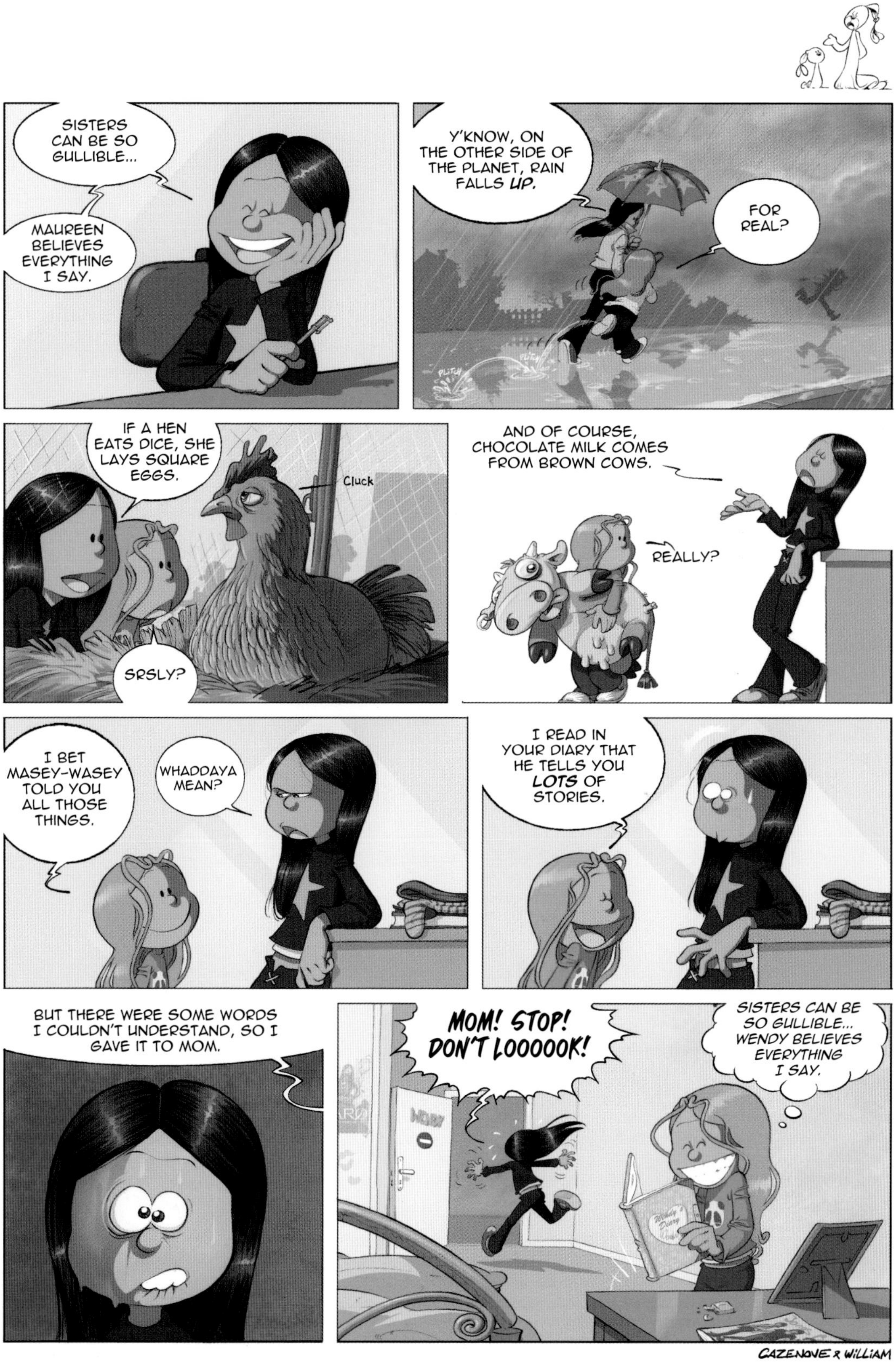

SISTERS CAN BE SO GULLIBLE...
MAUREEN BELIEVES EVERYTHING I SAY.
Y'KNOW, ON THE OTHER SIDE OF THE PLANET, RAIN FALLS *UP.*
FOR REAL?
IF A HEN EATS DICE, SHE LAYS SQUARE EGGS.
Cluck
SRSLY?
AND OF COURSE, CHOCOLATE MILK COMES FROM BROWN COWS.
REALLY?
I BET MASEY-WASEY TOLD YOU ALL THOSE THINGS.
WHADDAYA MEAN?
I READ IN YOUR DIARY THAT HE TELLS YOU **LOTS** OF STORIES.
BUT THERE WERE SOME WORDS I COULDN'T UNDERSTAND, SO I GAVE IT TO MOM.
MOM! STOP! DON'T LOOOOOK!
SISTERS CAN BE SO GULLIBLE... WENDY BELIEVES EVERYTHING I SAY.
CAZENOVE & WILLIAM

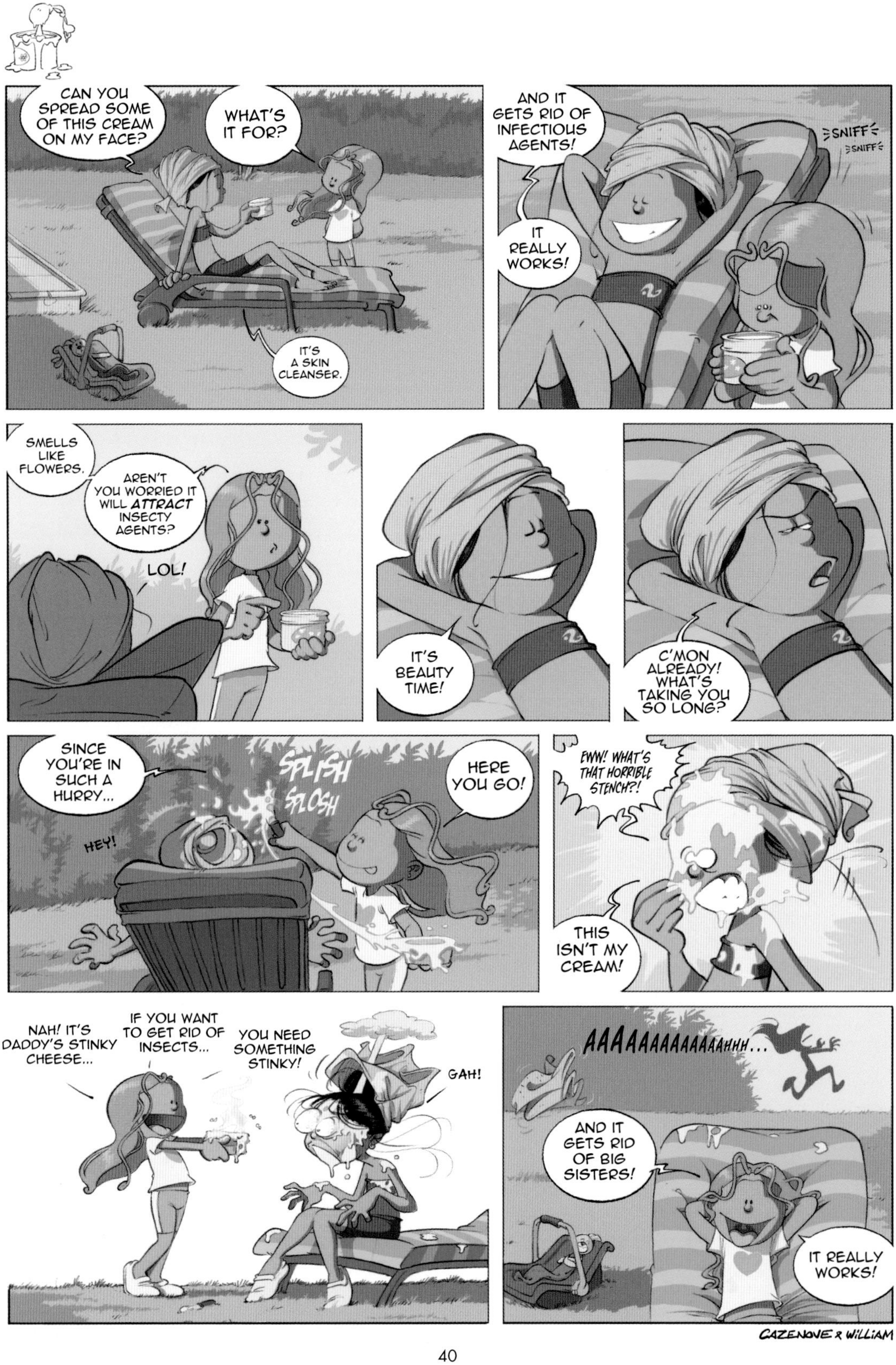
CAN YOU SPREAD SOME OF THIS CREAM ON MY FACE?
WHAT'S IT FOR?
IT'S A SKIN CLEANSER.
AND IT GETS RID OF INFECTIOUS AGENTS!
IT REALLY WORKS!
SNIFF
SNIFF
SMELLS LIKE FLOWERS.
AREN'T YOU WORRIED IT WILL ATTRACT INSECTY AGENTS?
LOL!
IT'S BEAUTY TIME!
C'MON ALREADY! WHAT'S TAKING YOU SO LONG?
SINCE YOU'RE IN SUCH A HURRY...
HEY!
SPLISH
SPLOSH
HERE YOU GO!
EWW! WHAT'S THAT HORRIBLE STENCH?!
THIS ISN'T MY CREAM!
NAH! IT'S DADDY'S STINKY CHEESE...
IF YOU WANT TO GET RID OF INSECTS...
YOU NEED SOMETHING STINKY!
GAH!
AAAAAAAAAAAAAHHH...
AND IT GETS RID OF BIG SISTERS!
IT REALLY WORKS!
CAZENOVE & WILLIAM

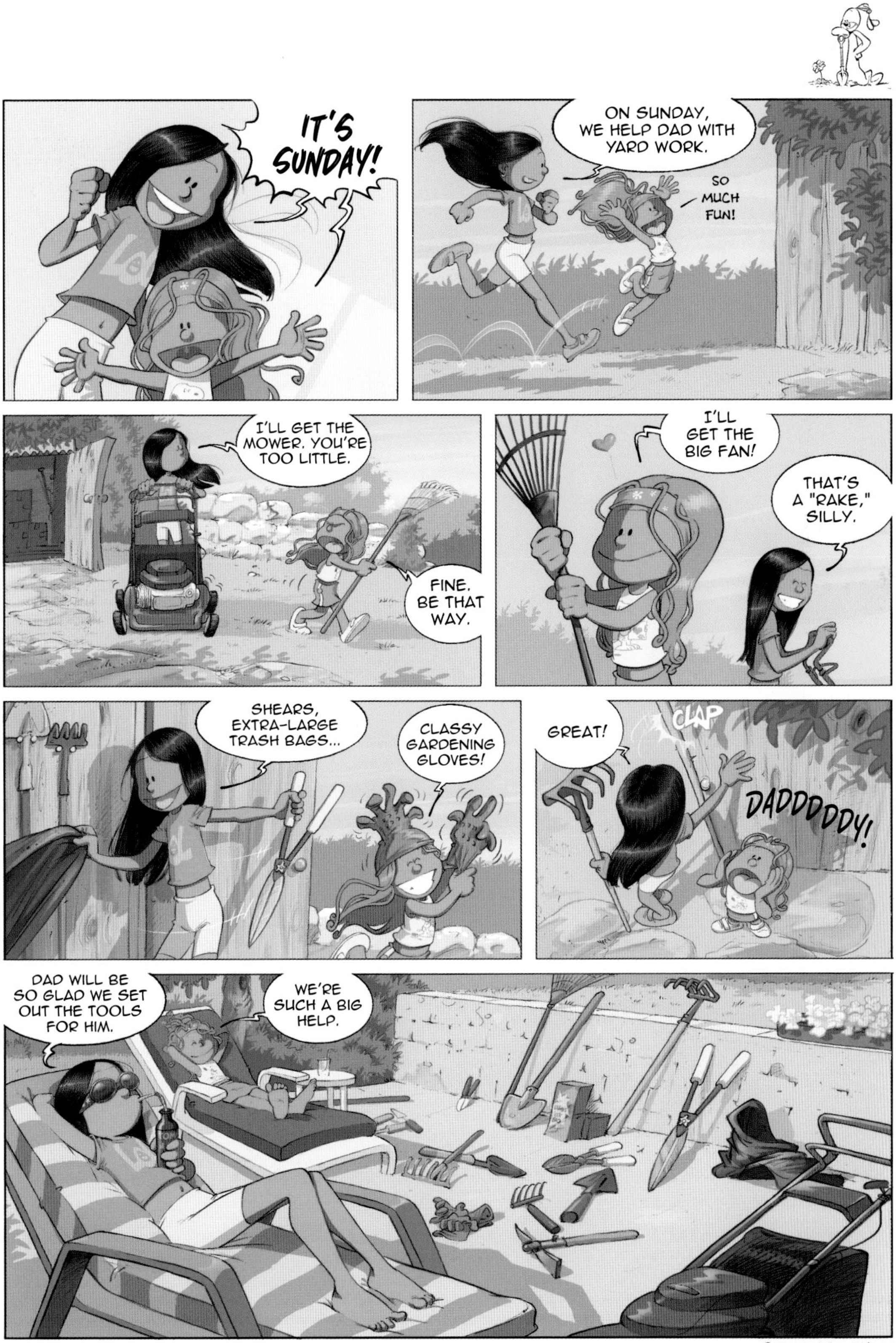
IT'S SUNDAY!
ON SUNDAY, WE HELP DAD WITH YARD WORK.
SO MUCH FUN!
I'LL GET THE MOWER. YOU'RE TOO LITTLE.
FINE. BE THAT WAY.
I'LL GET THE BIG FAN!
THAT'S A "RAKE," SILLY.
SHEARS, EXTRA-LARGE TRASH BAGS...
CLASSY GARDENING GLOVES!
GREAT!
CLAP
DADDDDDY!
DAD WILL BE SO GLAD WE SET OUT THE TOOLS FOR HIM.
WE'RE SUCH A BIG HELP.
CAZENOVE & WILLIAM

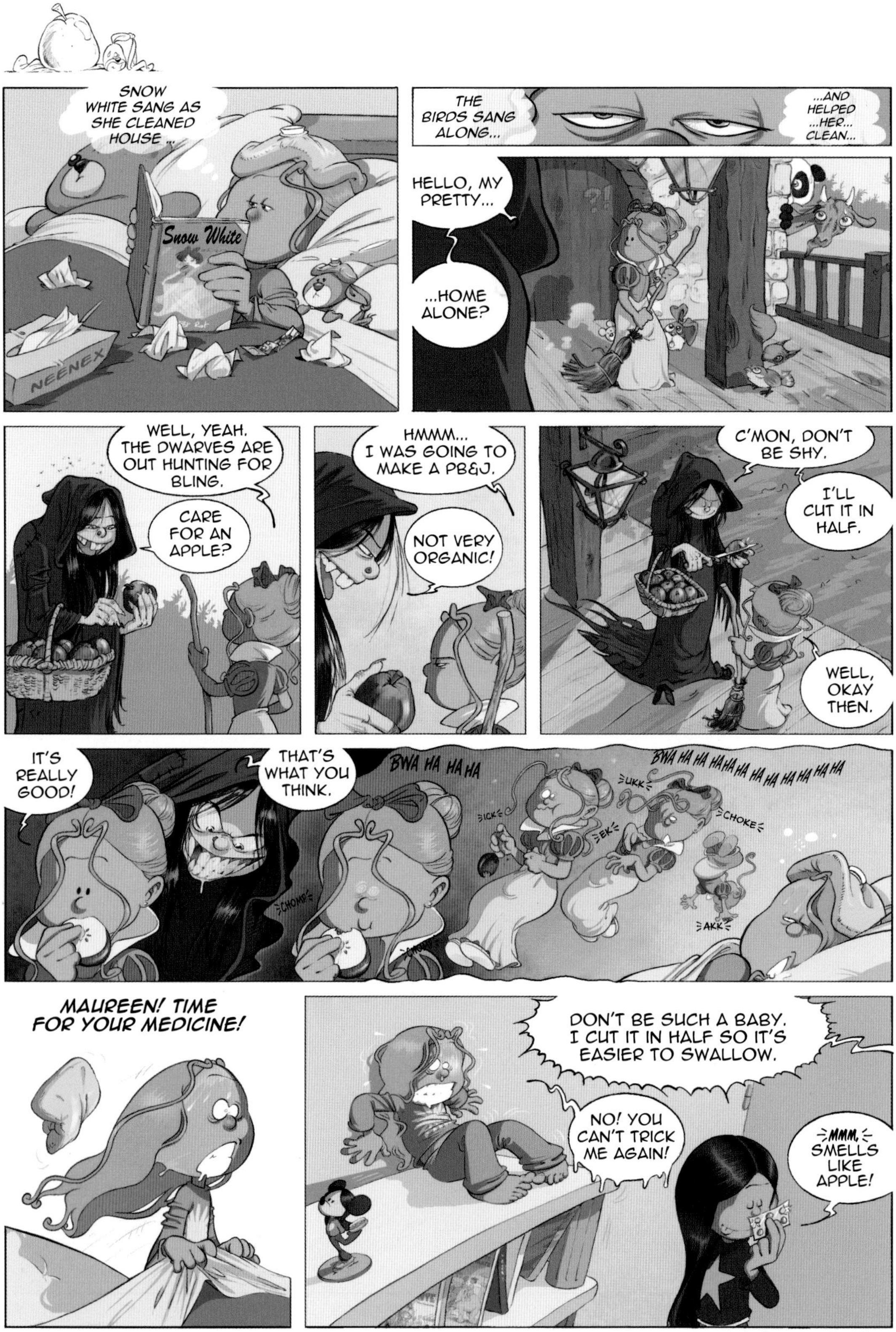
SNOW WHITE SANG AS SHE CLEANED HOUSE ...
Snow White
NEENEX
THE BIRDS SANG ALONG...
...AND HELPED ...HER... CLEAN...
HELLO, MY PRETTY...
...HOME ALONE?
WELL, YEAH. THE DWARVES ARE OUT HUNTING FOR BLING.
CARE FOR AN APPLE?
HMMM... I WAS GOING TO MAKE A PB&J.
NOT VERY ORGANIC!
C'MON, DON'T BE SHY.
I'LL CUT IT IN HALF.
WELL, OKAY THEN.
IT'S REALLY GOOD!
THAT'S WHAT YOU THINK.
BWA HA HA HA
CHOMP
BWA HA HA HA HA HA HA HA HA HA HA HA HA HA
ICK
UKK
EK
CHOKE
AKK
MAUREEN! TIME FOR YOUR MEDICINE!
DON'T BE SUCH A BABY. I CUT IT IN HALF SO IT'S EASIER TO SWALLOW.
NO! YOU CAN'T TRICK ME AGAIN!
MMM, SMELLS LIKE APPLE!
CAZENOVE & WILLIAM

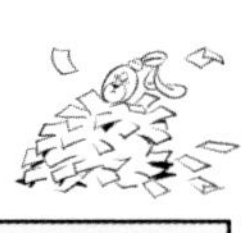

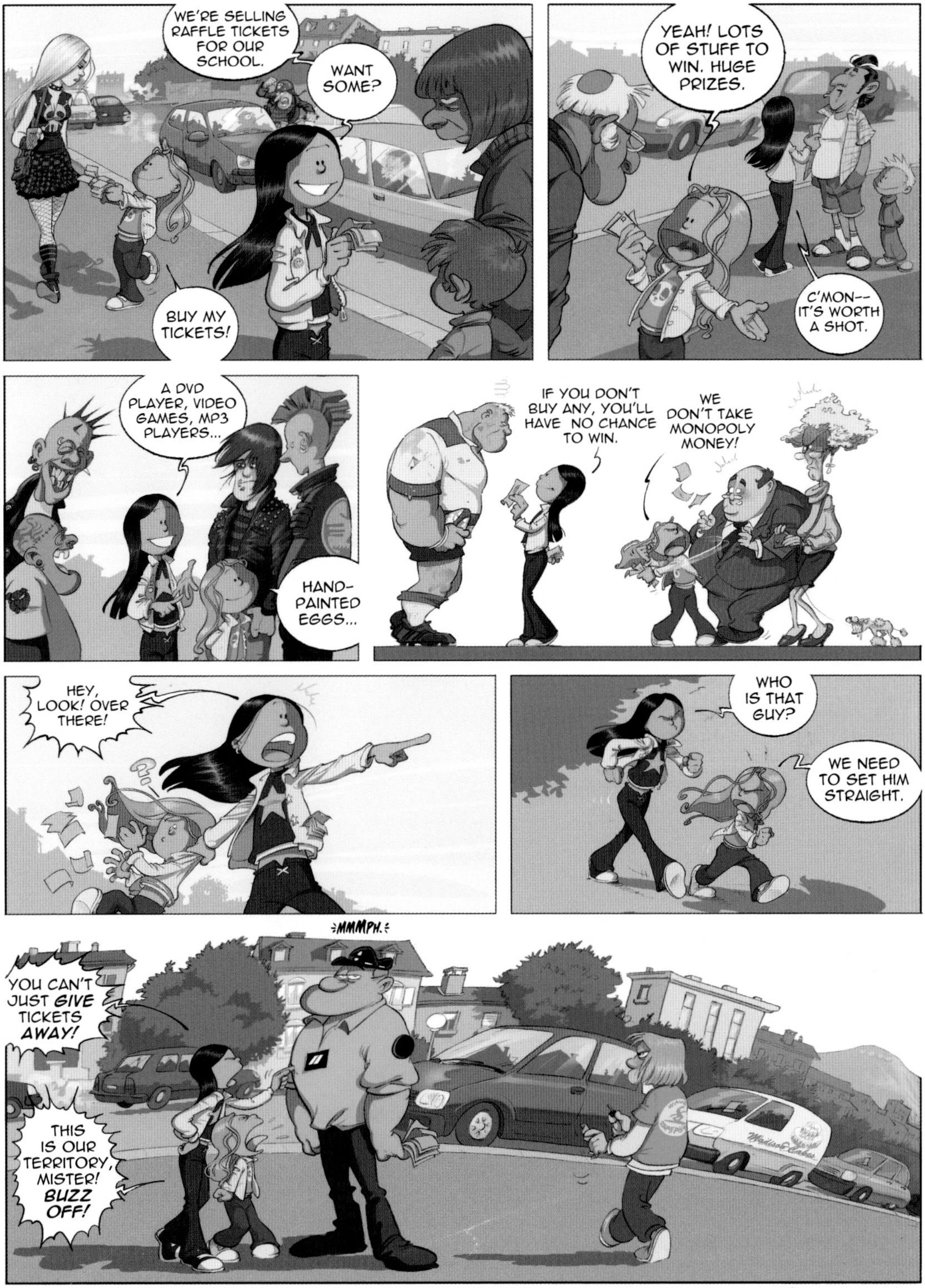

WE'RE SELLING RAFFLE TICKETS FOR OUR SCHOOL.
WANT SOME?
BUY MY TICKETS!
YEAH! LOTS OF STUFF TO WIN. HUGE PRIZES.
C'MON-- IT'S WORTH A SHOT.
A DVD PLAYER, VIDEO GAMES, MP3 PLAYERS...
HAND-PAINTED EGGS...
IF YOU DON'T BUY ANY, YOU'LL HAVE NO CHANCE TO WIN.
WE DON'T TAKE MONOPOLY MONEY!
HEY, LOOK! OVER THERE!
WHO IS THAT GUY?
WE NEED TO SET HIM STRAIGHT.
MMMPH.
YOU CAN'T JUST *GIVE* TICKETS *AWAY!*
THIS IS OUR TERRITORY, MISTER! ***BUZZ OFF!***

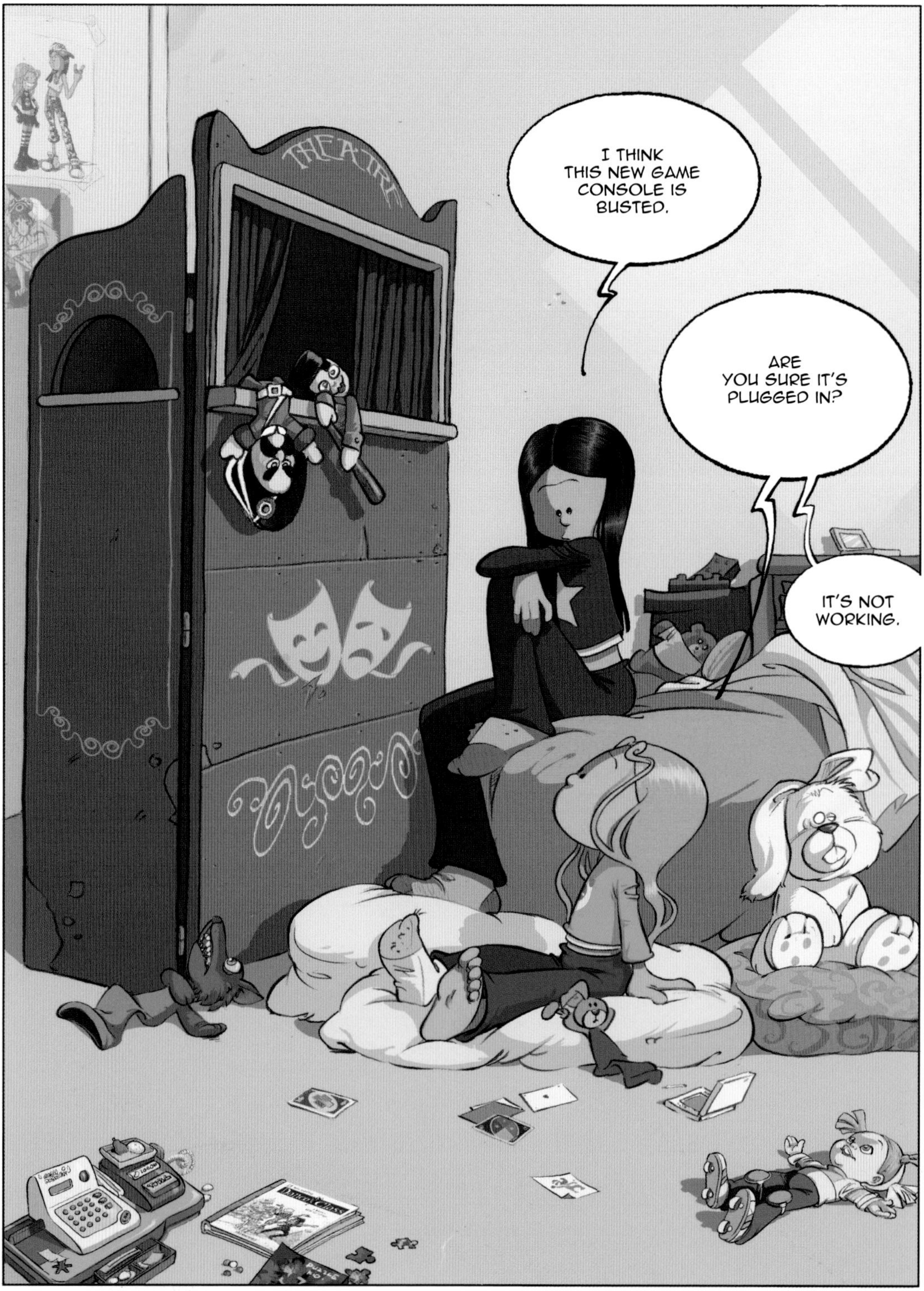
I THINK THIS NEW GAME CONSOLE IS BUSTED.
ARE YOU SURE IT'S PLUGGED IN?
IT'S NOT WORKING.

CAZENOVE & WILLIAM

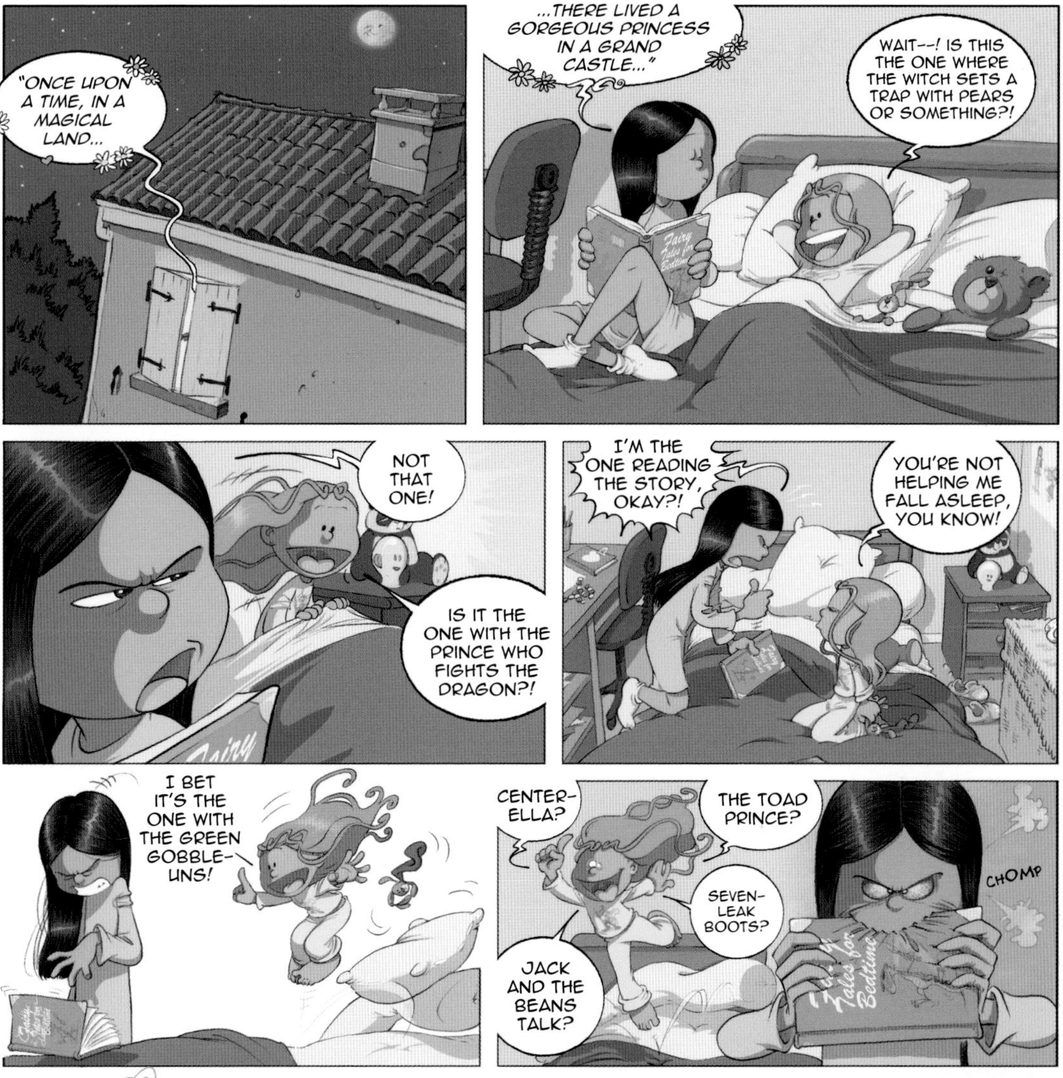
"ONCE UPON A TIME, IN A MAGICAL LAND...
...THERE LIVED A GORGEOUS PRINCESS IN A GRAND CASTLE..."
WAIT--! IS THIS THE ONE WHERE THE WITCH SETS A TRAP WITH PEARS OR SOMETHING?!
Fairy Tales for Bedtime
NOT THAT ONE!
IS IT THE ONE WITH THE PRINCE WHO FIGHTS THE DRAGON?!
I'M THE ONE READING THE STORY, OKAY?!
YOU'RE NOT HELPING ME FALL ASLEEP, YOU KNOW!
I BET IT'S THE ONE WITH THE GREEN GOBBLE-UNS!
CENTER-ELLA?
THE TOAD PRINCE?
SEVEN-LEAK BOOTS?
JACK AND THE BEANS TALK?
CHOMP
GRRRRR
I DUNNO... THE ONE WITH...ME?!
CAN'T FALL ASLEEP?
NAH! WENDY'S NO GOOD AT TELLING STORIES!

CAZENOVE & WILLIAM

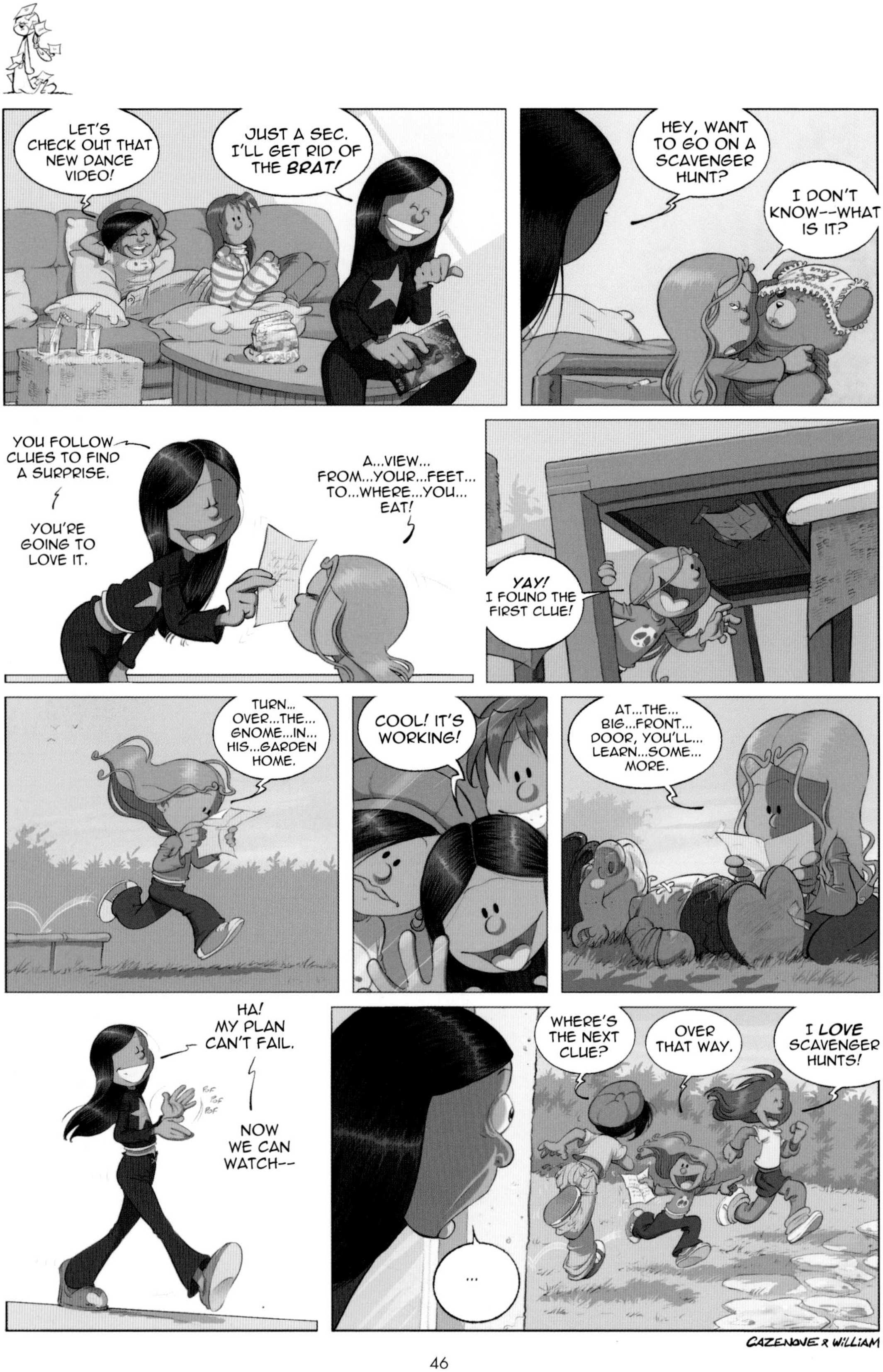
LET'S CHECK OUT THAT NEW DANCE VIDEO!
JUST A SEC. I'LL GET RID OF THE **BRAT!**
HEY, WANT TO GO ON A SCAVENGER HUNT?
I DON'T KNOW--WHAT IS IT?
YOU FOLLOW CLUES TO FIND A SURPRISE.
YOU'RE GOING TO LOVE IT.
A...VIEW... FROM...YOUR...FEET... TO...WHERE...YOU... EAT!
YAY! I FOUND THE FIRST CLUE!
TURN... OVER...THE... GNOME...IN... HIS...GARDEN HOME.
COOL! IT'S WORKING!
AT...THE... BIG...FRONT... DOOR, YOU'LL... LEARN...SOME... MORE.
HA! MY PLAN CAN'T FAIL.
NOW WE CAN WATCH--
...
WHERE'S THE NEXT CLUE?
OVER THAT WAY.
I *LOVE* SCAVENGER HUNTS!
CAZENOVE & WILLIAM

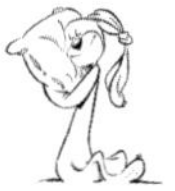

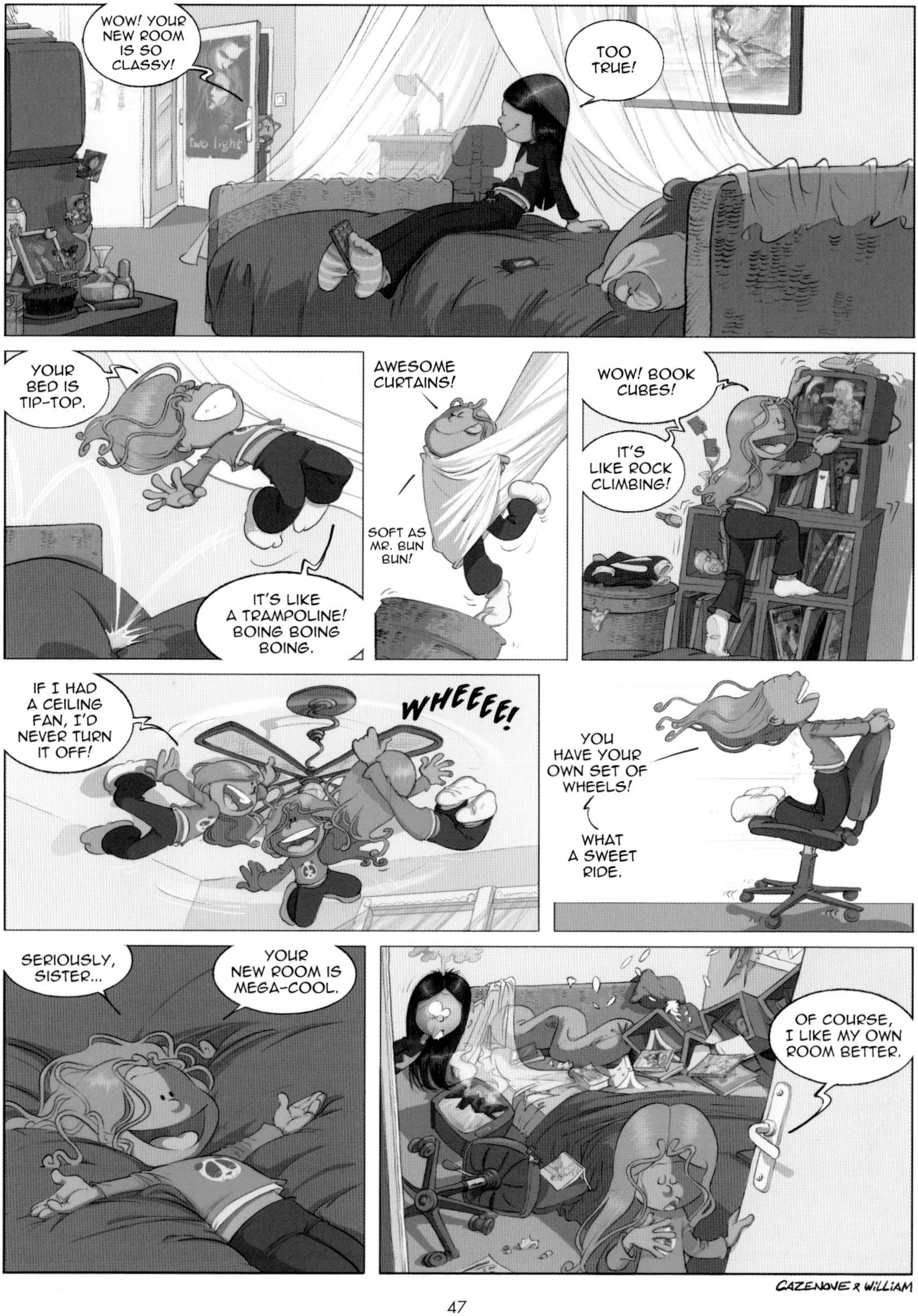
WOW! YOUR NEW ROOM IS SO CLASSY!
two light
TOO TRUE!
YOUR BED IS TIP-TOP.
IT'S LIKE A TRAMPOLINE! BOING BOING BOING.
AWESOME CURTAINS!
SOFT AS MR. BUN BUN!
WOW! BOOK CUBES!
IT'S LIKE ROCK CLIMBING!
IF I HAD A CEILING FAN, I'D NEVER TURN IT OFF!
WHEEEE!
YOU HAVE YOUR OWN SET OF WHEELS!
WHAT A SWEET RIDE.
SERIOUSLY, SISTER...
YOUR NEW ROOM IS MEGA-COOL.
OF COURSE, I LIKE MY OWN ROOM BETTER.

CAZENOVE & WILLIAM

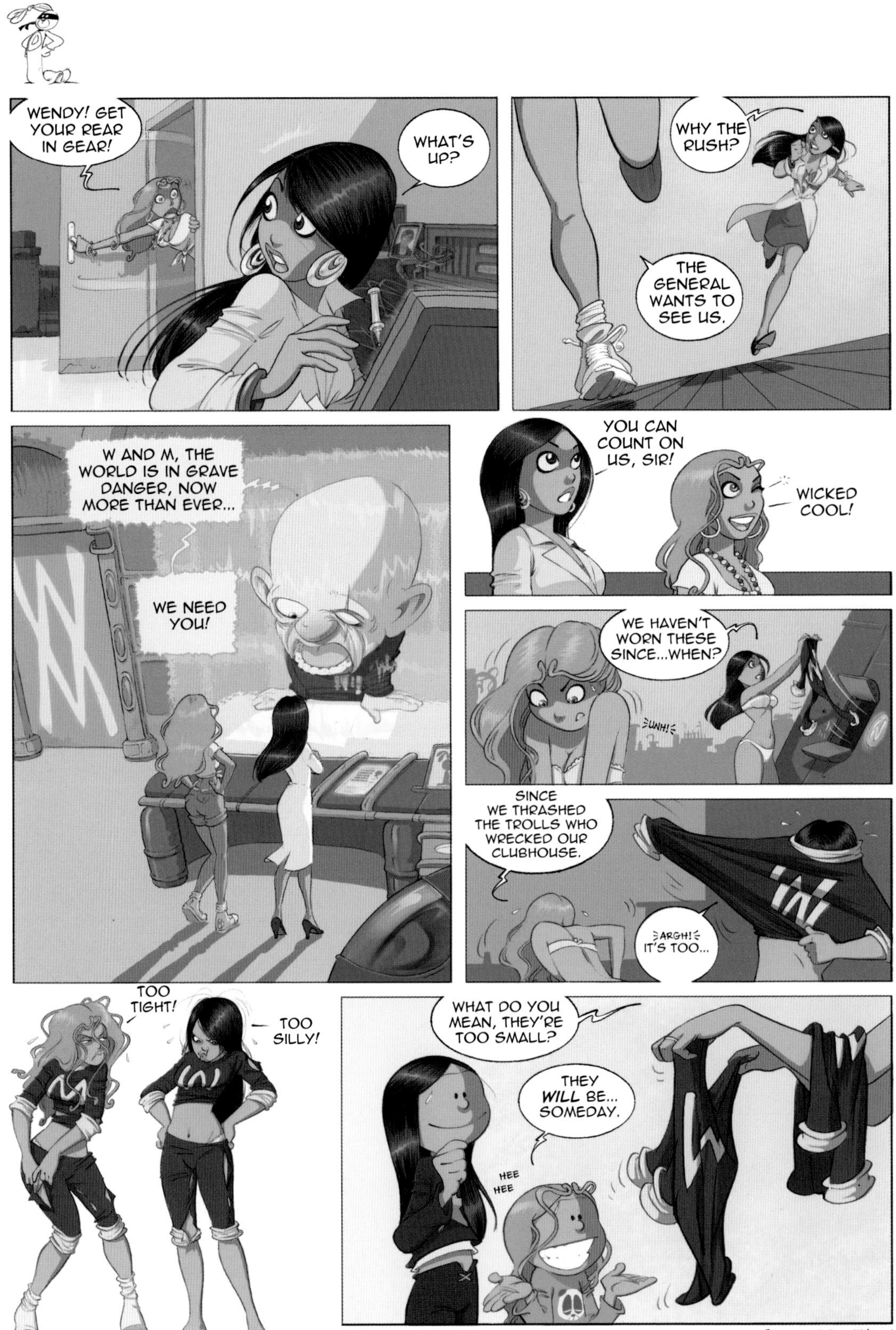
WENDY! GET YOUR REAR IN GEAR!
WHAT'S UP?
WHY THE RUSH?
THE GENERAL WANTS TO SEE US.
W AND M, THE WORLD IS IN GRAVE DANGER, NOW MORE THAN EVER...
WE NEED YOU!
YOU CAN COUNT ON US, SIR!
WICKED COOL!
WE HAVEN'T WORN THESE SINCE...WHEN?
UNH!
SINCE WE THRASHED THE TROLLS WHO WRECKED OUR CLUBHOUSE.
ARGH! IT'S TOO...
TOO TIGHT!
TOO SILLY!
WHAT DO YOU MEAN, THEY'RE TOO SMALL?
THEY *WILL* BE... SOMEDAY.
HEE HEE
CAZENOVE & WILLIAM

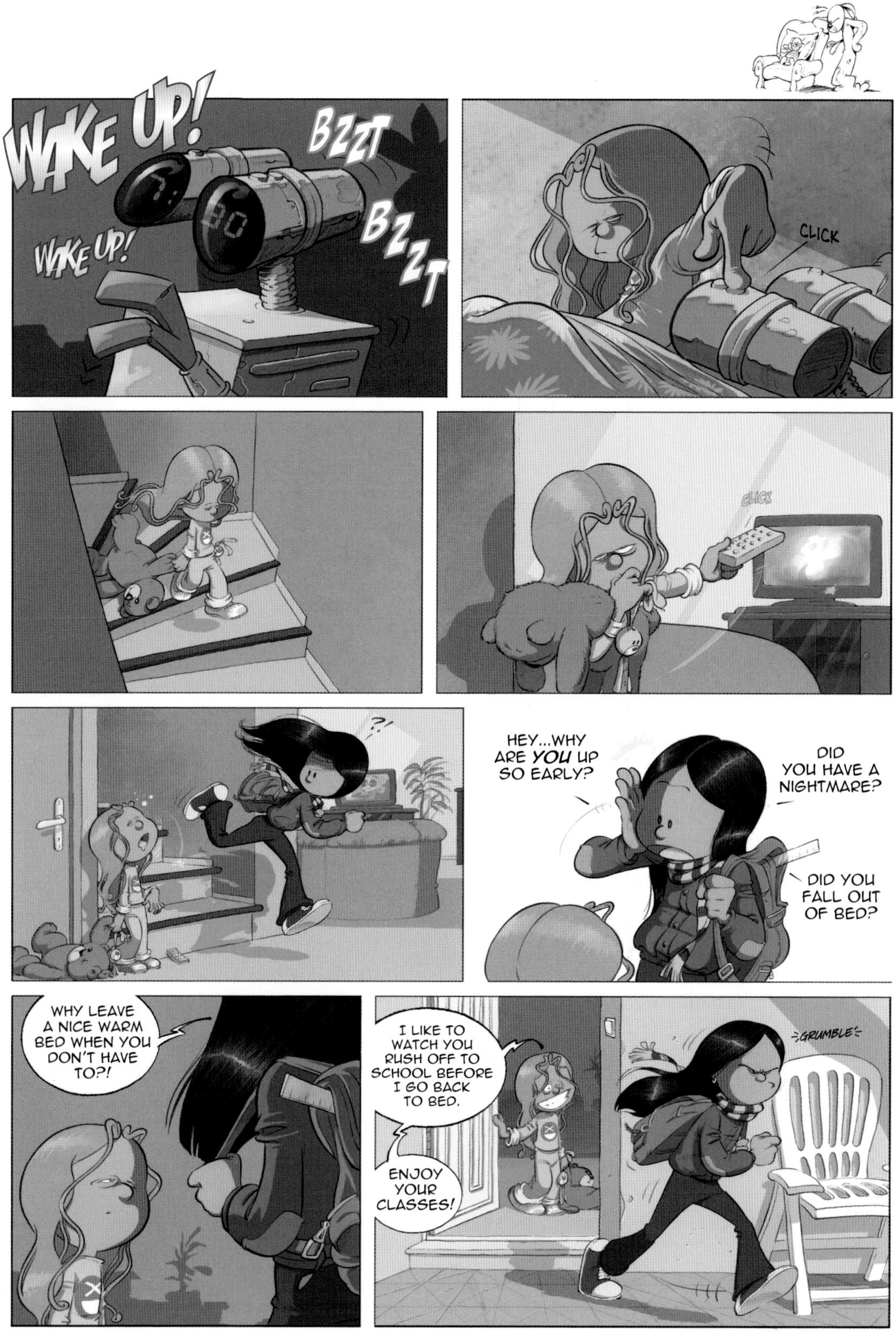
WAKE UP!
BZZT
WAKE UP!
BZZT
CLICK
CLICK
?!
HEY...WHY ARE *YOU* UP SO EARLY?
DID YOU HAVE A NIGHTMARE?
DID YOU FALL OUT OF BED?
WHY LEAVE A NICE WARM BED WHEN YOU DON'T HAVE TO?!
I LIKE TO WATCH YOU RUSH OFF TO SCHOOL BEFORE I GO BACK TO BED.
ENJOY YOUR CLASSES!
GRUMBLE
CAZENOVE & WILLIAM

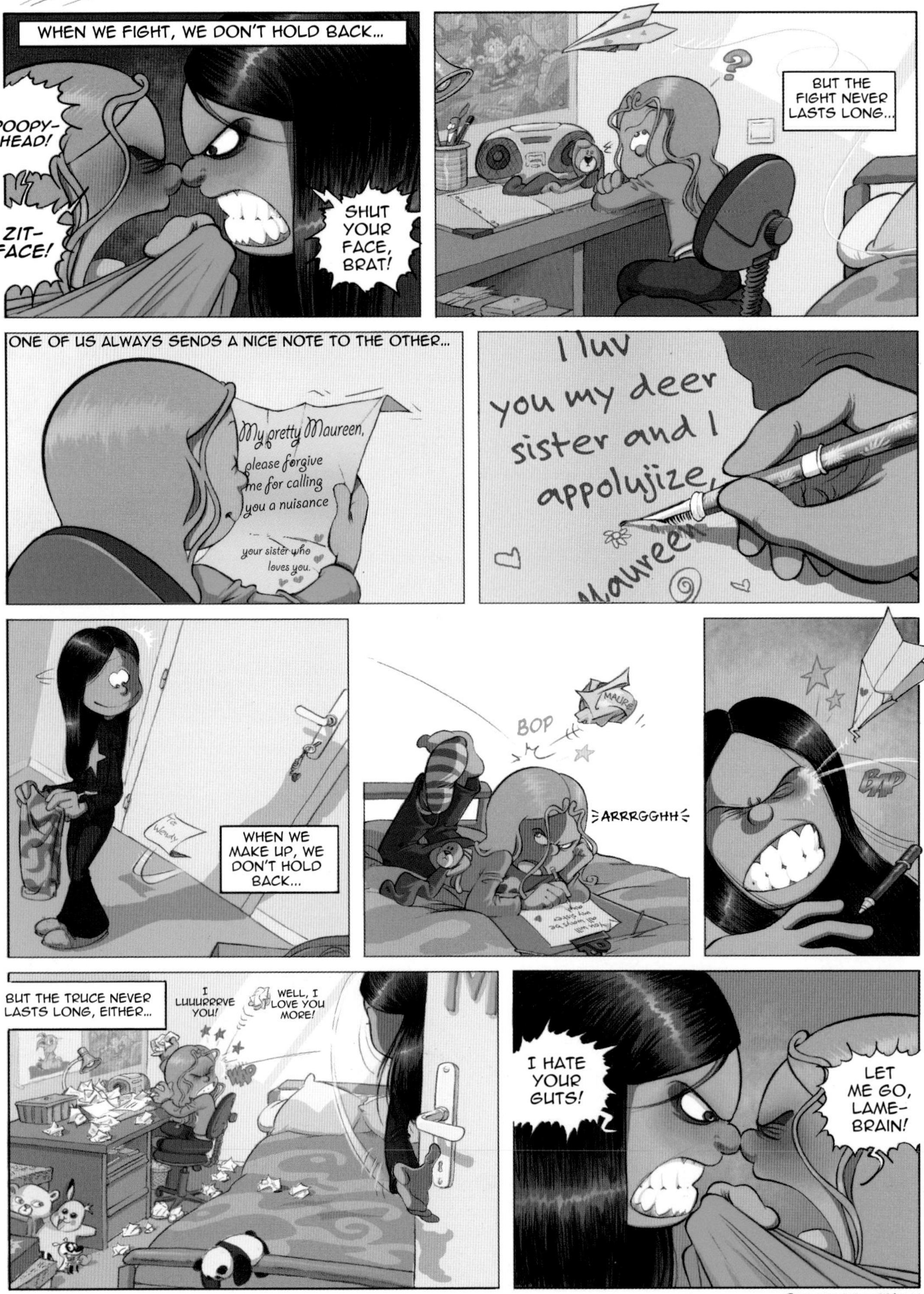
WHEN WE FIGHT, WE DON'T HOLD BACK...
POOPY-HEAD!
ZIT-FACE!
SHUT YOUR FACE, BRAT!
BUT THE FIGHT NEVER LASTS LONG...
ONE OF US ALWAYS SENDS A NICE NOTE TO THE OTHER...
My pretty Maureen, please forgive me for calling you a nuisance
your sister who loves you.
I luv you my deer sister and I appolujize,
Mauree
WHEN WE MAKE UP, WE DON'T HOLD BACK...
BOP
ARRRGGHH
BAP
BUT THE TRUCE NEVER LASTS LONG, EITHER...
I LUUURRRVE YOU!
WELL, I LOVE YOU MORE!
I HATE YOUR GUTS!
LET ME GO, LAME-BRAIN!

CAZENOVE & WILLIAM

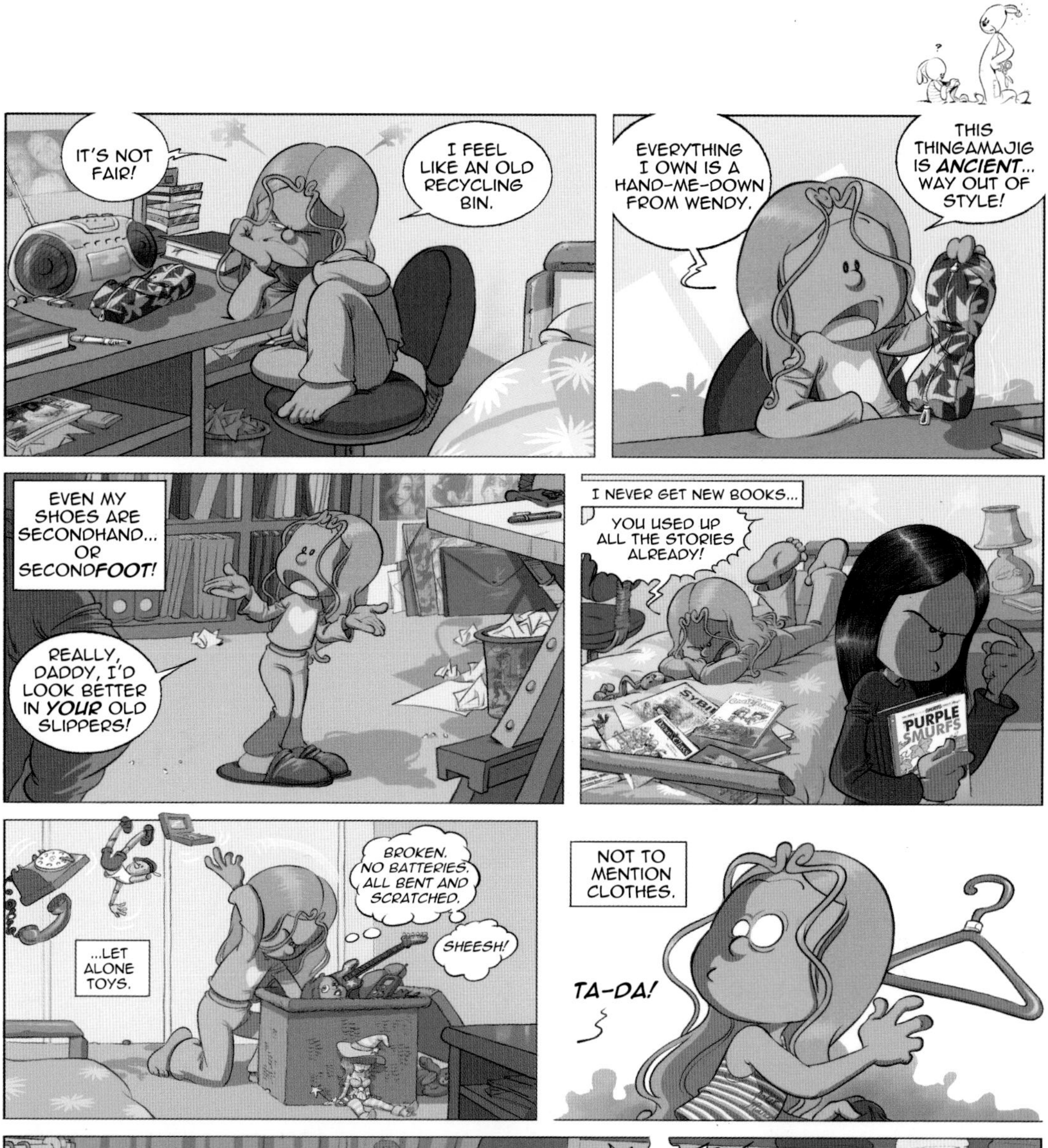
IT'S NOT FAIR!
I FEEL LIKE AN OLD RECYCLING BIN.
EVERYTHING I OWN IS A HAND-ME-DOWN FROM WENDY.
THIS THINGAMAJIG IS ***ANCIENT***... WAY OUT OF STYLE!
EVEN MY SHOES ARE SECONDHAND... OR SECOND***FOOT***!
REALLY, DADDY, I'D LOOK BETTER IN ***YOUR*** OLD SLIPPERS!
I NEVER GET NEW BOOKS...
YOU USED UP ALL THE STORIES ALREADY!
PURPLE SMURFS
...LET ALONE TOYS.
BROKEN. NO BATTERIES. ALL BENT AND SCRATCHED.
SHEESH!
NOT TO MENTION CLOTHES.
TA-DA!
NO WAY! DON'T YOU DARE BUY THAT OUTFIT...
I REFUSE TO WEAR IT!

CAZENOVE & WILLIAM

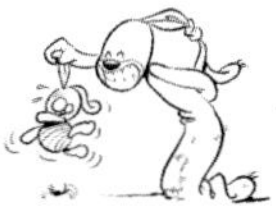

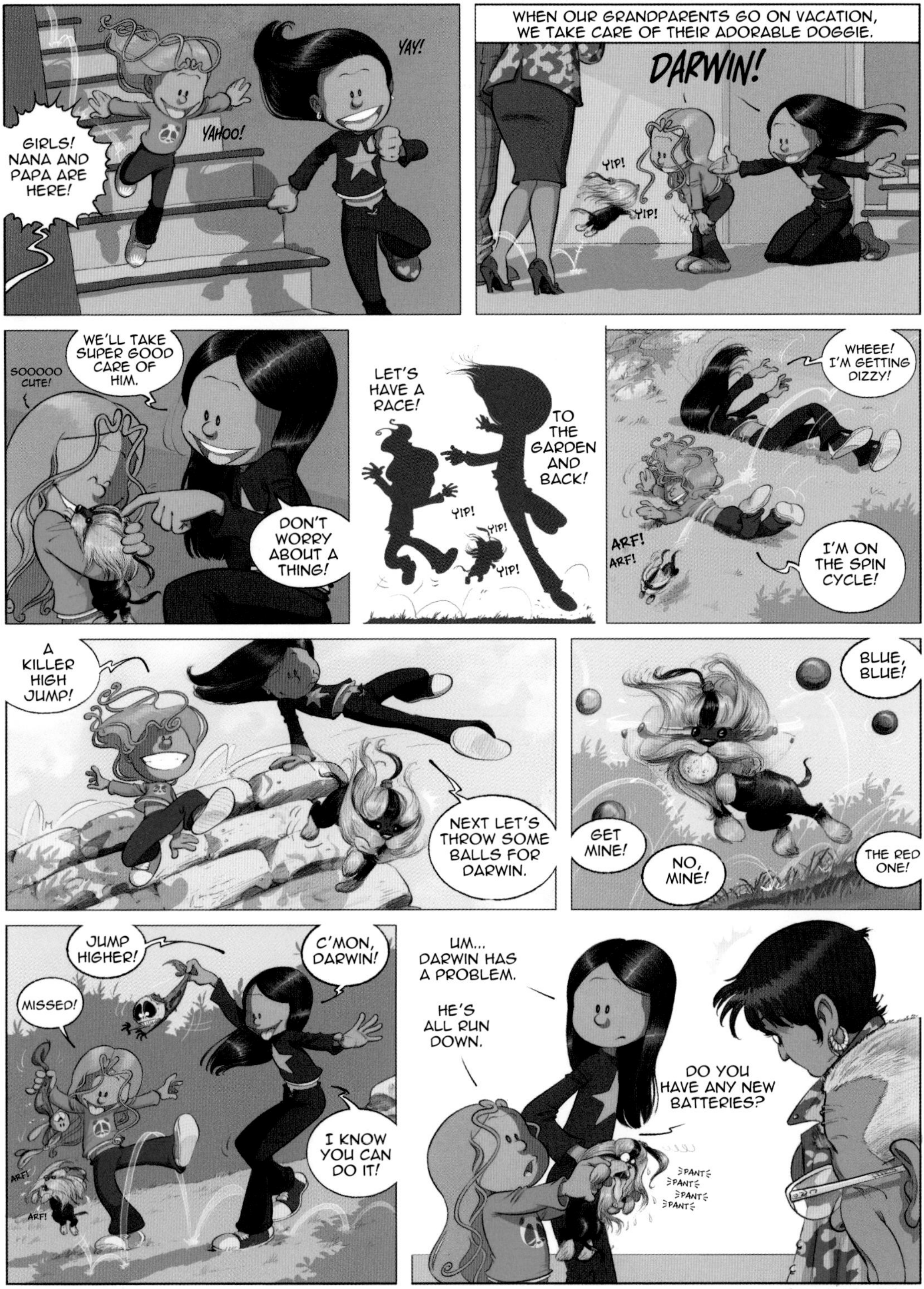
GIRLS! NANA AND PAPA ARE HERE!
YAHOO!
YAY!
WHEN OUR GRANDPARENTS GO ON VACATION, WE TAKE CARE OF THEIR ADORABLE DOGGIE.
DARWIN!
YIP!
YIP!
SOOOOO CUTE!
WE'LL TAKE SUPER GOOD CARE OF HIM.
DON'T WORRY ABOUT A THING!
LET'S HAVE A RACE!
TO THE GARDEN AND BACK!
YIP!
YIP!
YIP!
WHEEE! I'M GETTING DIZZY!
ARF! ARF!
I'M ON THE SPIN CYCLE!
A KILLER HIGH JUMP!
NEXT LET'S THROW SOME BALLS FOR DARWIN.
BLUE, BLUE!
GET MINE!
NO, MINE!
THE RED ONE!
JUMP HIGHER!
C'MON, DARWIN!
MISSED!
ARF!
ARF!
I KNOW YOU CAN DO IT!
UM... DARWIN HAS A PROBLEM.
HE'S ALL RUN DOWN.
DO YOU HAVE ANY NEW BATTERIES?
PANT
PANT
PANT
PANT

CAZENOVE & WILLIAM

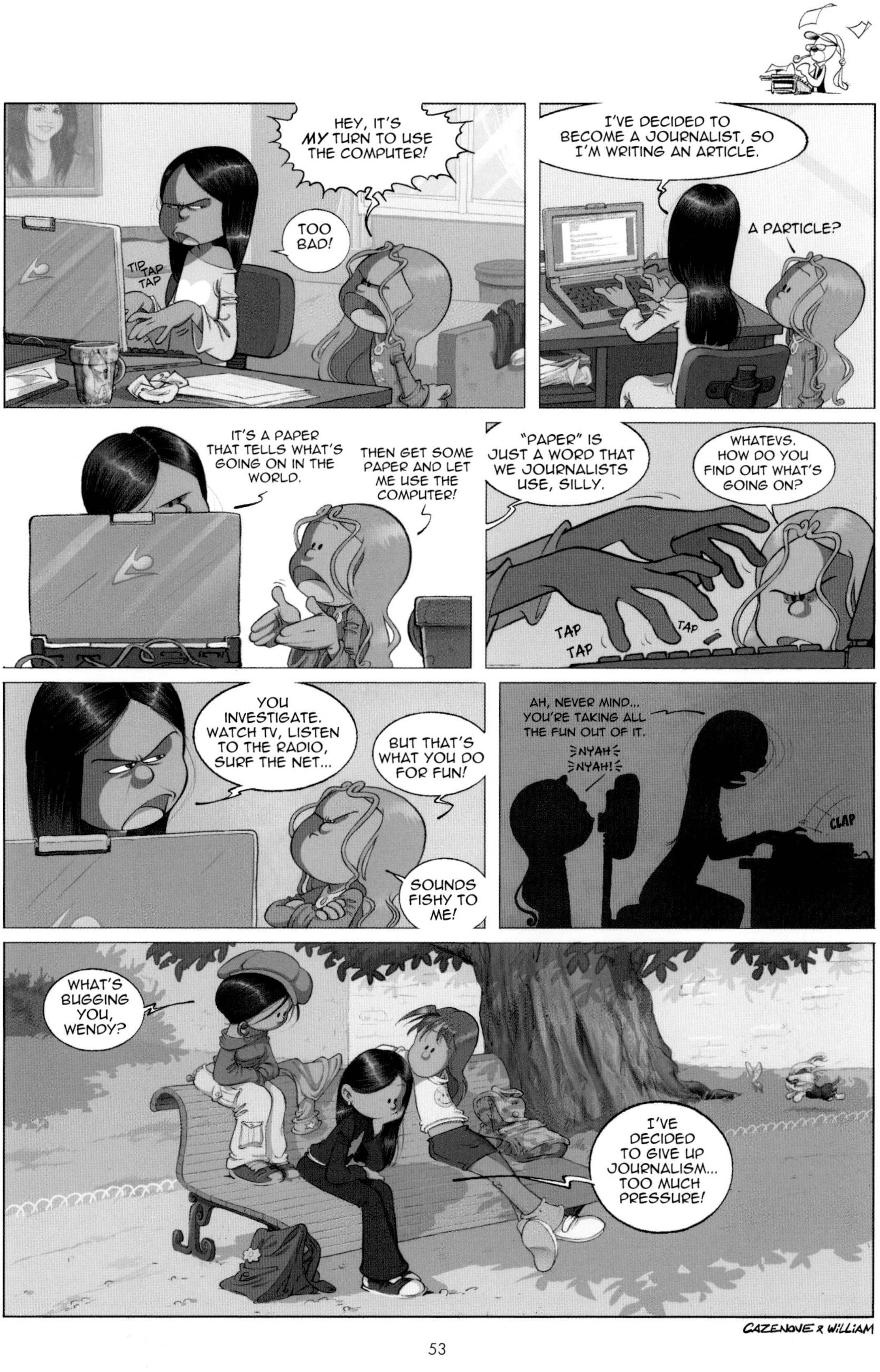
HEY, IT'S MY TURN TO USE THE COMPUTER!
TOO BAD!
TIP TAP TAP
I'VE DECIDED TO BECOME A JOURNALIST, SO I'M WRITING AN ARTICLE.
A PARTICLE?
IT'S A PAPER THAT TELLS WHAT'S GOING ON IN THE WORLD.
THEN GET SOME PAPER AND LET ME USE THE COMPUTER!
"PAPER" IS JUST A WORD THAT WE JOURNALISTS USE, SILLY.
WHATEVS. HOW DO YOU FIND OUT WHAT'S GOING ON?
TAP TAP
TAP
YOU INVESTIGATE. WATCH TV, LISTEN TO THE RADIO, SURF THE NET...
BUT THAT'S WHAT YOU DO FOR FUN!
SOUNDS FISHY TO ME!
AH, NEVER MIND... YOU'RE TAKING ALL THE FUN OUT OF IT.
NYAH NYAH!
CLAP
WHAT'S BUGGING YOU, WENDY?
I'VE DECIDED TO GIVE UP JOURNALISM... TOO MUCH PRESSURE!
CAZENOVE & WILLIAM

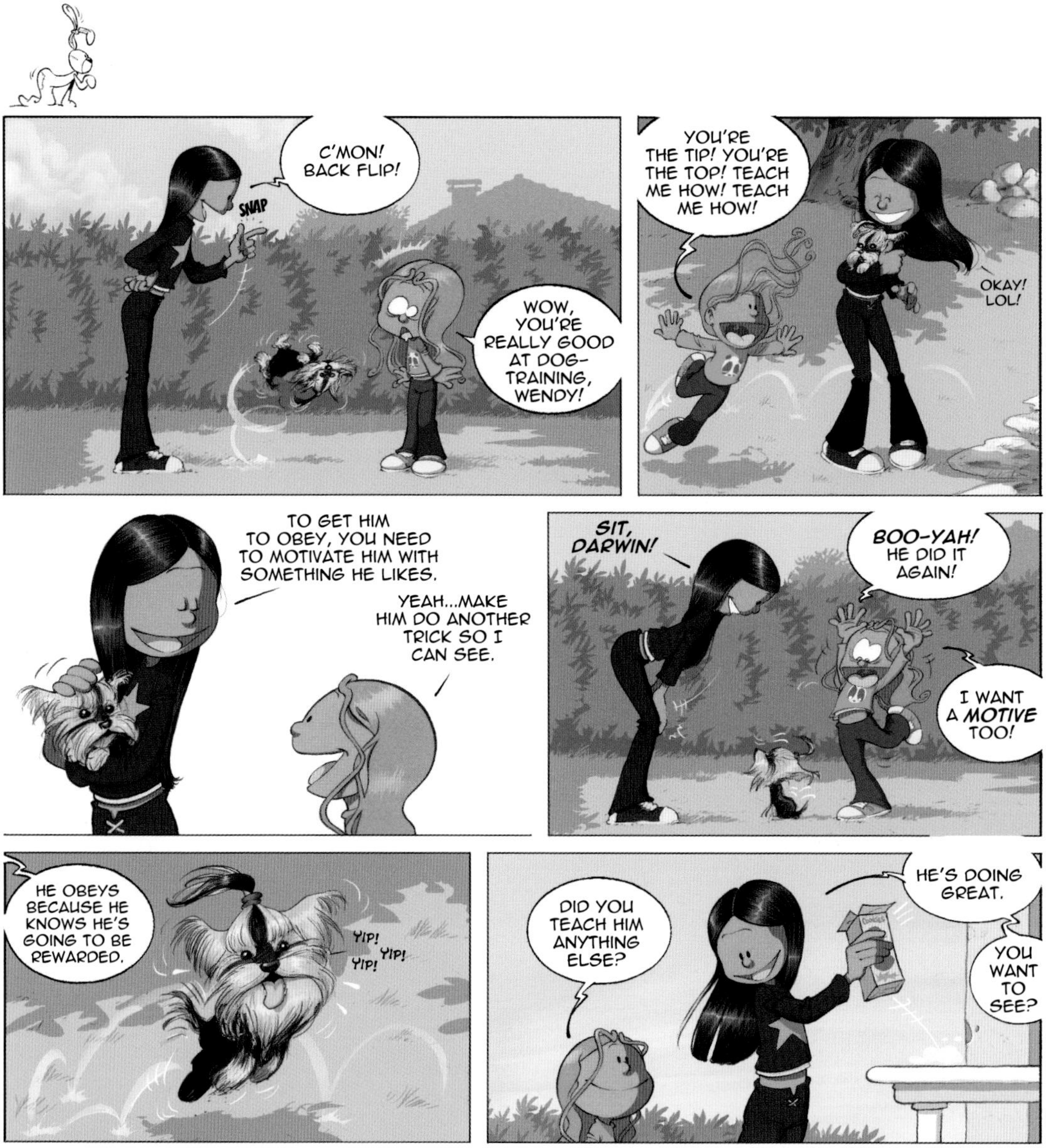
C'MON! BACK FLIP!
SNAP
WOW, YOU'RE REALLY GOOD AT DOG-TRAINING, WENDY!
YOU'RE THE TIP! YOU'RE THE TOP! TEACH ME HOW! TEACH ME HOW!
OKAY! LOL!
TO GET HIM TO OBEY, YOU NEED TO MOTIVATE HIM WITH SOMETHING HE LIKES.
YEAH...MAKE HIM DO ANOTHER TRICK SO I CAN SEE.
SIT, DARWIN!
BOO-YAH! HE DID IT AGAIN!
I WANT A MOTIVE TOO!
HE OBEYS BECAUSE HE KNOWS HE'S GOING TO BE REWARDED.
YIP! YIP! YIP!
HE'S DOING GREAT.
DID YOU TEACH HIM ANYTHING ELSE?
YOU WANT TO SEE?
A CAROB CHIP COOKIE WILL BRING SUCCESS!
COOKIES
GUARANTEED!
ARF!
ARF!
CAZENOVE & WILLIAM

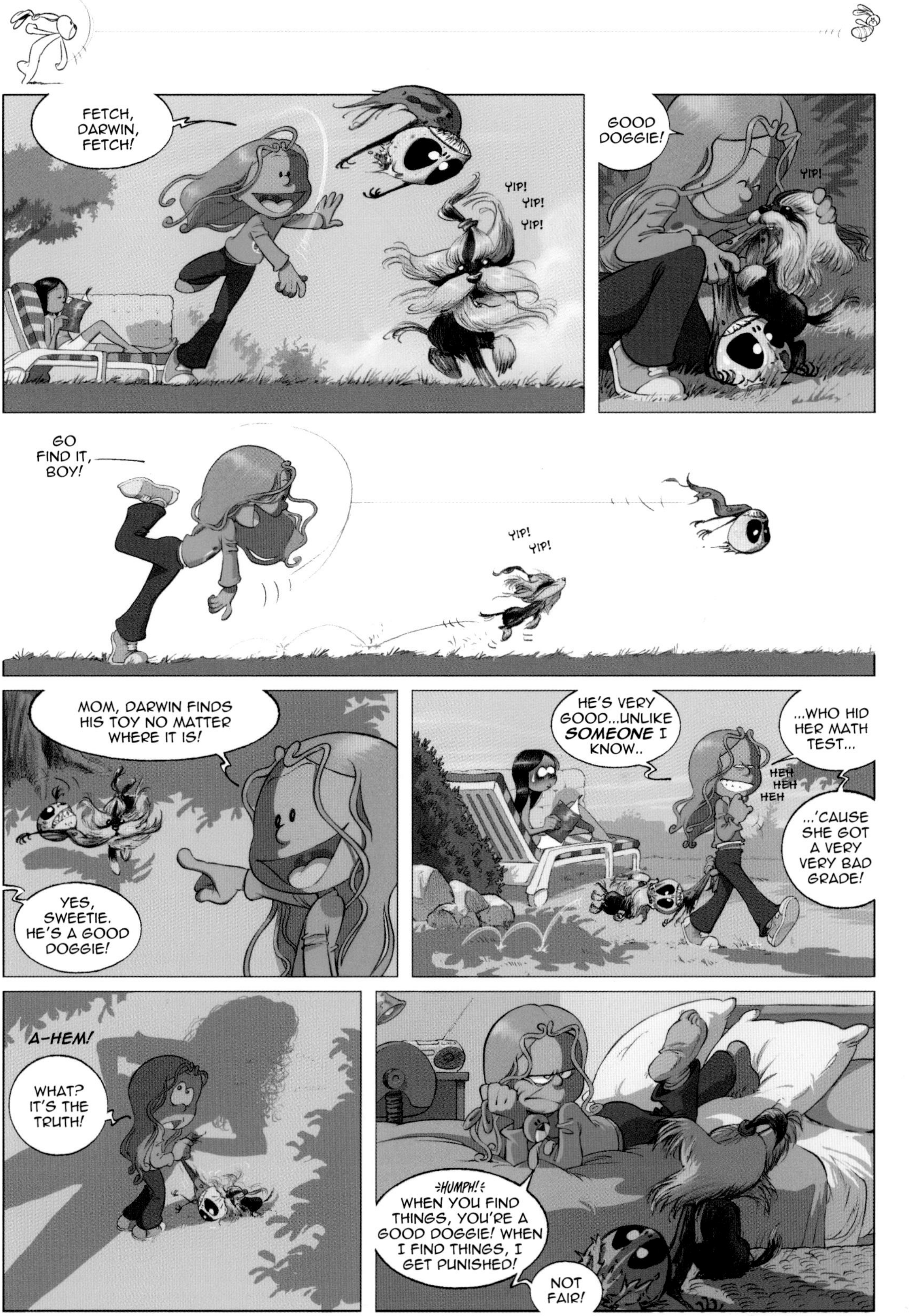
FETCH, DARWIN, FETCH!
YIP! YIP! YIP!
GOOD DOGGIE!
YIP!
GO FIND IT, BOY!
YIP! YIP!
MOM, DARWIN FINDS HIS TOY NO MATTER WHERE IT IS!
YES, SWEETIE. HE'S A GOOD DOGGIE!
HE'S VERY GOOD...UNLIKE SOMEONE I KNOW..
...WHO HID HER MATH TEST...
HEH HEH HEH
...'CAUSE SHE GOT A VERY VERY BAD GRADE!
A-HEM!
WHAT? IT'S THE TRUTH!
HUMPH!
WHEN YOU FIND THINGS, YOU'RE A GOOD DOGGIE! WHEN I FIND THINGS, I GET PUNISHED!
NOT FAIR!
CAZENOVE & WILLIAM

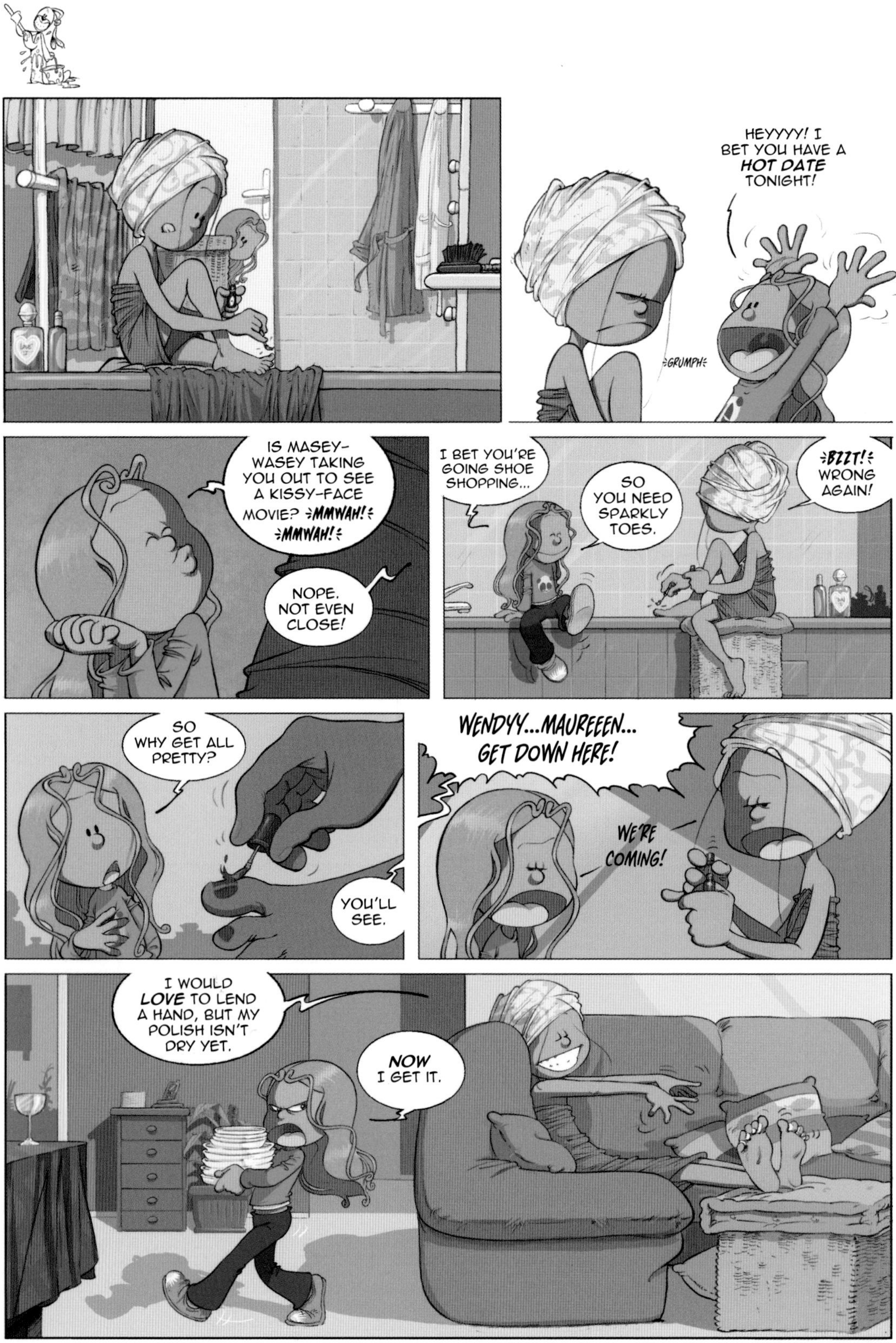
HEYYYY! I BET YOU HAVE A **HOT DATE** TONIGHT!
GRUMPH
IS MASEY-WASEY TAKING YOU OUT TO SEE A KISSY-FACE MOVIE? MMWAH! MMWAH!
NOPE. NOT EVEN CLOSE!
I BET YOU'RE GOING SHOE SHOPPING...
SO YOU NEED SPARKLY TOES.
BZZT! WRONG AGAIN!
SO WHY GET ALL PRETTY?
YOU'LL SEE.
WENDYY...MAUREEEN... GET DOWN HERE!
WE'RE COMING!
I WOULD **LOVE** TO LEND A HAND, BUT MY POLISH ISN'T DRY YET.
NOW I GET IT.
CAZENOVE & WILLIAM

CAZENOVE & WILLIAM

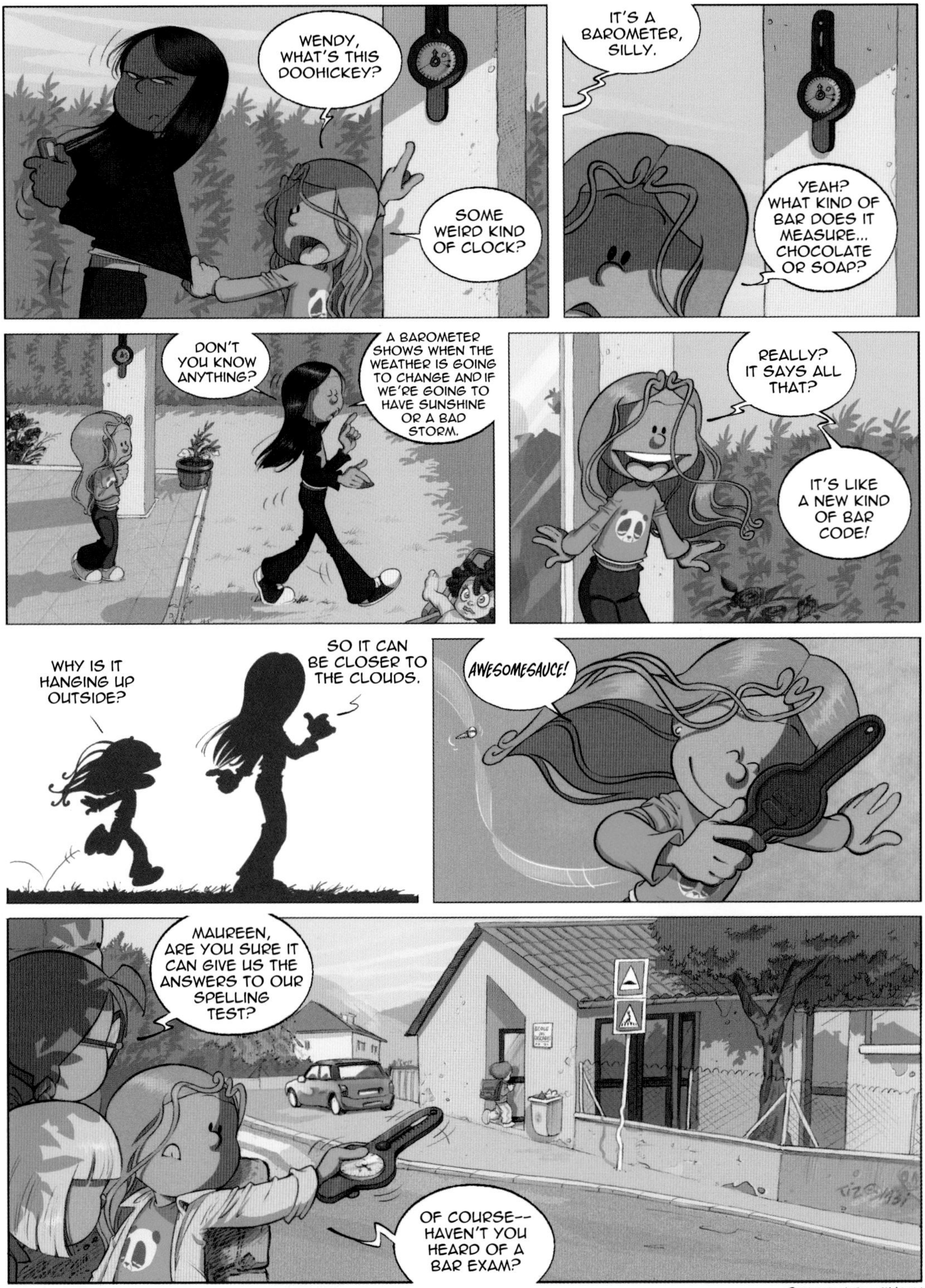

WENDY, WHAT'S THIS DOOHICKEY?
SOME WEIRD KIND OF CLOCK?
IT'S A BAROMETER, SILLY.
YEAH? WHAT KIND OF BAR DOES IT MEASURE... CHOCOLATE OR SOAP?
DON'T YOU KNOW ANYTHING?
A BAROMETER SHOWS WHEN THE WEATHER IS GOING TO CHANGE AND IF WE'RE GOING TO HAVE SUNSHINE OR A BAD STORM.
REALLY? IT SAYS ALL THAT?
IT'S LIKE A NEW KIND OF BAR CODE!
WHY IS IT HANGING UP OUTSIDE?
SO IT CAN BE CLOSER TO THE CLOUDS.
AWESOMESAUCE!
MAUREEN, ARE YOU SURE IT CAN GIVE US THE ANSWERS TO OUR SPELLING TEST?
OF COURSE-- HAVEN'T YOU HEARD OF A BAR EXAM?

CAZENOVE & WILLIAM

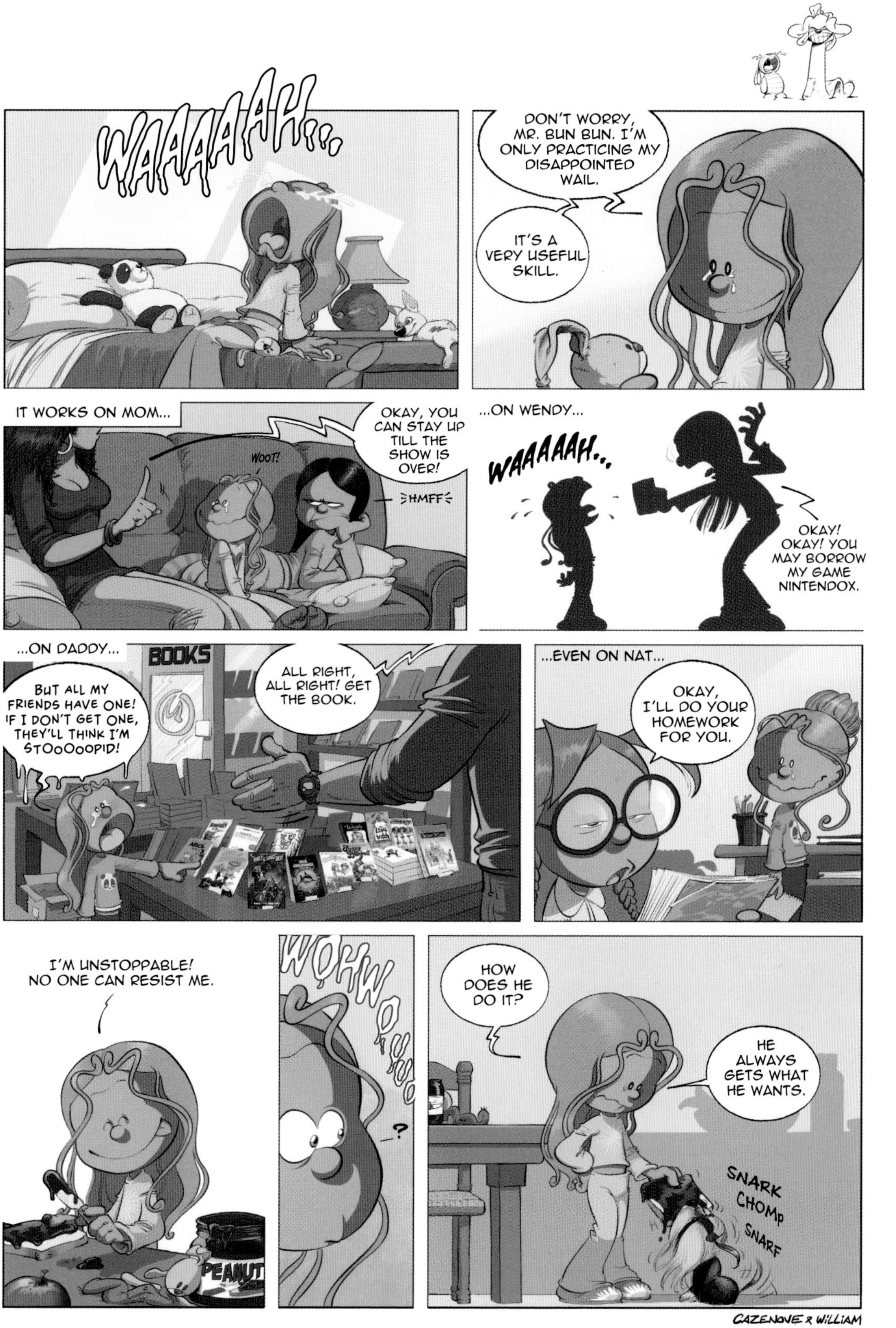
WAAAAAH...
DON'T WORRY, MR. BUN BUN. I'M ONLY PRACTICING MY DISAPPOINTED WAIL.
IT'S A VERY USEFUL SKILL.
IT WORKS ON MOM...
OKAY, YOU CAN STAY UP TILL THE SHOW IS OVER!
WOOT!
HMFF
...ON WENDY...
WAAAAAH...
OKAY! OKAY! YOU MAY BORROW MY GAME NINTENDOX.
...ON DADDY...
BOOKS
BUT ALL MY FRIENDS HAVE ONE! IF I DON'T GET ONE, THEY'LL THINK I'M STOOOOOPID!
ALL RIGHT, ALL RIGHT! GET THE BOOK.
...EVEN ON NAT...
OKAY, I'LL DO YOUR HOMEWORK FOR YOU.
I'M UNSTOPPABLE! NO ONE CAN RESIST ME.
PEANUT
WOHWOUUU
?
HOW DOES HE DO IT?
HE ALWAYS GETS WHAT HE WANTS.
SNARK
CHOMP
SNARF
CAZENOVE & WILLIAM

CAZENOVE & WILLIAM

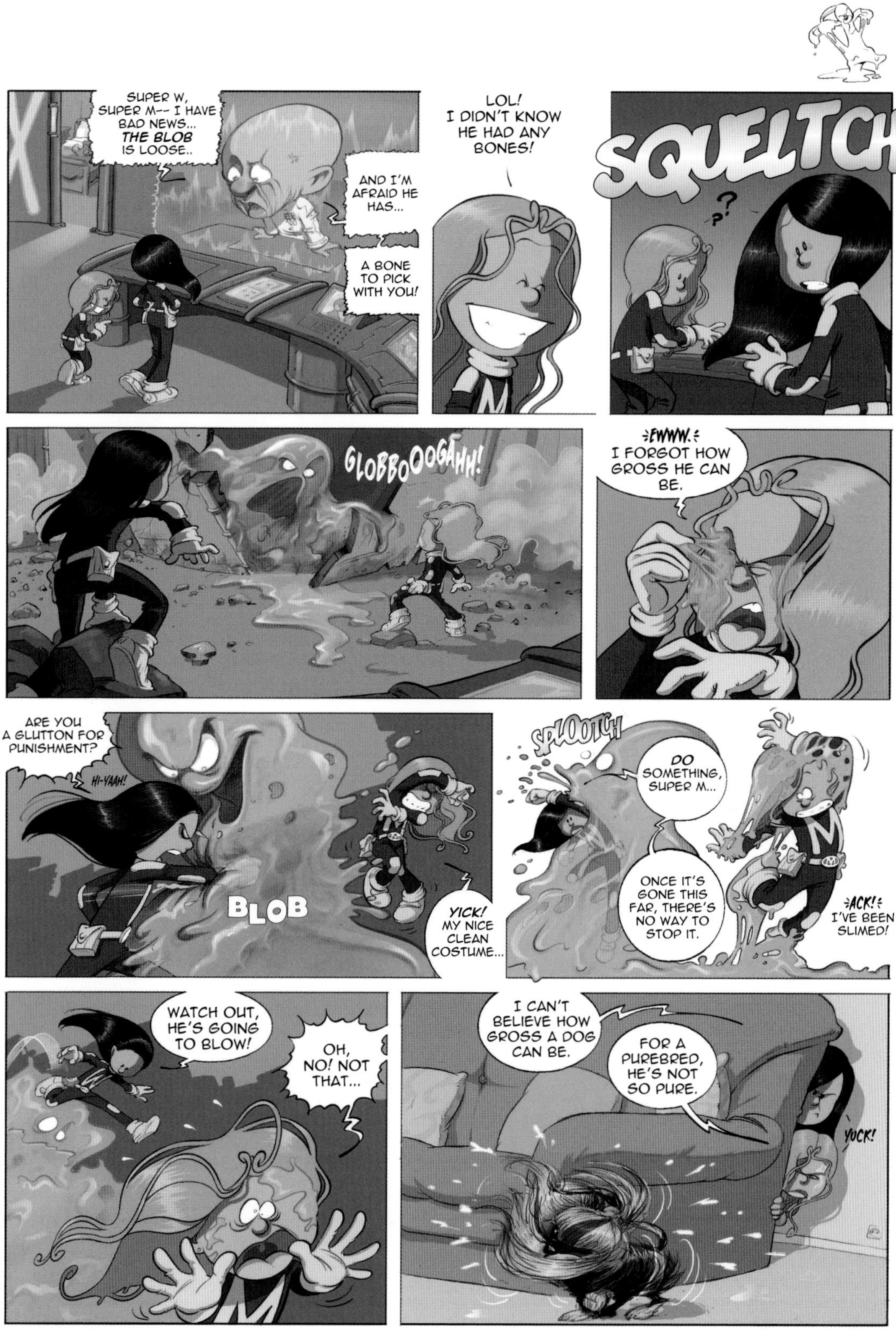
SUPER W, SUPER M-- I HAVE BAD NEWS... THE BLOB IS LOOSE..
AND I'M AFRAID HE HAS...
A BONE TO PICK WITH YOU!
LOL! I DIDN'T KNOW HE HAD ANY BONES!
SQUELTCH
GLOBBOOOGAHH!
EWWW. I FORGOT HOW GROSS HE CAN BE.
ARE YOU A GLUTTON FOR PUNISHMENT?
HI-YAAH!
BLOB
YICK! MY NICE CLEAN COSTUME...
SPLOOTCH
DO SOMETHING, SUPER M...
ONCE IT'S GONE THIS FAR, THERE'S NO WAY TO STOP IT.
ACK! I'VE BEEN SLIMED!
WATCH OUT, HE'S GOING TO BLOW!
OH, NO! NOT THAT...
I CAN'T BELIEVE HOW GROSS A DOG CAN BE.
FOR A PUREBRED, HE'S NOT SO PURE.
YUCK!

CAZENOVE & WILLIAM

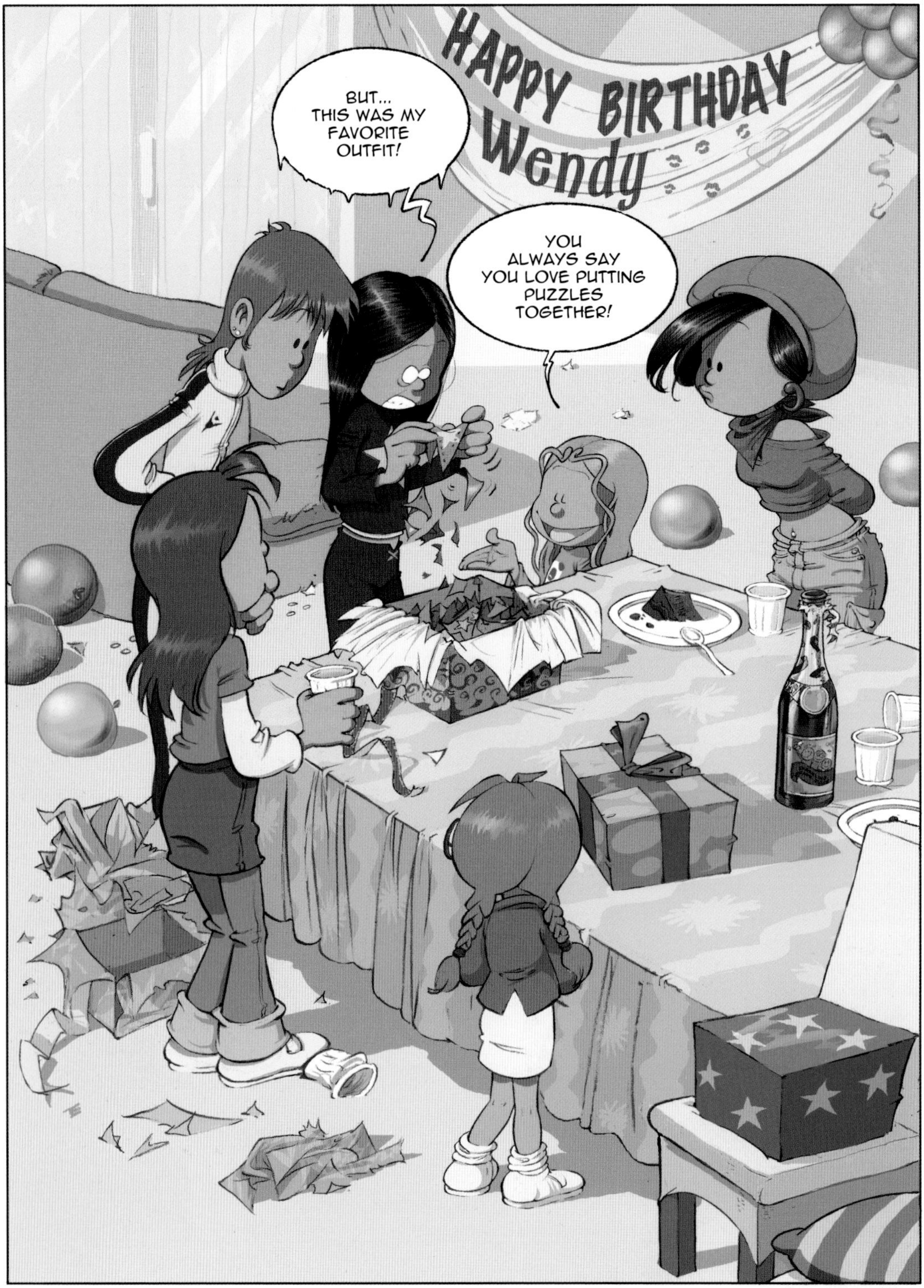
HAPPY BIRTHDAY Wendy
BUT... THIS WAS MY FAVORITE OUTFIT!
YOU ALWAYS SAY YOU LOVE PUTTING PUZZLES TOGETHER!

CAZENOVE & WILLIAM

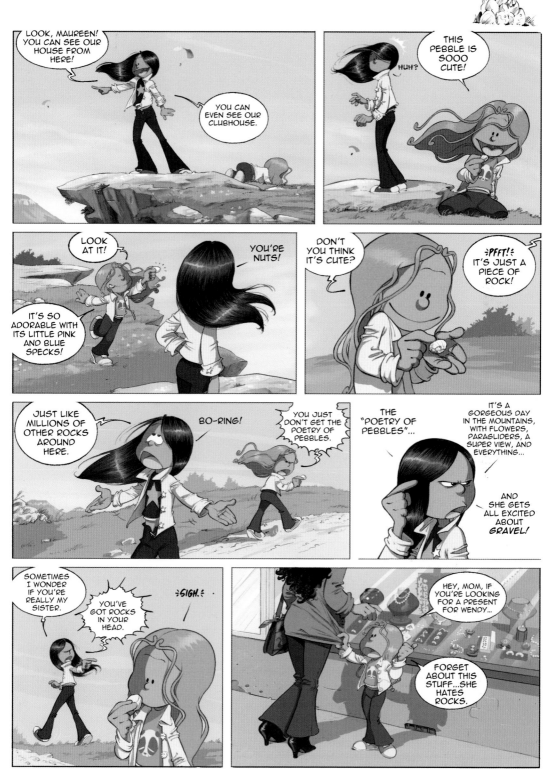

CAZENOVE & WILLIAM

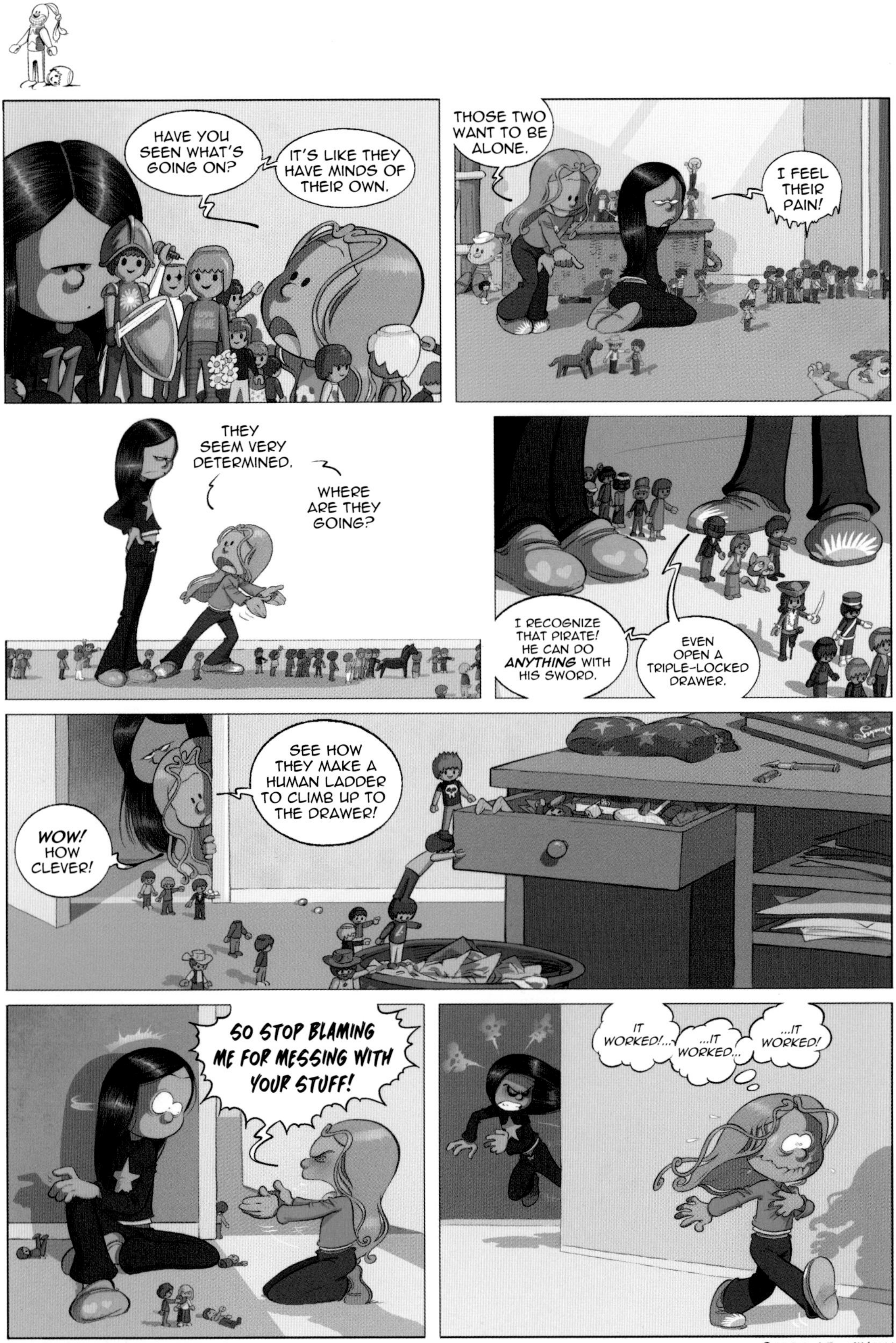
HAVE YOU SEEN WHAT'S GOING ON?
IT'S LIKE THEY HAVE MINDS OF THEIR OWN.
THOSE TWO WANT TO BE ALONE.
I FEEL THEIR PAIN!
THEY SEEM VERY DETERMINED.
WHERE ARE THEY GOING?
I RECOGNIZE THAT PIRATE! HE CAN DO ANYTHING WITH HIS SWORD.
EVEN OPEN A TRIPLE-LOCKED DRAWER.
SEE HOW THEY MAKE A HUMAN LADDER TO CLIMB UP TO THE DRAWER!
WOW! HOW CLEVER!
SO STOP BLAMING ME FOR MESSING WITH YOUR STUFF!
IT WORKED!...
...IT WORKED...
...IT WORKED!
CAZENOVE & WILLIAM

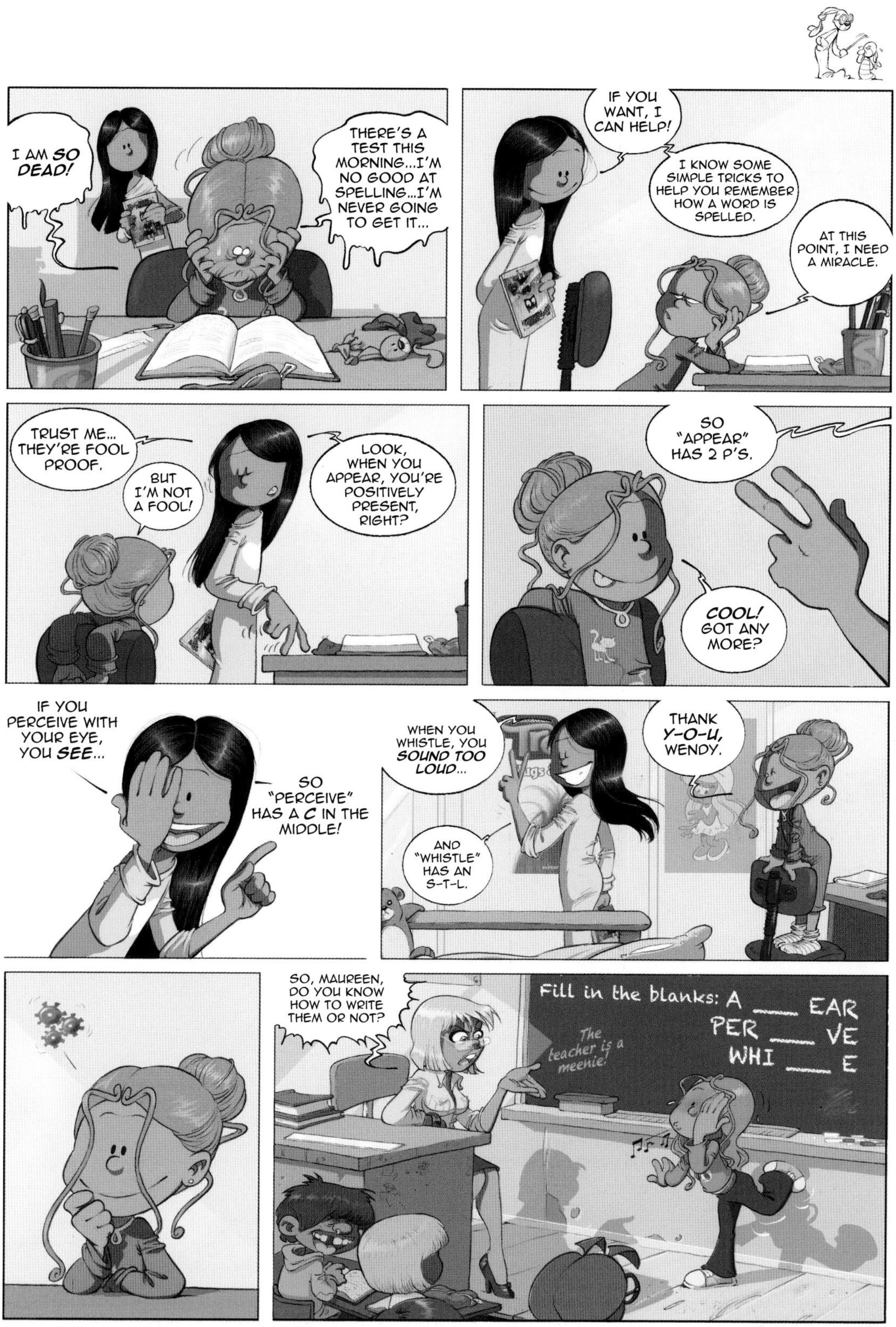
I AM **SO DEAD!**
THERE'S A TEST THIS MORNING...I'M NO GOOD AT SPELLING...I'M NEVER GOING TO GET IT...
IF YOU WANT, I CAN HELP!
I KNOW SOME SIMPLE TRICKS TO HELP YOU REMEMBER HOW A WORD IS SPELLED.
AT THIS POINT, I NEED A MIRACLE.
TRUST ME... THEY'RE FOOL PROOF.
BUT I'M NOT A FOOL!
LOOK, WHEN YOU APPEAR, YOU'RE POSITIVELY PRESENT, RIGHT?
SO "APPEAR" HAS 2 P'S.
COOL! GOT ANY MORE?
IF YOU PERCEIVE WITH YOUR EYE, YOU **SEE**...
SO "PERCEIVE" HAS A **C** IN THE MIDDLE!
WHEN YOU WHISTLE, YOU **SOUND TOO LOUD**...
AND "WHISTLE" HAS AN S-T-L.
THANK **Y-O-U,** WENDY.
SO, MAUREEN, DO YOU KNOW HOW TO WRITE THEM OR NOT?
Fill in the blanks: A ___ EAR
PER ___ VE
WHI ___ E
The teacher is a meenie!
CAZENOVE & WILLIAM

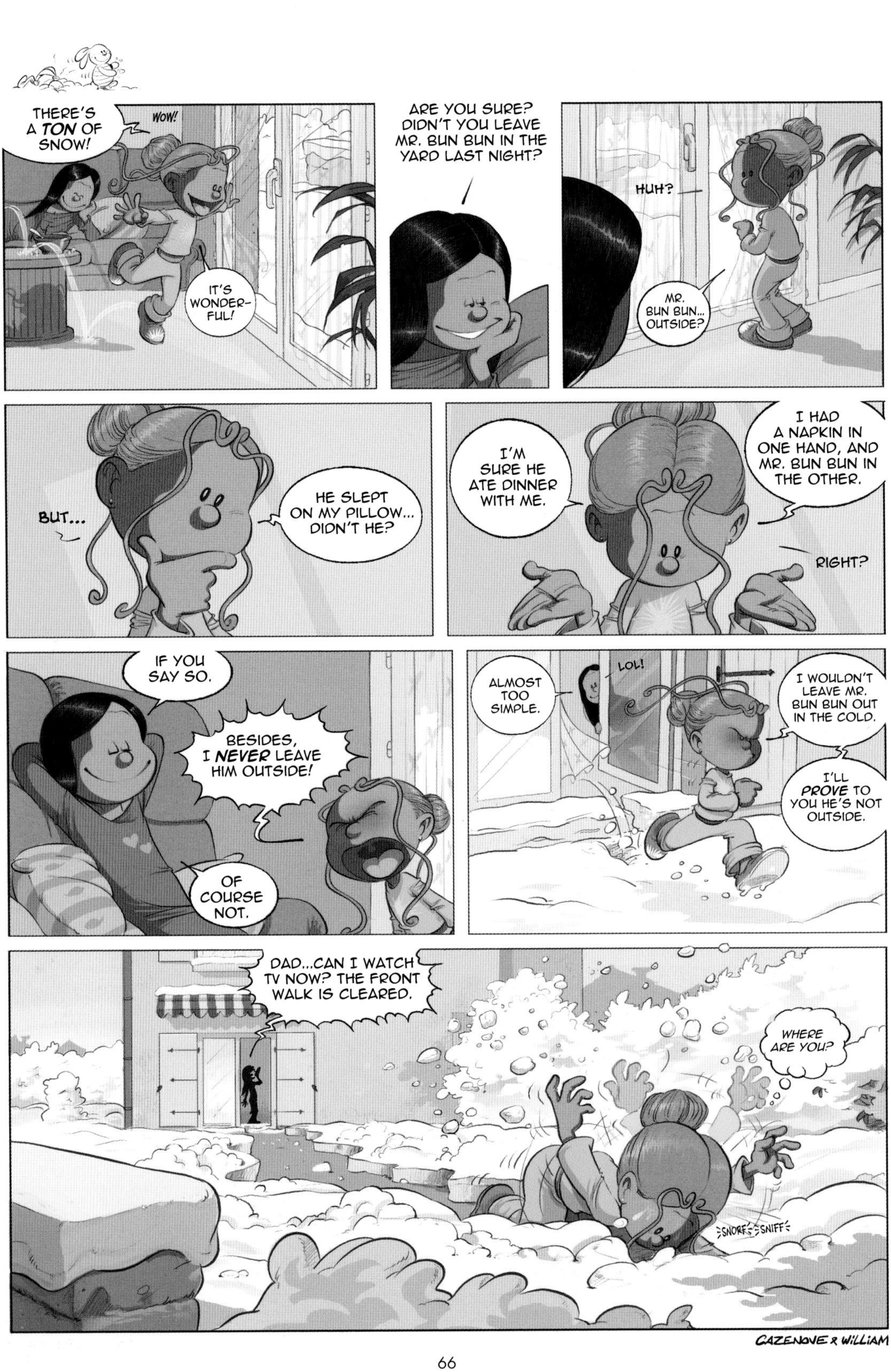
THERE'S A TON OF SNOW!
WOW!
IT'S WONDERFUL!
ARE YOU SURE? DIDN'T YOU LEAVE MR. BUN BUN IN THE YARD LAST NIGHT?
HUH?
MR. BUN BUN... OUTSIDE?
BUT...
HE SLEPT ON MY PILLOW... DIDN'T HE?
I'M SURE HE ATE DINNER WITH ME.
I HAD A NAPKIN IN ONE HAND, AND MR. BUN BUN IN THE OTHER.
RIGHT?
IF YOU SAY SO.
BESIDES, I NEVER LEAVE HIM OUTSIDE!
OF COURSE NOT.
ALMOST TOO SIMPLE.
LOL!
I WOULDN'T LEAVE MR. BUN BUN OUT IN THE COLD.
I'LL PROVE TO YOU HE'S NOT OUTSIDE.
DAD...CAN I WATCH TV NOW? THE FRONT WALK IS CLEARED.
WHERE ARE YOU?
SNORF SNIFF
CAZENOVE & WILLIAM

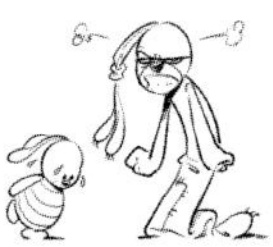

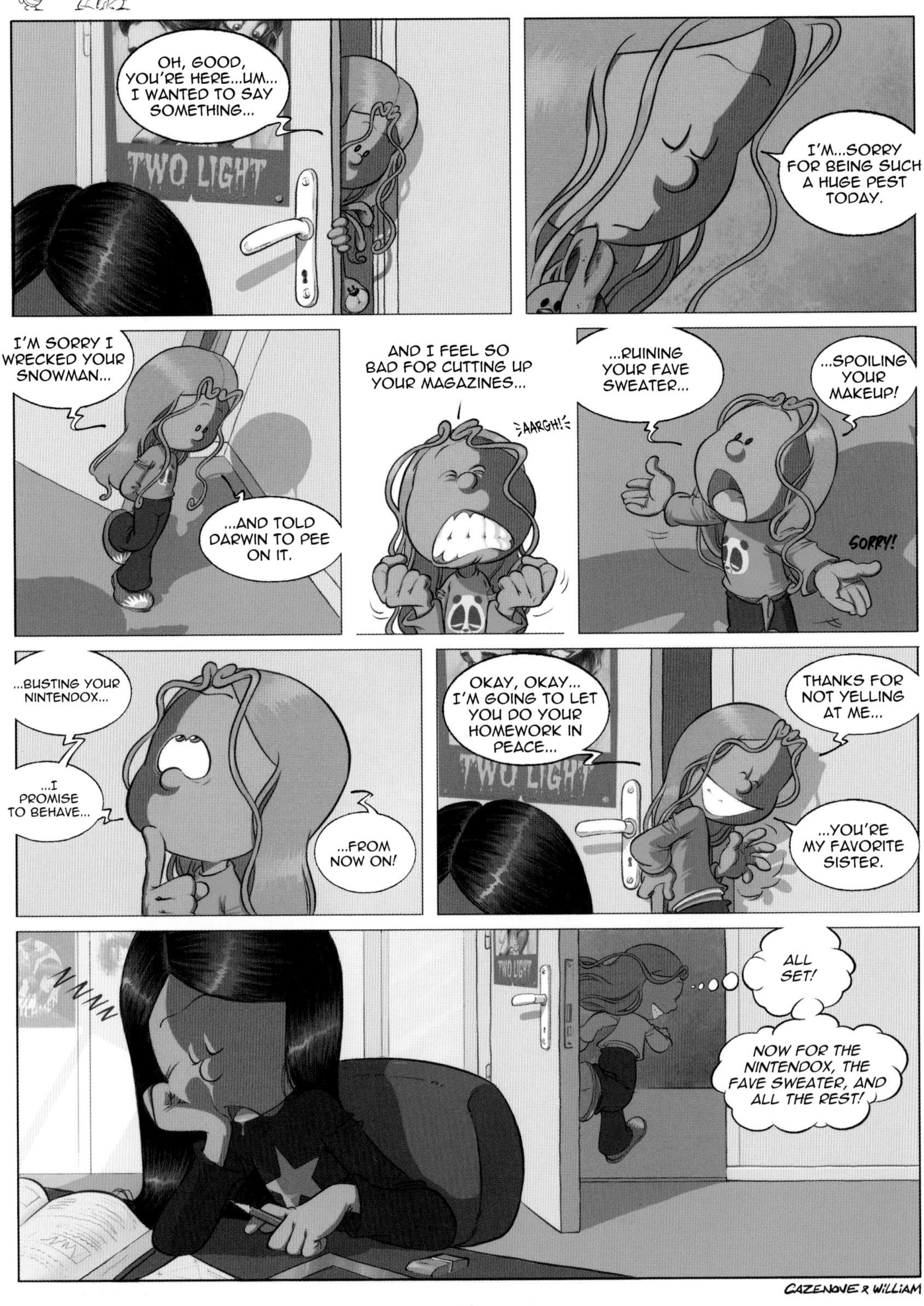

OH, GOOD, YOU'RE HERE...UM... I WANTED TO SAY SOMETHING...
TWO LIGHT
I'M...SORRY FOR BEING SUCH A HUGE PEST TODAY.
I'M SORRY I WRECKED YOUR SNOWMAN...
...AND TOLD DARWIN TO PEE ON IT.
AND I FEEL SO BAD FOR CUTTING UP YOUR MAGAZINES...
AARGH!
...RUINING YOUR FAVE SWEATER...
...SPOILING YOUR MAKEUP!
SORRY!
...BUSTING YOUR NINTENDOX...
...I PROMISE TO BEHAVE...
...FROM NOW ON!
OKAY, OKAY... I'M GOING TO LET YOU DO YOUR HOMEWORK IN PEACE...
TWO LIGHT
THANKS FOR NOT YELLING AT ME...
...YOU'RE MY FAVORITE SISTER.
NNNN
TWO LIGHT
ALL SET!
NOW FOR THE NINTENDOX, THE FAVE SWEATER, AND ALL THE REST!
CAZENOVE & WILLIAM

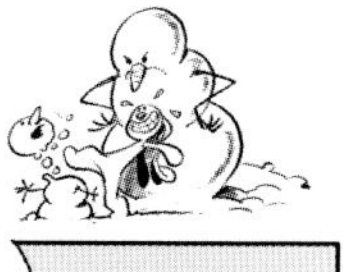

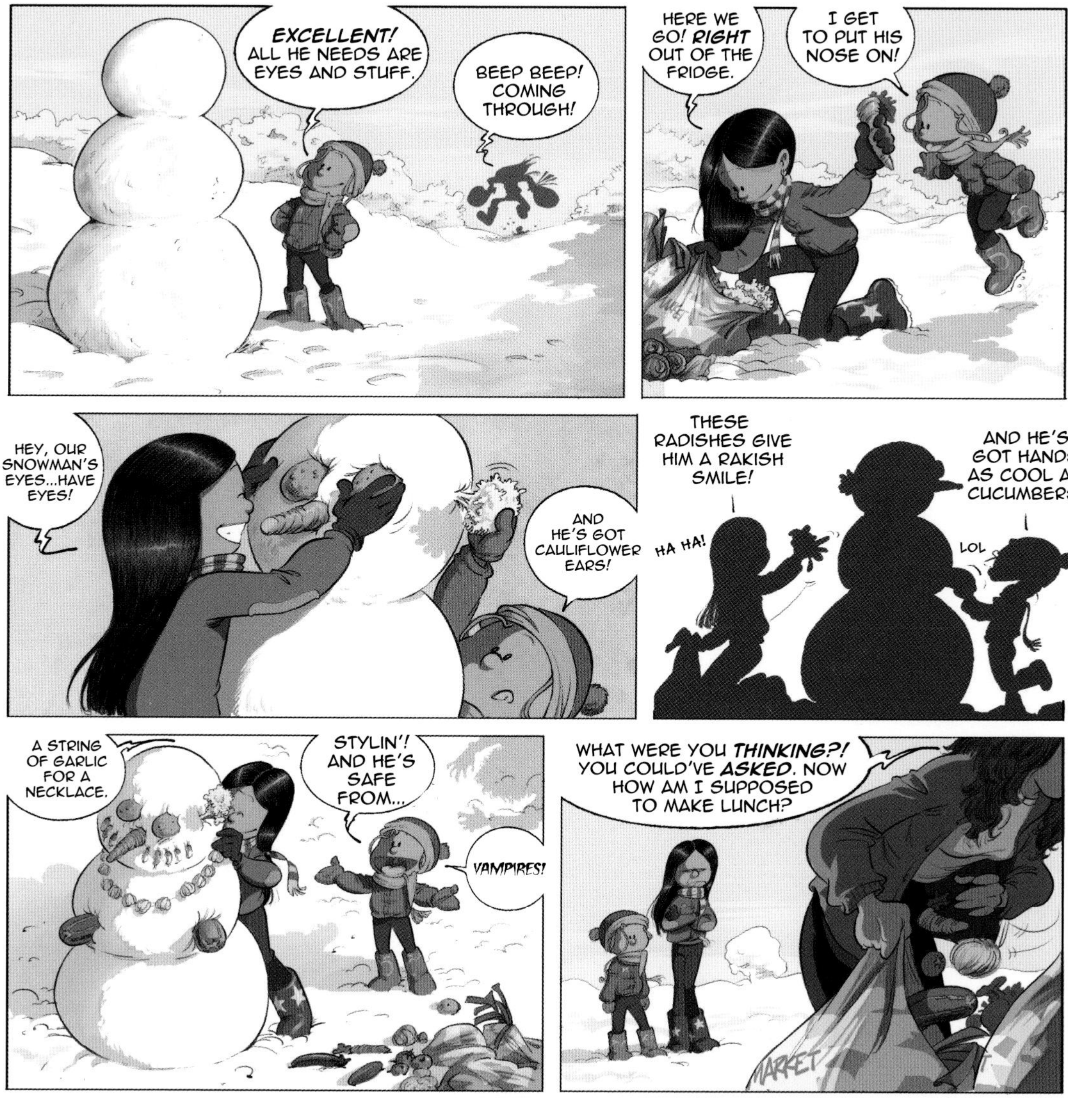
EXCELLENT! ALL HE NEEDS ARE EYES AND STUFF.
BEEP BEEP! COMING THROUGH!
HERE WE GO! RIGHT OUT OF THE FRIDGE.
I GET TO PUT HIS NOSE ON!
HEY, OUR SNOWMAN'S EYES...HAVE EYES!
AND HE'S GOT CAULIFLOWER EARS!
THESE RADISHES GIVE HIM A RAKISH SMILE!
HA HA!
AND HE'S GOT HANDS AS COOL AS CUCUMBERS.
LOL
A STRING OF GARLIC FOR A NECKLACE.
STYLIN'! AND HE'S SAFE FROM...
VAMPIRES!
WHAT WERE YOU THINKING?! YOU COULD'VE ASKED. NOW HOW AM I SUPPOSED TO MAKE LUNCH?
MARKET
LOST YOUR APPETITE, GIRLS?
OF COURSE! YOU'VE GOT TO UNDERSTAND, MOM--WE'RE NOT CANNIBALS!

CAZENOVE & WILLIAM

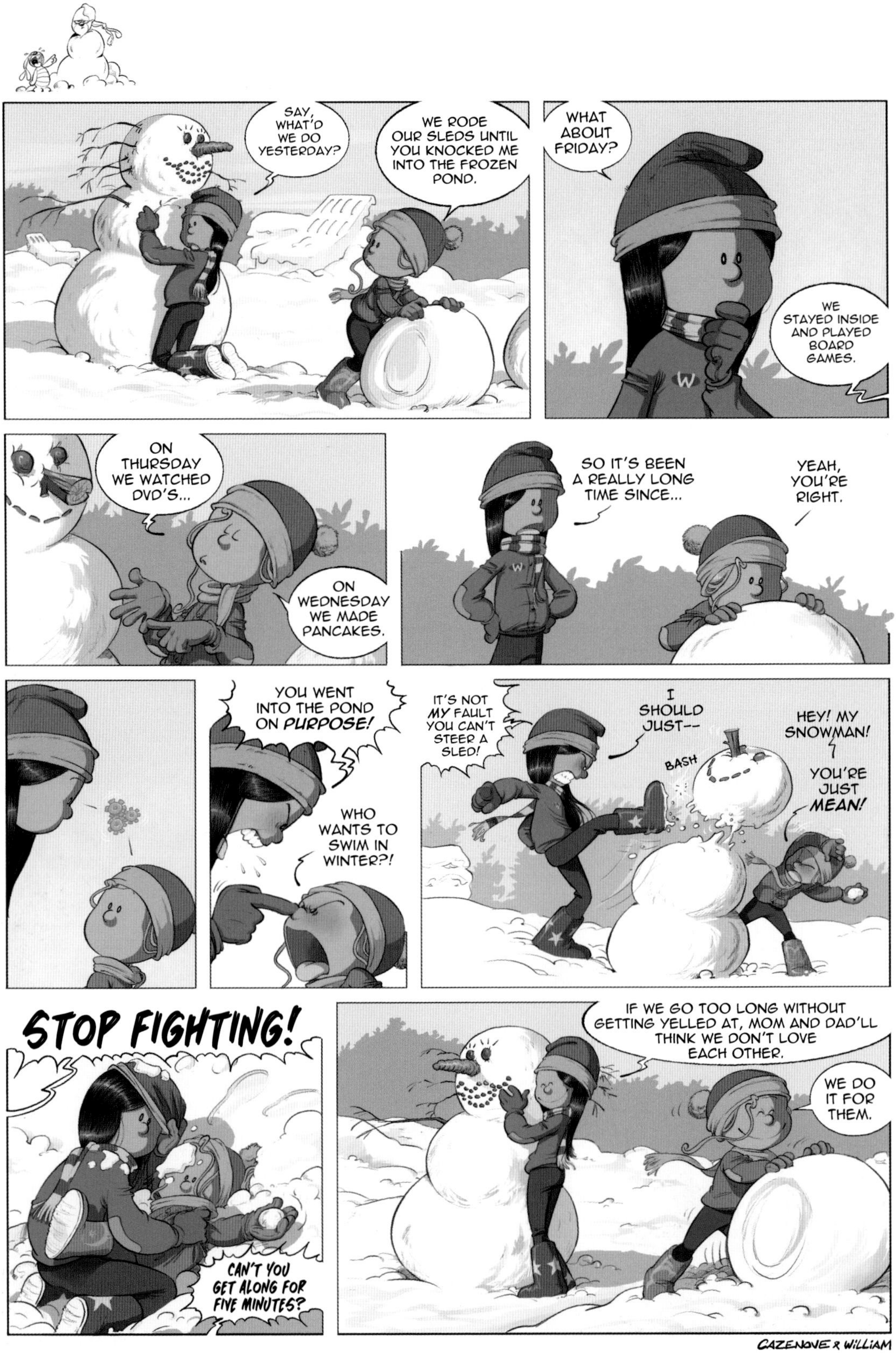
SAY, WHAT'D WE DO YESTERDAY?
WE RODE OUR SLEDS UNTIL YOU KNOCKED ME INTO THE FROZEN POND.
WHAT ABOUT FRIDAY?
WE STAYED INSIDE AND PLAYED BOARD GAMES.
ON THURSDAY WE WATCHED DVD'S...
ON WEDNESDAY WE MADE PANCAKES.
SO IT'S BEEN A REALLY LONG TIME SINCE...
YEAH, YOU'RE RIGHT.
YOU WENT INTO THE POND ON PURPOSE!
WHO WANTS TO SWIM IN WINTER?!
IT'S NOT MY FAULT YOU CAN'T STEER A SLED!
I SHOULD JUST--
BASH
HEY! MY SNOWMAN!
YOU'RE JUST MEAN!
STOP FIGHTING!
CAN'T YOU GET ALONG FOR FIVE MINUTES?
IF WE GO TOO LONG WITHOUT GETTING YELLED AT, MOM AND DAD'LL THINK WE DON'T LOVE EACH OTHER.
WE DO IT FOR THEM.
CAZENOVE & WILLIAM

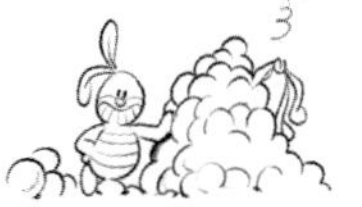

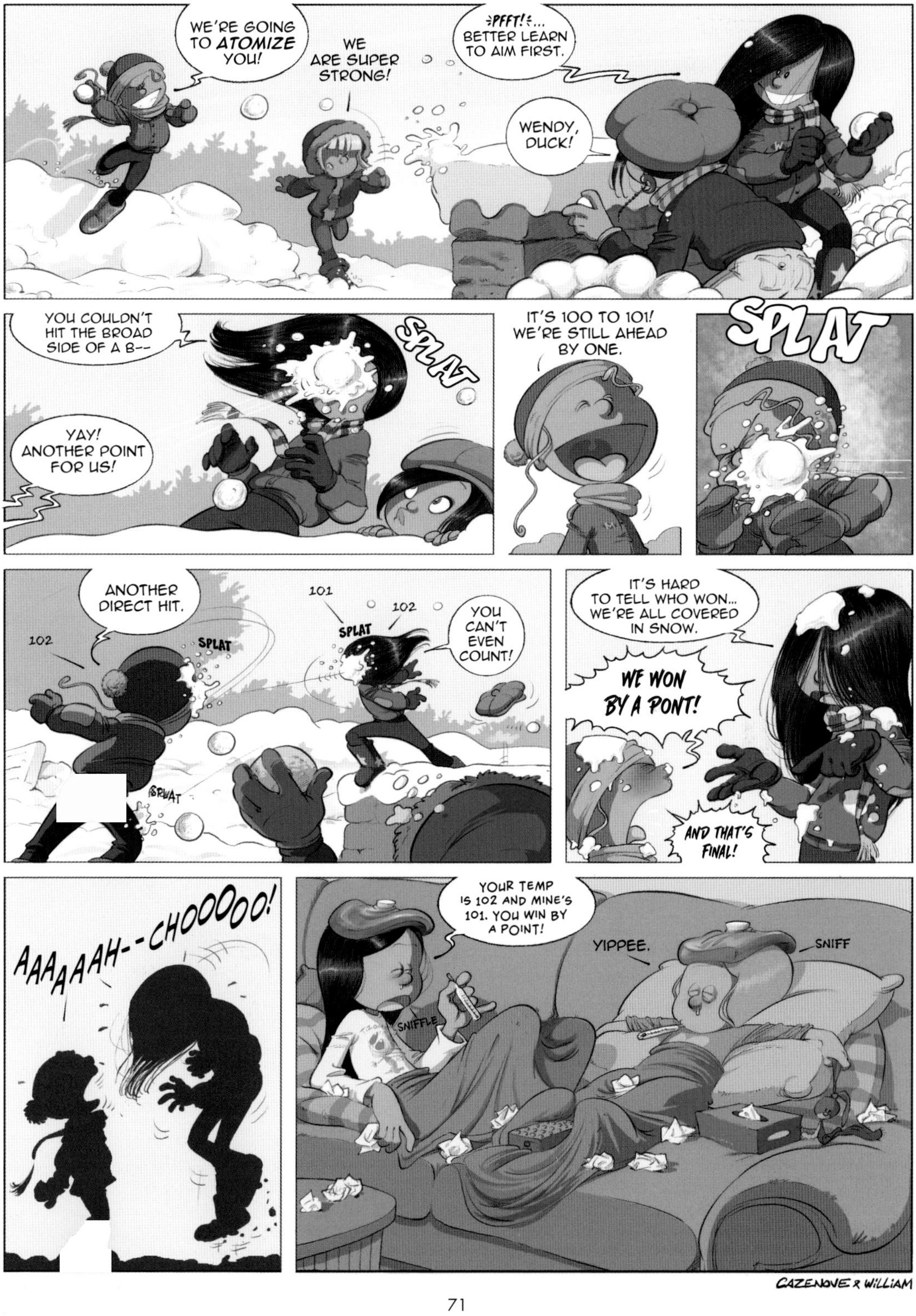

WE'RE GOING TO ATOMIZE YOU!
WE ARE SUPER STRONG!
PFFT!... BETTER LEARN TO AIM FIRST.
WENDY, DUCK!
YOU COULDN'T HIT THE BROAD SIDE OF A B--
SPLAT
YAY! ANOTHER POINT FOR US!
IT'S 100 TO 101! WE'RE STILL AHEAD BY ONE.
SPLAT
ANOTHER DIRECT HIT.
102
SPLAT
101
102
SPLAT
YOU CAN'T EVEN COUNT!
SPLAT
IT'S HARD TO TELL WHO WON... WE'RE ALL COVERED IN SNOW.
WE WON BY A POINT!
AND THAT'S FINAL!
AAAAAAH--CHOOOOO!
YOUR TEMP IS 102 AND MINE'S 101. YOU WIN BY A POINT!
SNIFFLE
YIPPEE.
SNIFF

CAZENOVE & WILLIAM

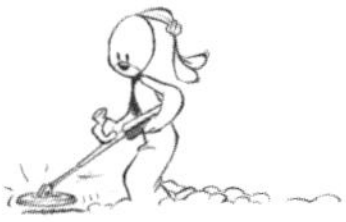

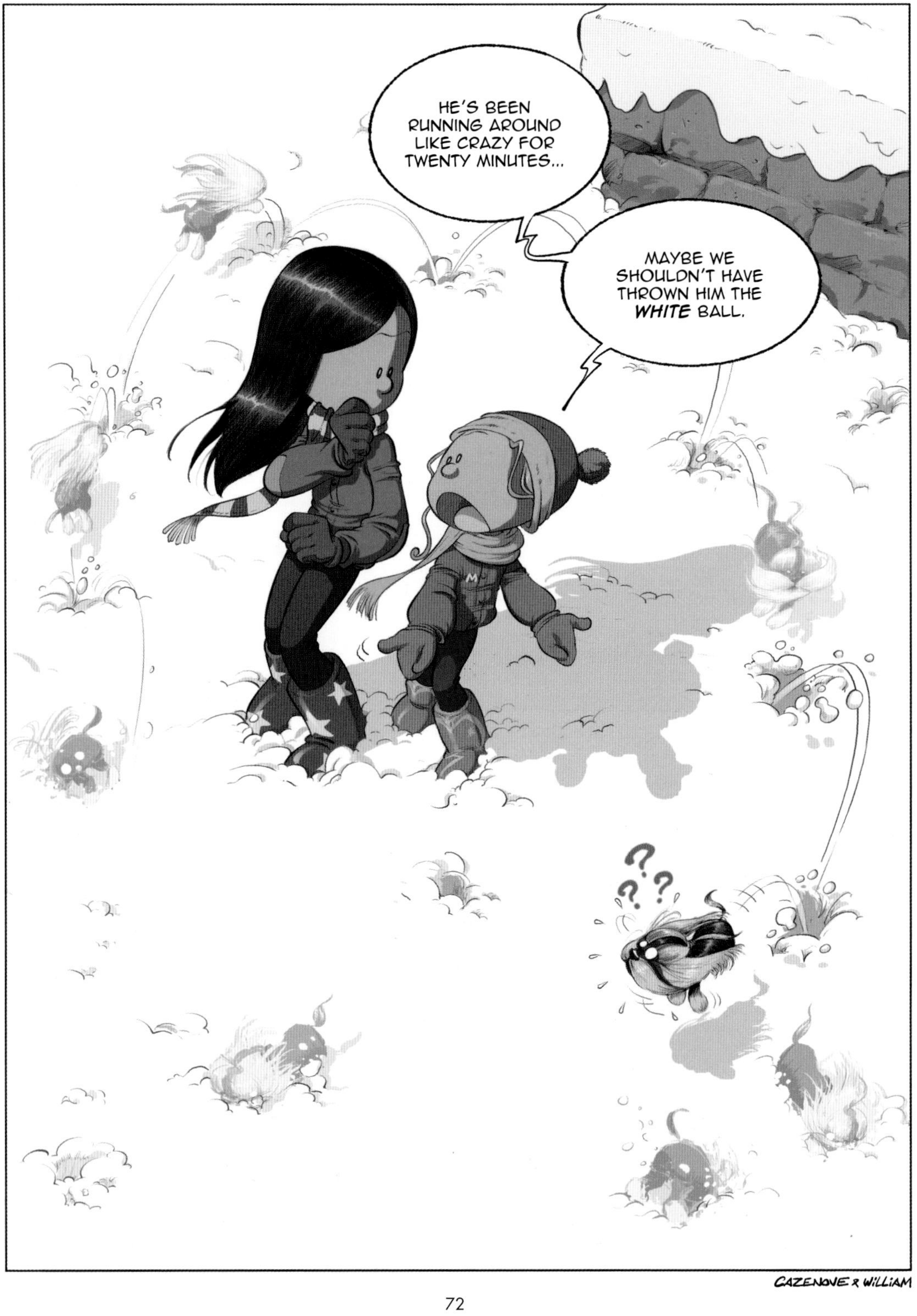
HE'S BEEN RUNNING AROUND LIKE CRAZY FOR TWENTY MINUTES...
MAYBE WE SHOULDN'T HAVE THROWN HIM THE *WHITE* BALL.

CAZENOVE & WILLIAM

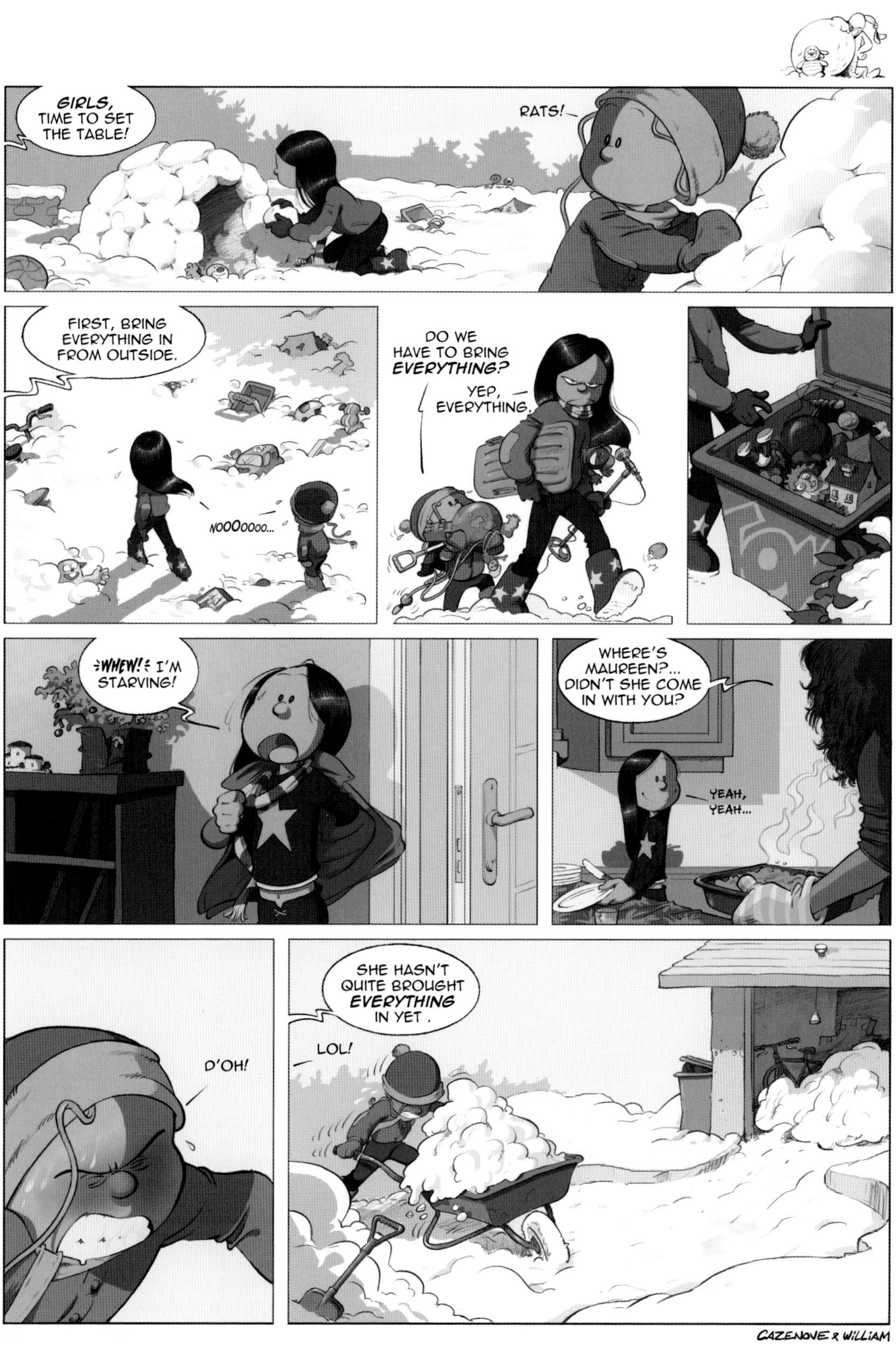
GIRLS, TIME TO SET THE TABLE!
RATS!
FIRST, BRING EVERYTHING IN FROM OUTSIDE.
NOOOoooo...
DO WE HAVE TO BRING EVERYTHING?
YEP, EVERYTHING.
WHEW! I'M STARVING!
WHERE'S MAUREEN?... DIDN'T SHE COME IN WITH YOU?
YEAH, YEAH...
D'OH!
SHE HASN'T QUITE BROUGHT EVERYTHING IN YET .
LOL!
CAZENOVE & WILLIAM

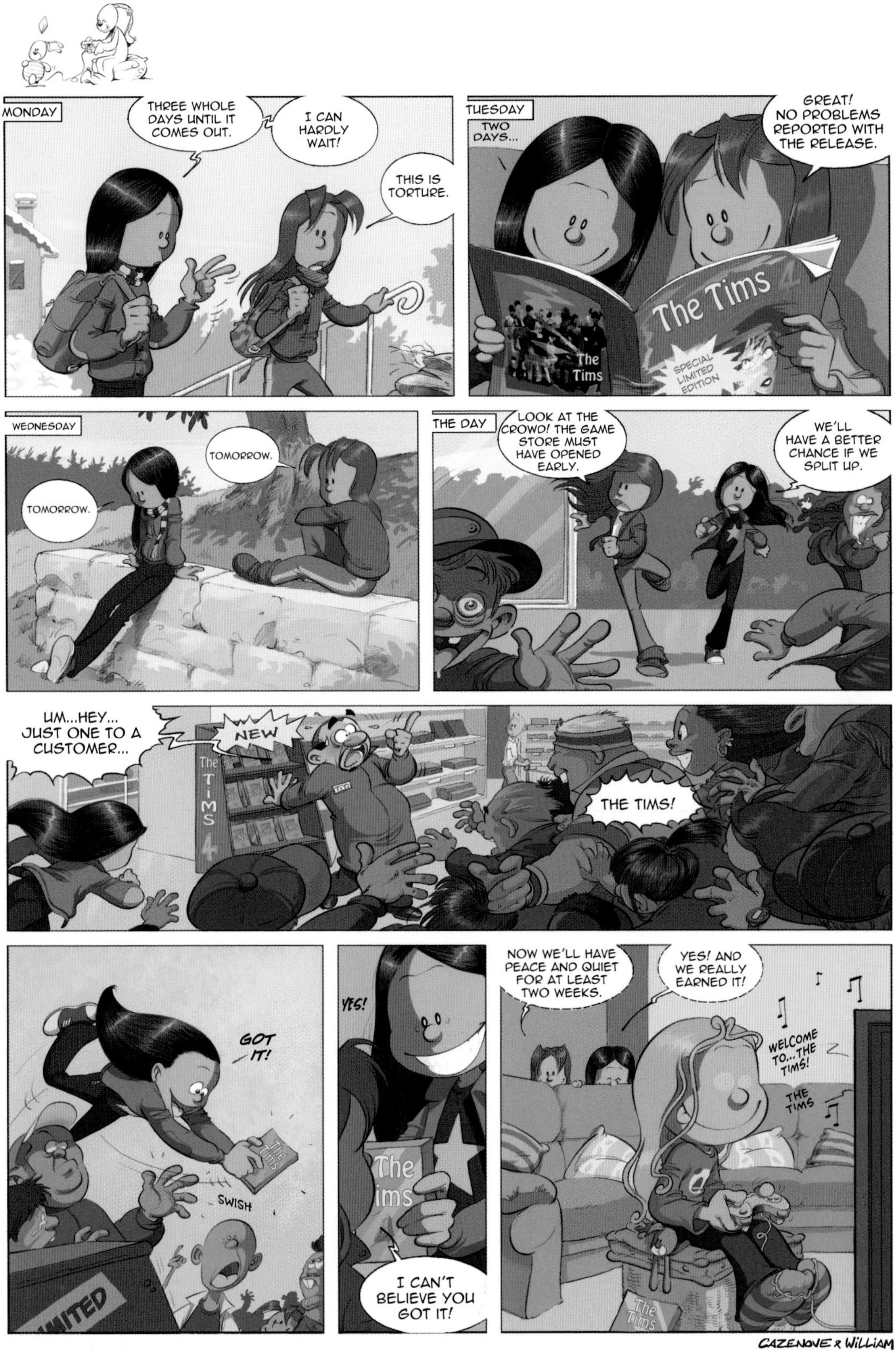
MONDAY
THREE WHOLE DAYS UNTIL IT COMES OUT.
I CAN HARDLY WAIT!
THIS IS TORTURE.
TUESDAY
TWO DAYS...
GREAT! NO PROBLEMS REPORTED WITH THE RELEASE.
The Tims 4
SPECIAL LIMITED EDITION
The Tims
WEDNESDAY
TOMORROW.
TOMORROW.
THE DAY
LOOK AT THE CROWD! THE GAME STORE MUST HAVE OPENED EARLY.
WE'LL HAVE A BETTER CHANCE IF WE SPLIT UP.
UM...HEY... JUST ONE TO A CUSTOMER...
NEW
The Tims 4
THE TIMS!
GOT IT!
SWISH
The Tims
LIMITED
YES!
The ims
I CAN'T BELIEVE YOU GOT IT!
NOW WE'LL HAVE PEACE AND QUIET FOR AT LEAST TWO WEEKS.
YES! AND WE REALLY EARNED IT!
WELCOME TO...THE TIMS!
THE TIMS
The Tims
CAZENOVE & WILLIAM

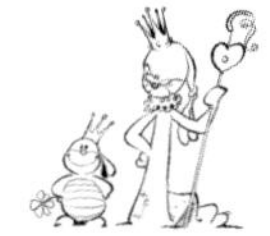

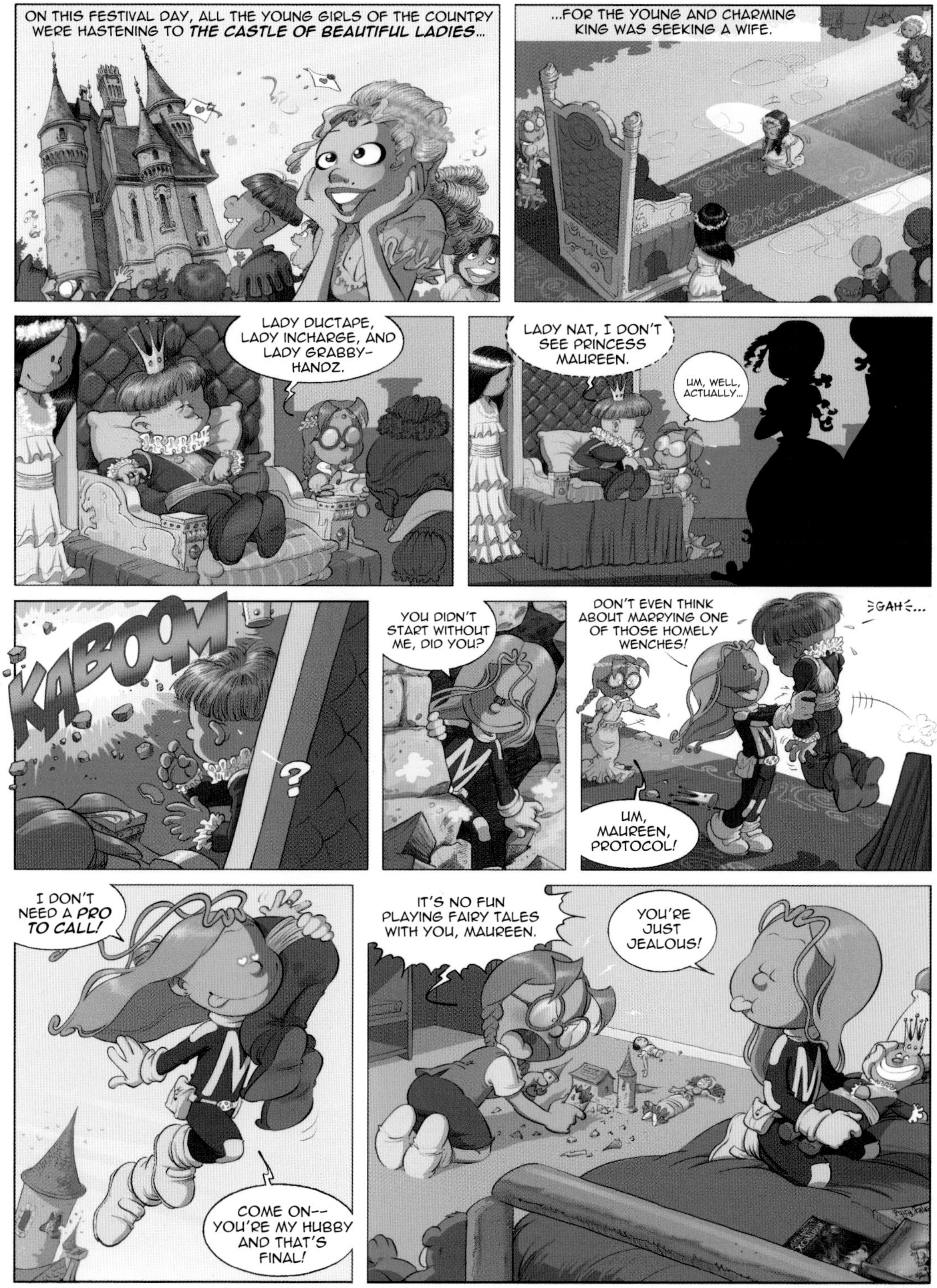

ON THIS FESTIVAL DAY, ALL THE YOUNG GIRLS OF THE COUNTRY WERE HASTENING TO THE CASTLE OF BEAUTIFUL LADIES...
...FOR THE YOUNG AND CHARMING KING WAS SEEKING A WIFE.
LADY DUCTAPE, LADY INCHARGE, AND LADY GRABBY-HANDZ.
LADY NAT, I DON'T SEE PRINCESS MAUREEN.
UM, WELL, ACTUALLY...
KABOOM
?
YOU DIDN'T START WITHOUT ME, DID YOU?
DON'T EVEN THINK ABOUT MARRYING ONE OF THOSE HOMELY WENCHES!
GAH...
UM, MAUREEN, PROTOCOL!
I DON'T NEED A PRO TO CALL!
COME ON-- YOU'RE MY HUBBY AND THAT'S FINAL!
IT'S NO FUN PLAYING FAIRY TALES WITH YOU, MAUREEN.
YOU'RE JUST JEALOUS!

CAZENOVE & WILLIAM

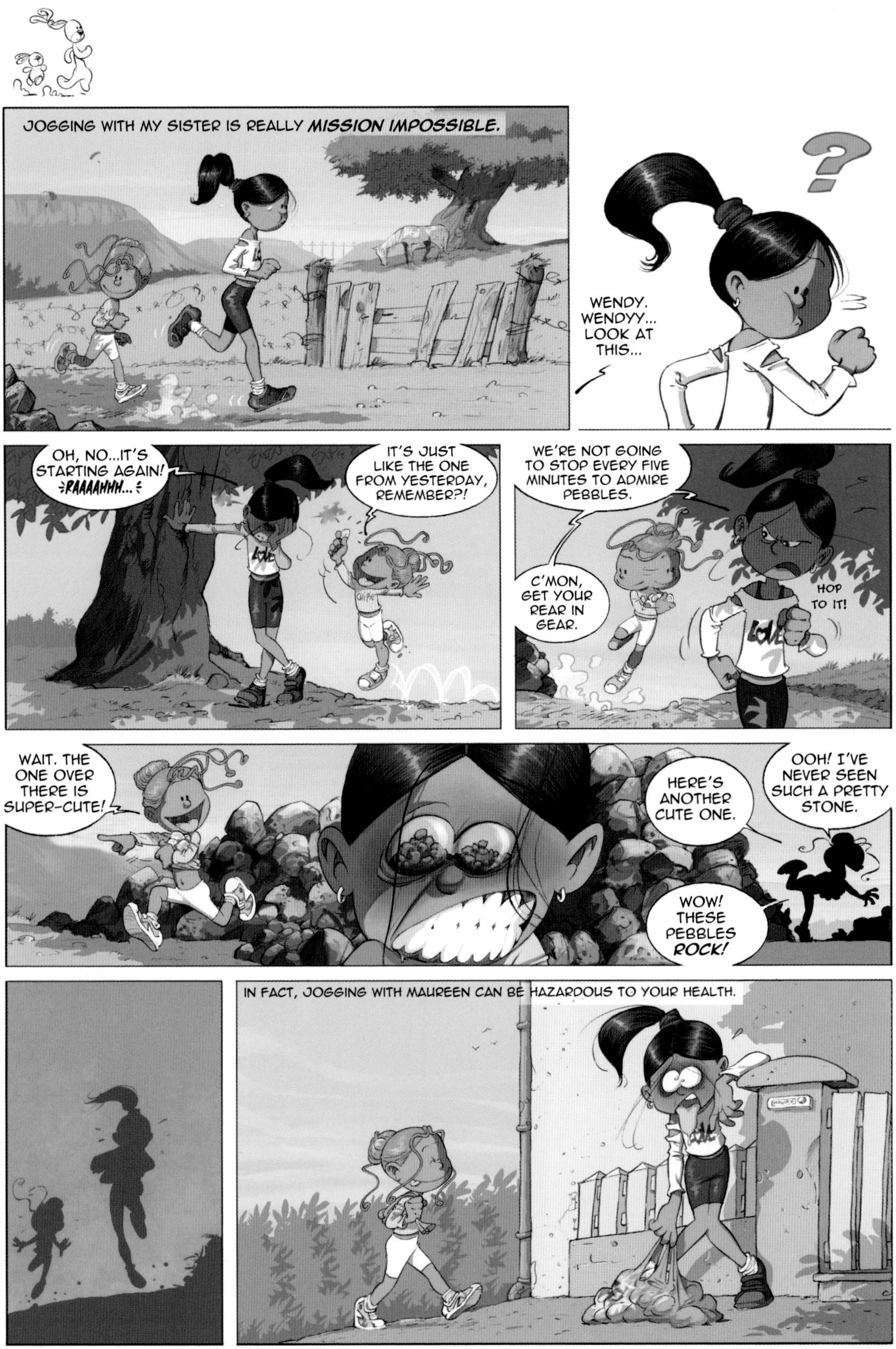
JOGGING WITH MY SISTER IS REALLY MISSION IMPOSSIBLE.
?
WENDY. WENDYY... LOOK AT THIS...
OH, NO...IT'S STARTING AGAIN! RAAAAHHH...
IT'S JUST LIKE THE ONE FROM YESTERDAY, REMEMBER?!
WE'RE NOT GOING TO STOP EVERY FIVE MINUTES TO ADMIRE PEBBLES.
C'MON, GET YOUR REAR IN GEAR.
HOP TO IT!
WAIT. THE ONE OVER THERE IS SUPER-CUTE!
HERE'S ANOTHER CUTE ONE.
OOH! I'VE NEVER SEEN SUCH A PRETTY STONE.
WOW! THESE PEBBLES ROCK!
IN FACT, JOGGING WITH MAUREEN CAN BE HAZARDOUS TO YOUR HEALTH.
CAZENOVE & WILLIAM

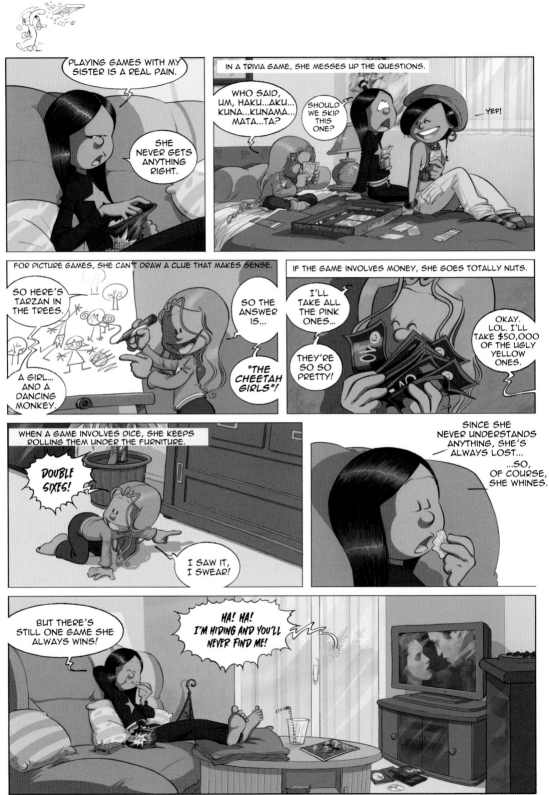

CAZENOVE & WILLIAM

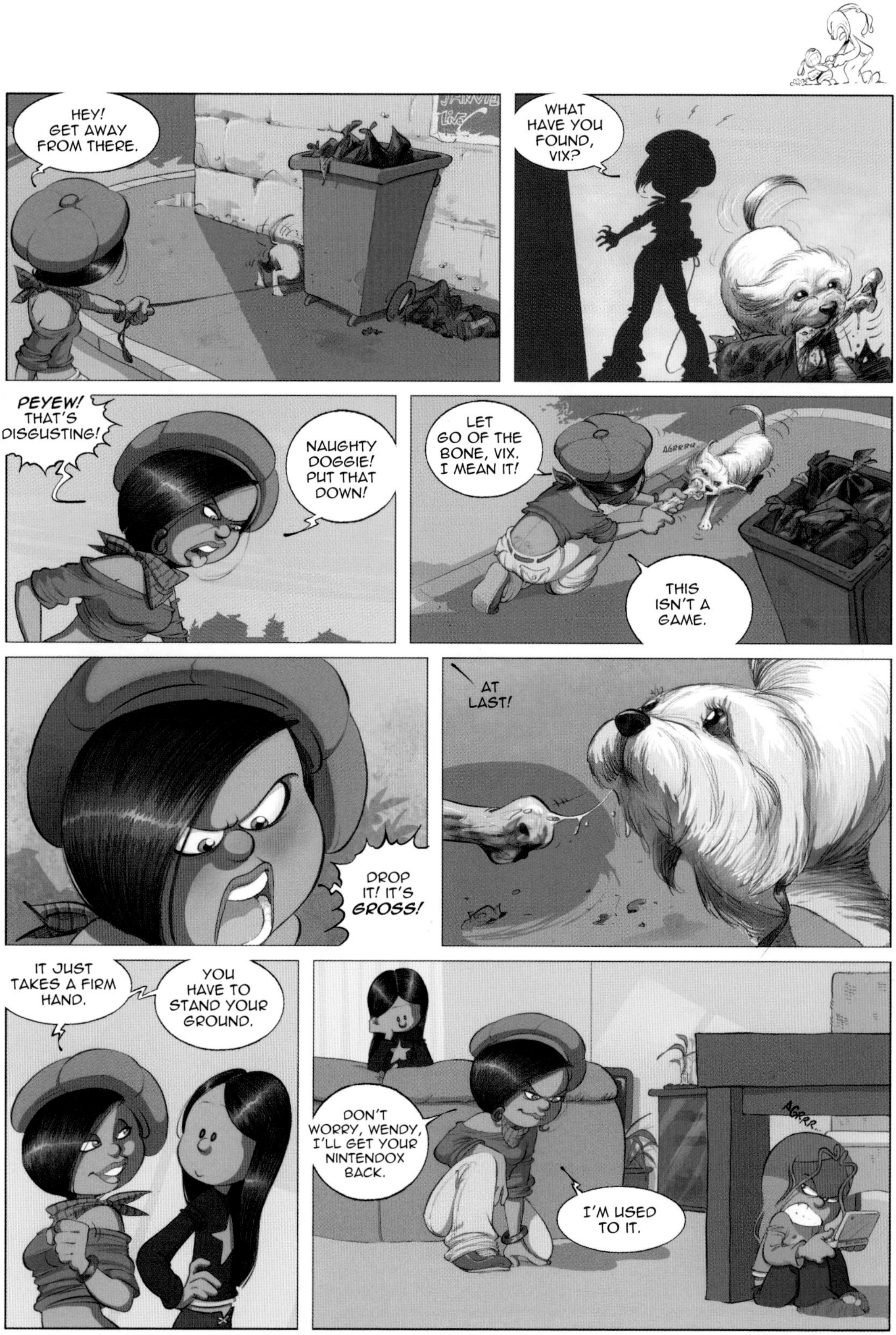

HEY! GET AWAY FROM THERE.
WHAT HAVE YOU FOUND, VIX?
PEYEW! THAT'S DISGUSTING!
NAUGHTY DOGGIE! PUT THAT DOWN!
LET GO OF THE BONE, VIX. I MEAN IT!
AGRRRR...
THIS ISN'T A GAME.
DROP IT! IT'S GROSS!
AT LAST!
IT JUST TAKES A FIRM HAND.
YOU HAVE TO STAND YOUR GROUND.
DON'T WORRY, WENDY, I'LL GET YOUR NINTENDOX BACK.
AGRRR...
I'M USED TO IT.

CAZENOVE & WILLIAM

CAZENOVE & WILLIAM

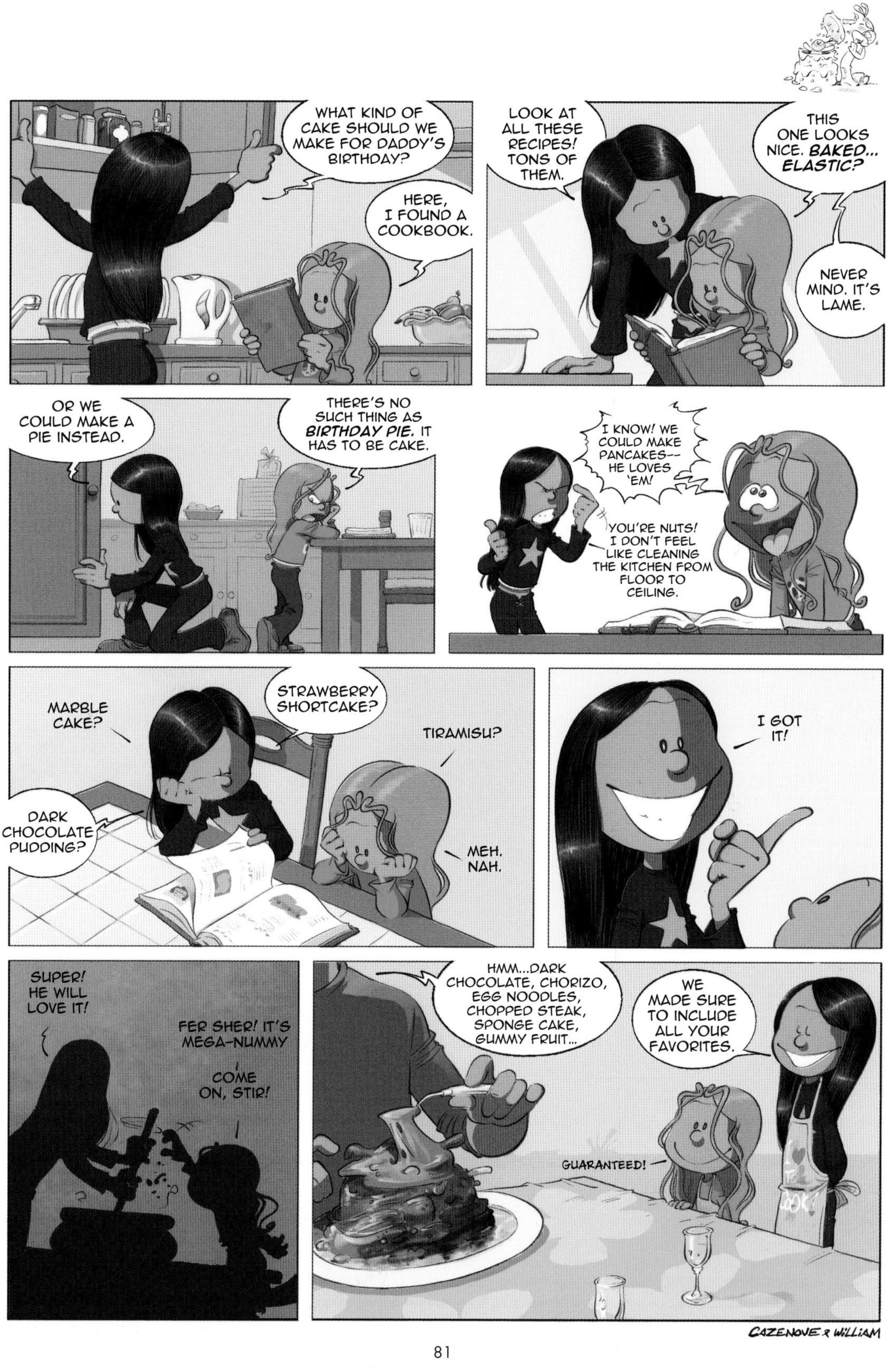
WHAT KIND OF CAKE SHOULD WE MAKE FOR DADDY'S BIRTHDAY?
HERE, I FOUND A COOKBOOK.
LOOK AT ALL THESE RECIPES! TONS OF THEM.
THIS ONE LOOKS NICE. BAKED... ELASTIC?
NEVER MIND. IT'S LAME.
OR WE COULD MAKE A PIE INSTEAD.
THERE'S NO SUCH THING AS BIRTHDAY PIE. IT HAS TO BE CAKE.
I KNOW! WE COULD MAKE PANCAKES-- HE LOVES 'EM!
YOU'RE NUTS! I DON'T FEEL LIKE CLEANING THE KITCHEN FROM FLOOR TO CEILING.
MARBLE CAKE?
STRAWBERRY SHORTCAKE?
TIRAMISU?
DARK CHOCOLATE PUDDING?
MEH. NAH.
I GOT IT!
SUPER! HE WILL LOVE IT!
FER SHER! IT'S MEGA-NUMMY
COME ON, STIR!
HMM...DARK CHOCOLATE, CHORIZO, EGG NOODLES, CHOPPED STEAK, SPONGE CAKE, GUMMY FRUIT...
WE MADE SURE TO INCLUDE ALL YOUR FAVORITES.
GUARANTEED!
CAZENOVE & WILLIAM

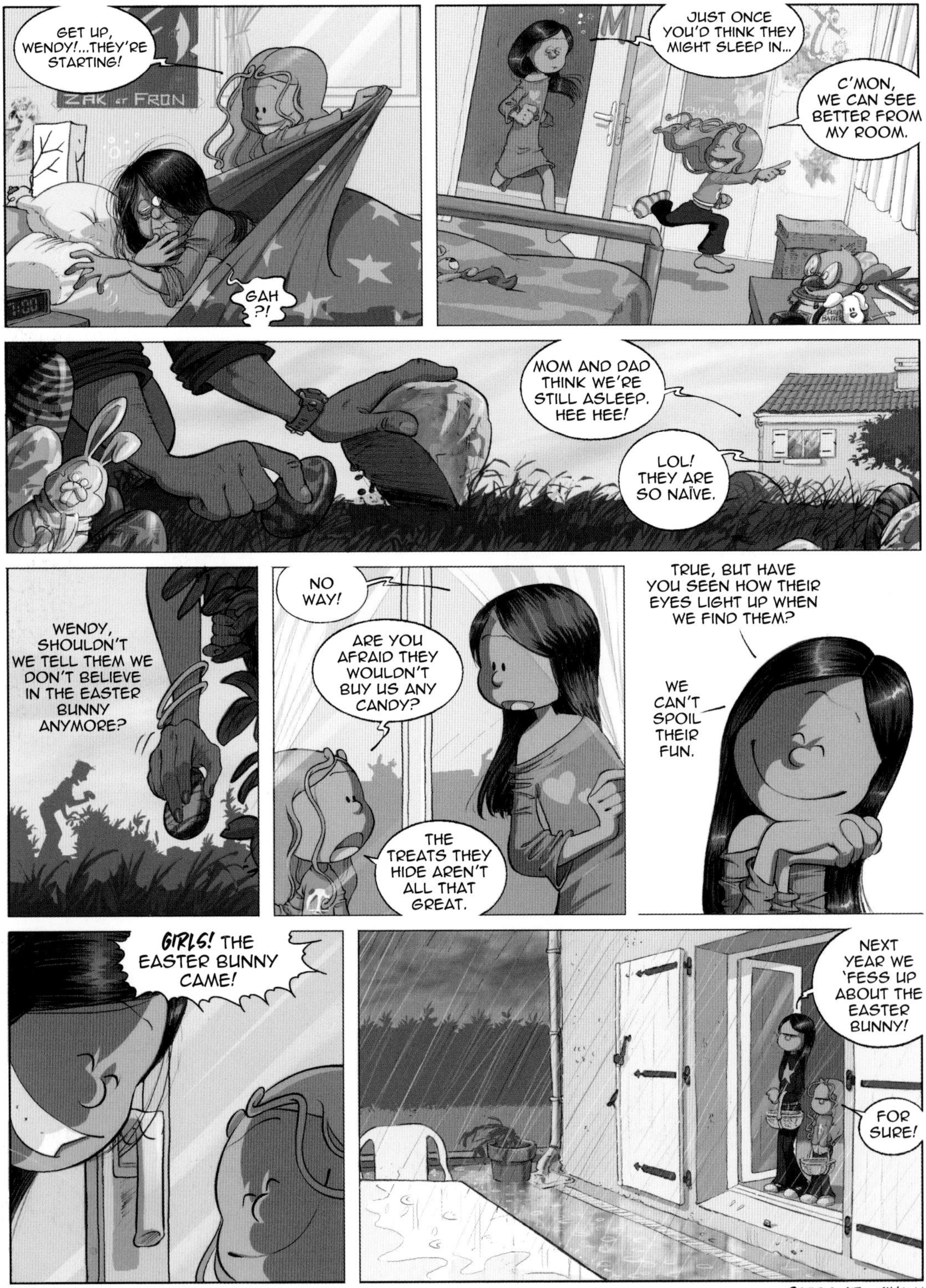
GET UP, WENDY!...THEY'RE STARTING!
ZAK et FRON
GAH ?!
JUST ONCE YOU'D THINK THEY MIGHT SLEEP IN...
C'MON, WE CAN SEE BETTER FROM MY ROOM.
MOM AND DAD THINK WE'RE STILL ASLEEP. HEE HEE!
LOL! THEY ARE SO NAÏVE.
WENDY, SHOULDN'T WE TELL THEM WE DON'T BELIEVE IN THE EASTER BUNNY ANYMORE?
NO WAY!
ARE YOU AFRAID THEY WOULDN'T BUY US ANY CANDY?
THE TREATS THEY HIDE AREN'T ALL THAT GREAT.
TRUE, BUT HAVE YOU SEEN HOW THEIR EYES LIGHT UP WHEN WE FIND THEM?
WE CAN'T SPOIL THEIR FUN.
GIRLS! THE EASTER BUNNY CAME!
NEXT YEAR WE 'FESS UP ABOUT THE EASTER BUNNY!
FOR SURE!

CAZENOVE & WILLIAM

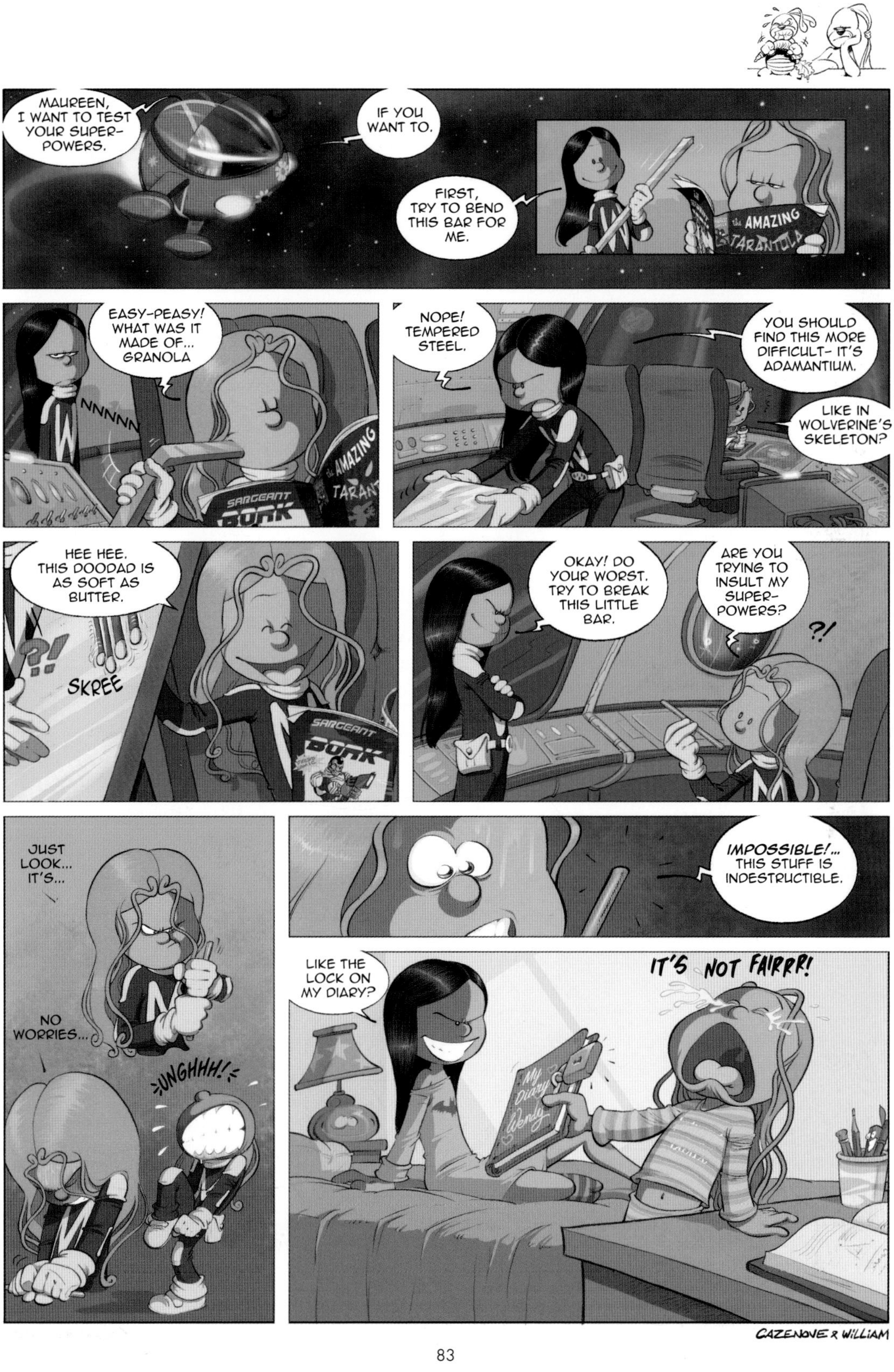
MAUREEN, I WANT TO TEST YOUR SUPER-POWERS.
IF YOU WANT TO.
FIRST, TRY TO BEND THIS BAR FOR ME.
the AMAZING TARANTOLA
EASY-PEASY! WHAT WAS IT MADE OF... GRANOLA
NNNNNN
SARGEANT BORK
NOPE! TEMPERED STEEL.
YOU SHOULD FIND THIS MORE DIFFICULT- IT'S ADAMANTIUM.
LIKE IN WOLVERINE'S SKELETON?
HEE HEE. THIS DOODAD IS AS SOFT AS BUTTER.
?!
SKREE
OKAY! DO YOUR WORST. TRY TO BREAK THIS LITTLE BAR.
ARE YOU TRYING TO INSULT MY SUPER-POWERS?
?!
JUST LOOK... IT'S...
NO WORRIES...
UNGHHH!
IMPOSSIBLE!... THIS STUFF IS INDESTRUCTIBLE.
LIKE THE LOCK ON MY DIARY?
IT'S NOT FAIRRR!
My Diary Wendy
CAZENOVE & WILLIAM

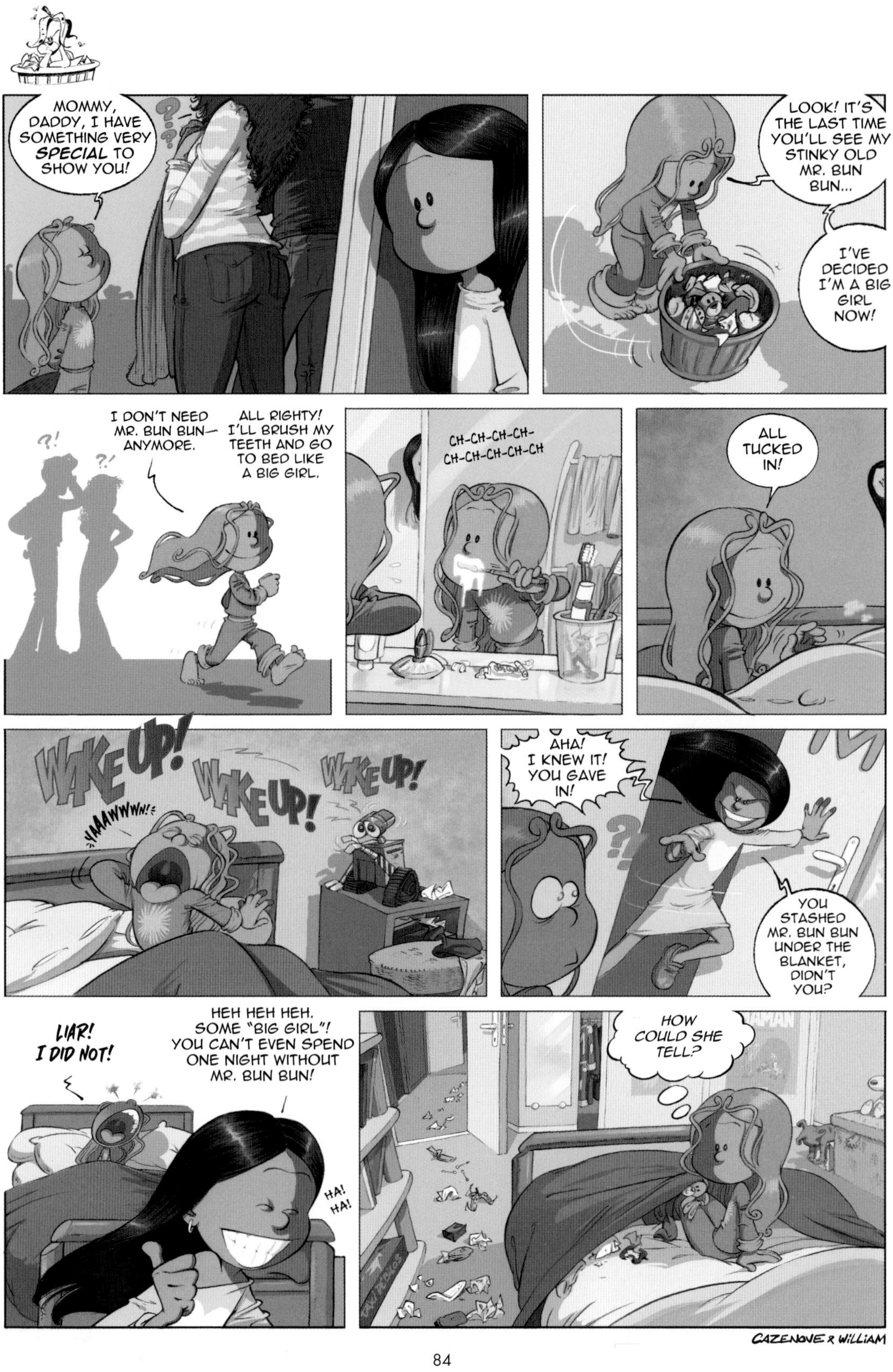

MOMMY, DADDY, I HAVE SOMETHING VERY **SPECIAL** TO SHOW YOU!
?
??
LOOK! IT'S THE LAST TIME YOU'LL SEE MY STINKY OLD MR. BUN BUN...
I'VE DECIDED I'M A BIG GIRL NOW!
?!
?!
I DON'T NEED MR. BUN BUN— ANYMORE.
ALL RIGHTY! I'LL BRUSH MY TEETH AND GO TO BED LIKE A BIG GIRL.
CH-CH-CH-CH-CH-CH-CH-CH-CH
ALL TUCKED IN!
WAKE UP!
WAKE UP!
WAKE UP!
YAAAWWWN!
AHA! I KNEW IT! YOU GAVE IN!
?
YOU STASHED MR. BUN BUN UNDER THE BLANKET, DIDN'T YOU?
LIAR! I DID NOT!
HEH HEH HEH. SOME "BIG GIRL"! YOU CAN'T EVEN SPEND ONE NIGHT WITHOUT MR. BUN BUN!
HA! HA!
HOW COULD SHE TELL?

CAZENOVE & WILLIAM

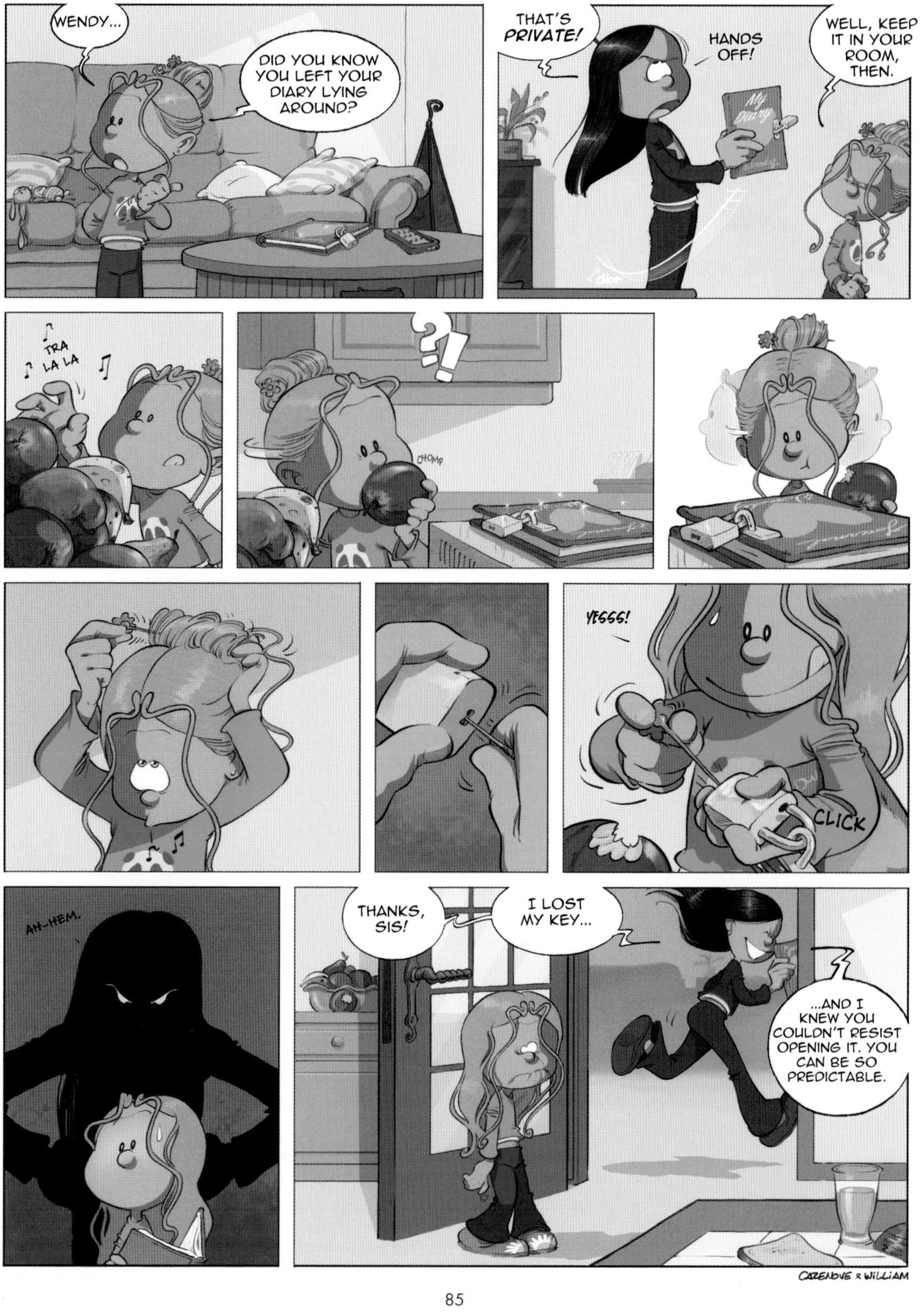
WENDY...
DID YOU KNOW YOU LEFT YOUR DIARY LYING AROUND?
THAT'S *PRIVATE!*
HANDS OFF!
My Diary
WELL, KEEP IT IN YOUR ROOM, THEN.
TRA LA LA
CHOMP
YESSS!
CLICK
AH-HEM.
THANKS, SIS!
I LOST MY KEY...
...AND I KNEW YOU COULDN'T RESIST OPENING IT. YOU CAN BE SO PREDICTABLE.

CAZENOVE & WILLIAM

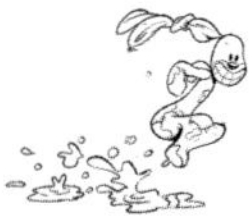

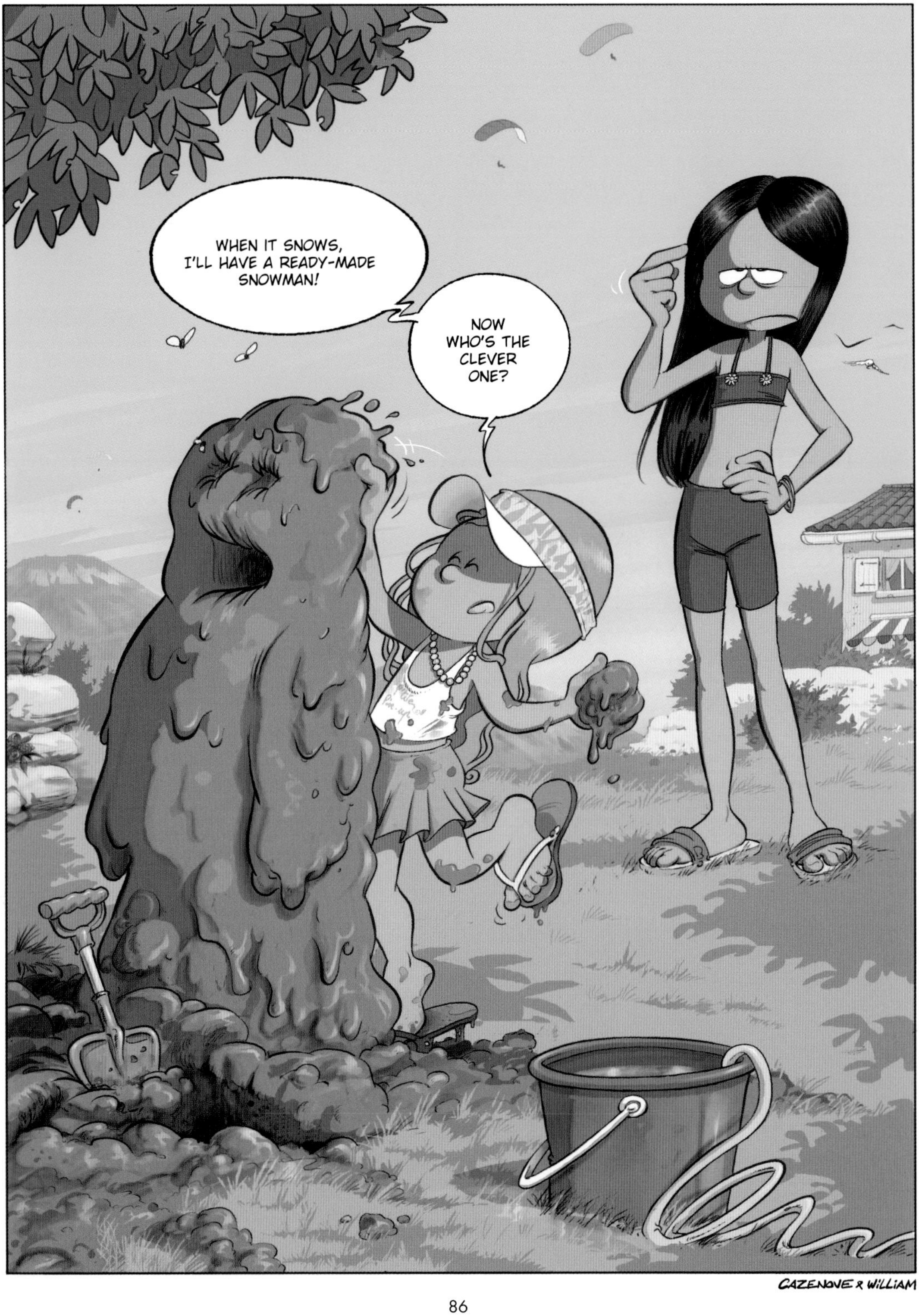
WHEN IT SNOWS, I'LL HAVE A READY-MADE SNOWMAN!
NOW WHO'S THE CLEVER ONE?

CAZENOVE & WILLIAM

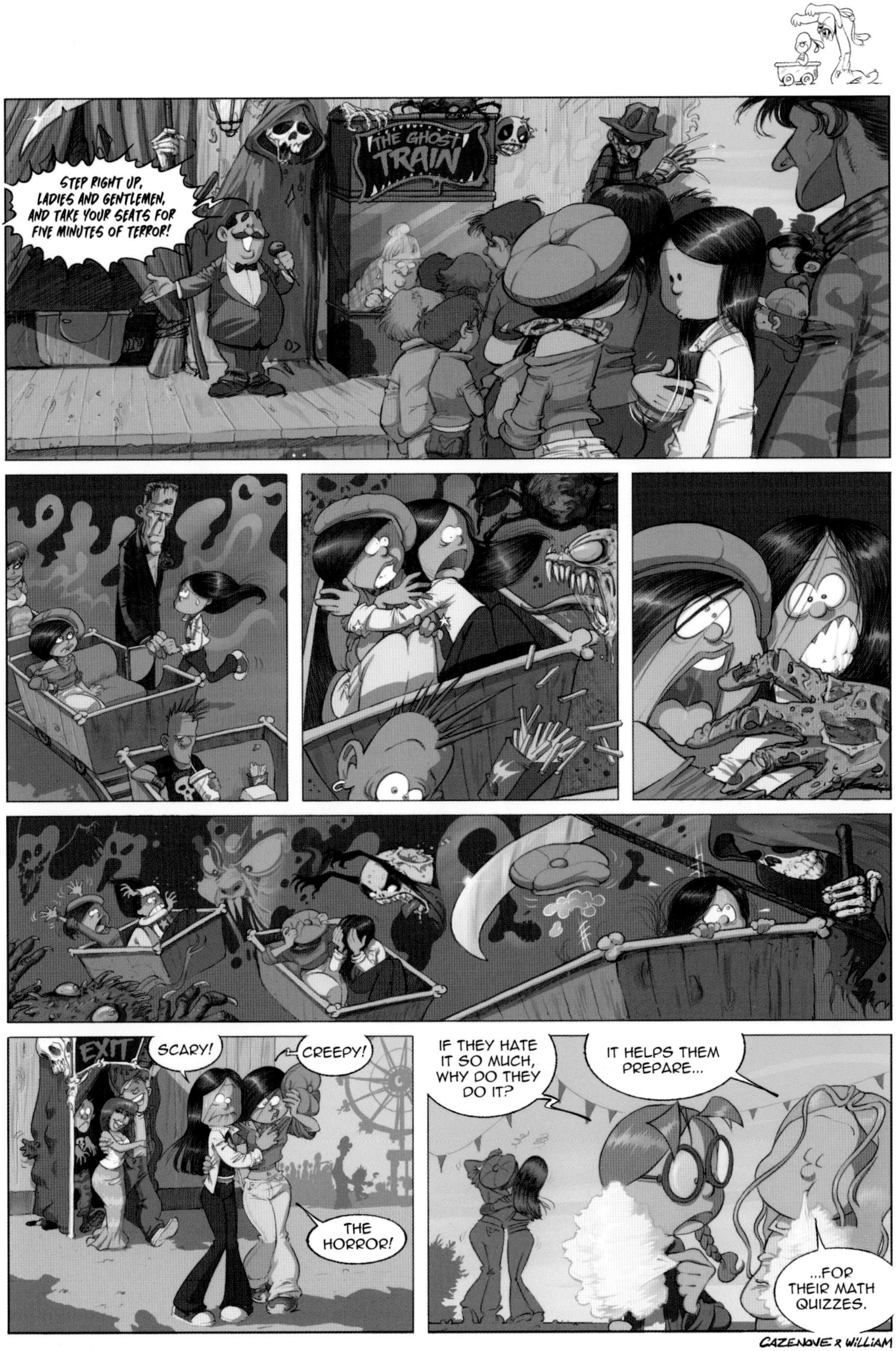
STEP RIGHT UP, LADIES AND GENTLEMEN, AND TAKE YOUR SEATS FOR FIVE MINUTES OF TERROR!
THE GHOST TRAIN
EXIT
SCARY!
CREEPY!
THE HORROR!
IF THEY HATE IT SO MUCH, WHY DO THEY DO IT?
IT HELPS THEM PREPARE...
...FOR THEIR MATH QUIZZES.
CAZENOVE & WILLIAM

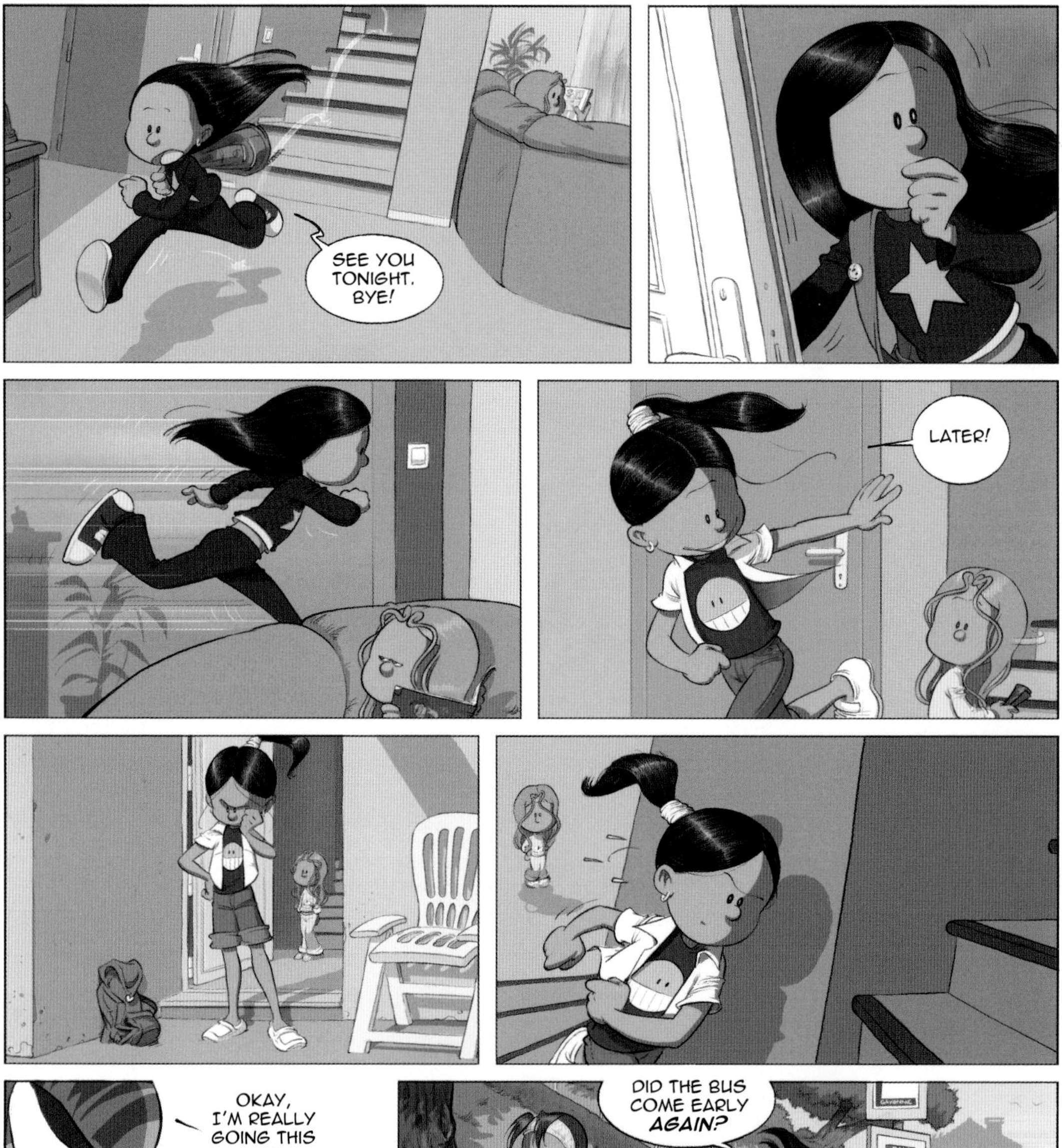
SEE YOU TONIGHT. BYE!
LATER!
OKAY, I'M REALLY GOING THIS TIME.
TAP TAP
DID THE BUS COME EARLY *AGAIN?*
BUS STOP
HOW DO THEY EXPECT US TO CATCH IT?
BUS

CAZENOVE & WILLIAM

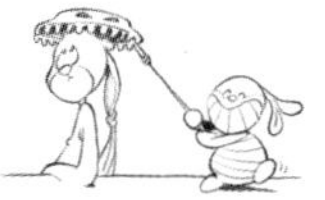

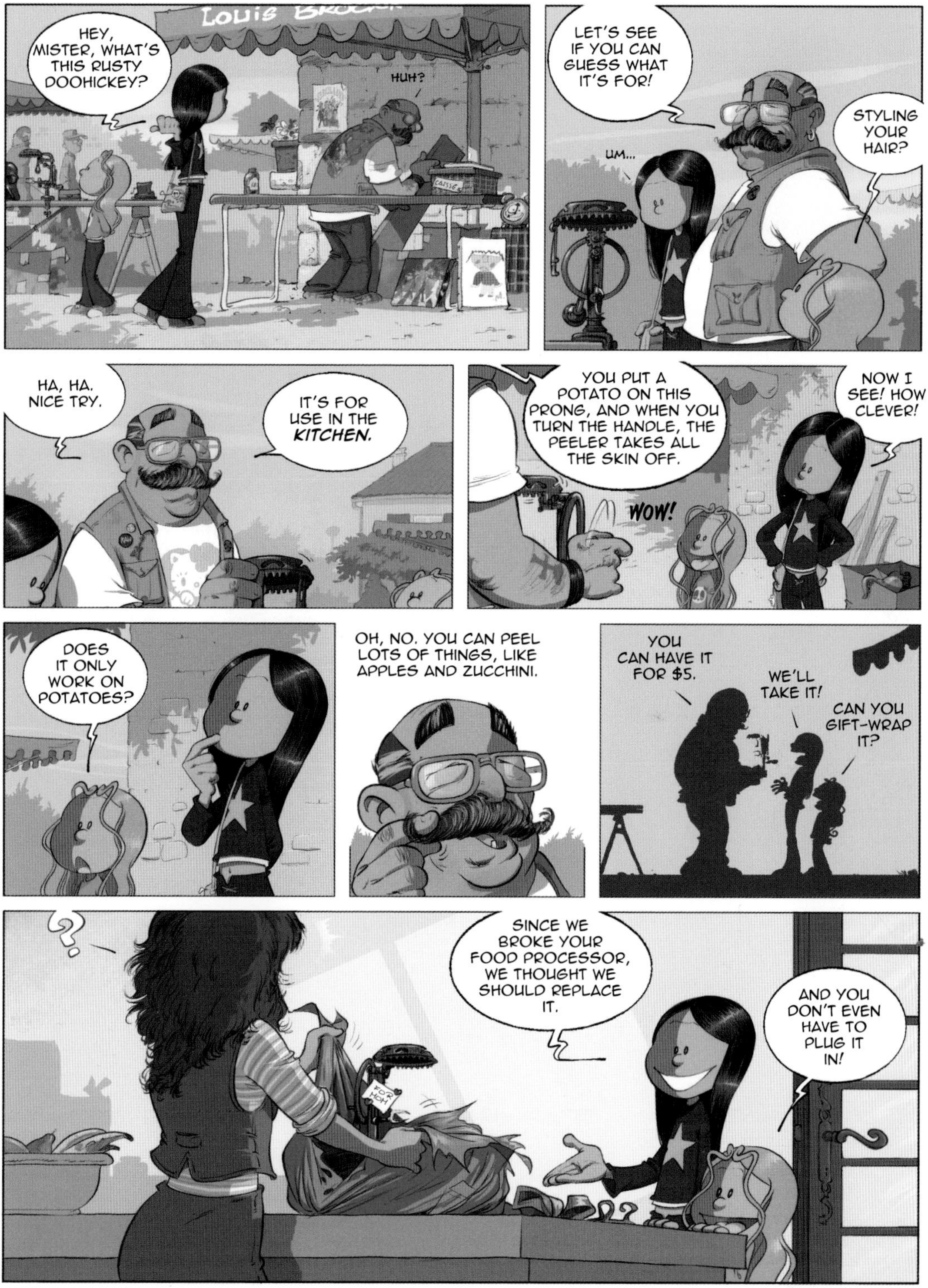

HEY, MISTER, WHAT'S THIS RUSTY DOOHICKEY?
HUH?
LET'S SEE IF YOU CAN GUESS WHAT IT'S FOR!
UM...
STYLING YOUR HAIR?
HA, HA. NICE TRY.
IT'S FOR USE IN THE *KITCHEN.*
YOU PUT A POTATO ON THIS PRONG, AND WHEN YOU TURN THE HANDLE, THE PEELER TAKES ALL THE SKIN OFF.
NOW I SEE! HOW CLEVER!
WOW!
DOES IT ONLY WORK ON POTATOES?
OH, NO. YOU CAN PEEL LOTS OF THINGS, LIKE APPLES AND ZUCCHINI.
YOU CAN HAVE IT FOR $5.
WE'LL TAKE IT!
CAN YOU GIFT-WRAP IT?
?
SINCE WE BROKE YOUR FOOD PROCESSOR, WE THOUGHT WE SHOULD REPLACE IT.
FOR MOM
AND YOU DON'T EVEN HAVE TO PLUG IT IN!

CAZENOVE & WILLIAM

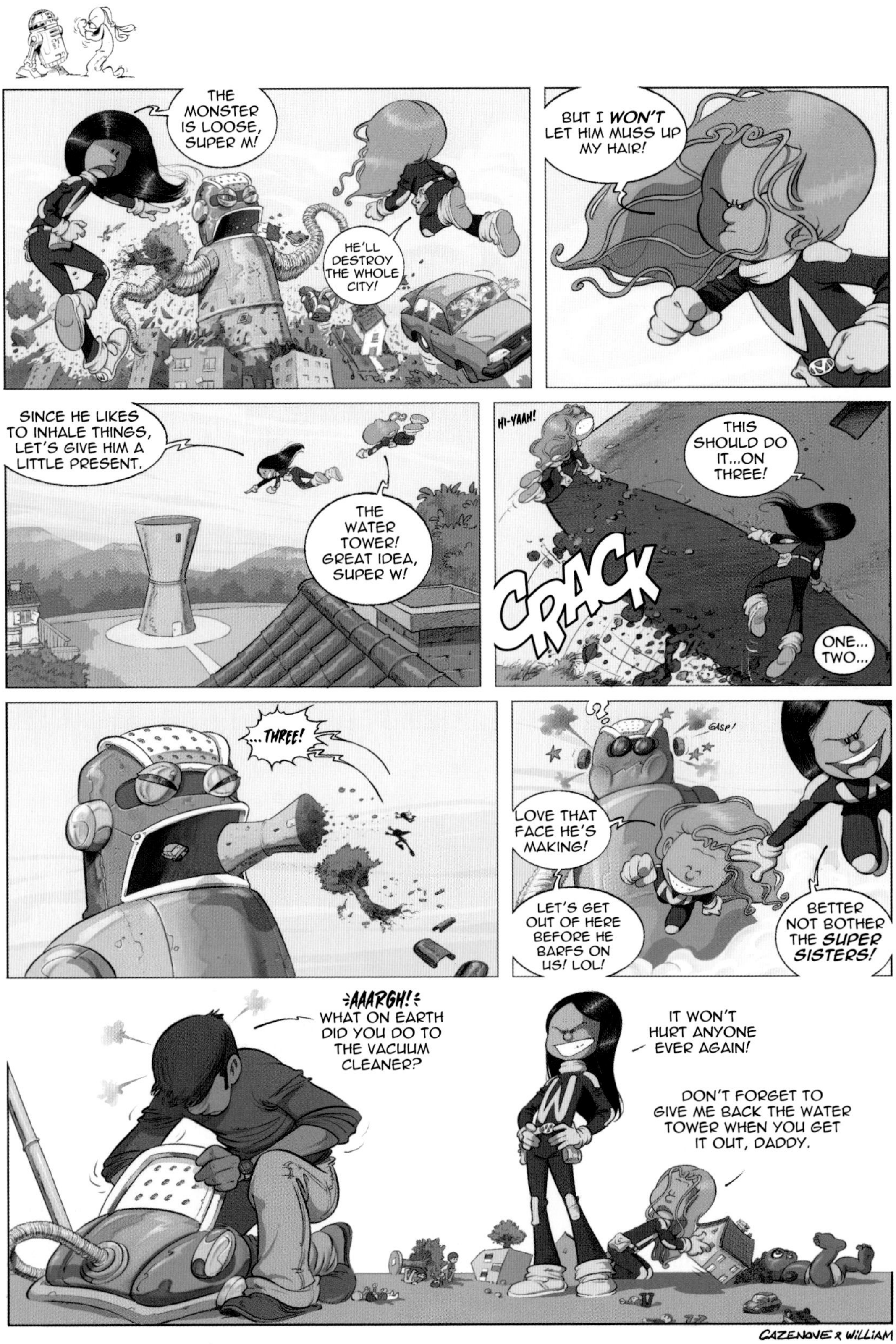
THE MONSTER IS LOOSE, SUPER M!
HE'LL DESTROY THE WHOLE CITY!
BUT I WON'T LET HIM MUSS UP MY HAIR!
SINCE HE LIKES TO INHALE THINGS, LET'S GIVE HIM A LITTLE PRESENT.
THE WATER TOWER! GREAT IDEA, SUPER W!
HI-YAAH!
THIS SHOULD DO IT...ON THREE!
CRACK
ONE... TWO...
...THREE!
GASP!
LOVE THAT FACE HE'S MAKING!
LET'S GET OUT OF HERE BEFORE HE BARFS ON US! LOL!
BETTER NOT BOTHER THE SUPER SISTERS!
AAARGH! WHAT ON EARTH DID YOU DO TO THE VACUUM CLEANER?
IT WON'T HURT ANYONE EVER AGAIN!
DON'T FORGET TO GIVE ME BACK THE WATER TOWER WHEN YOU GET IT OUT, DADDY.
CAZENOVE & WILLIAM

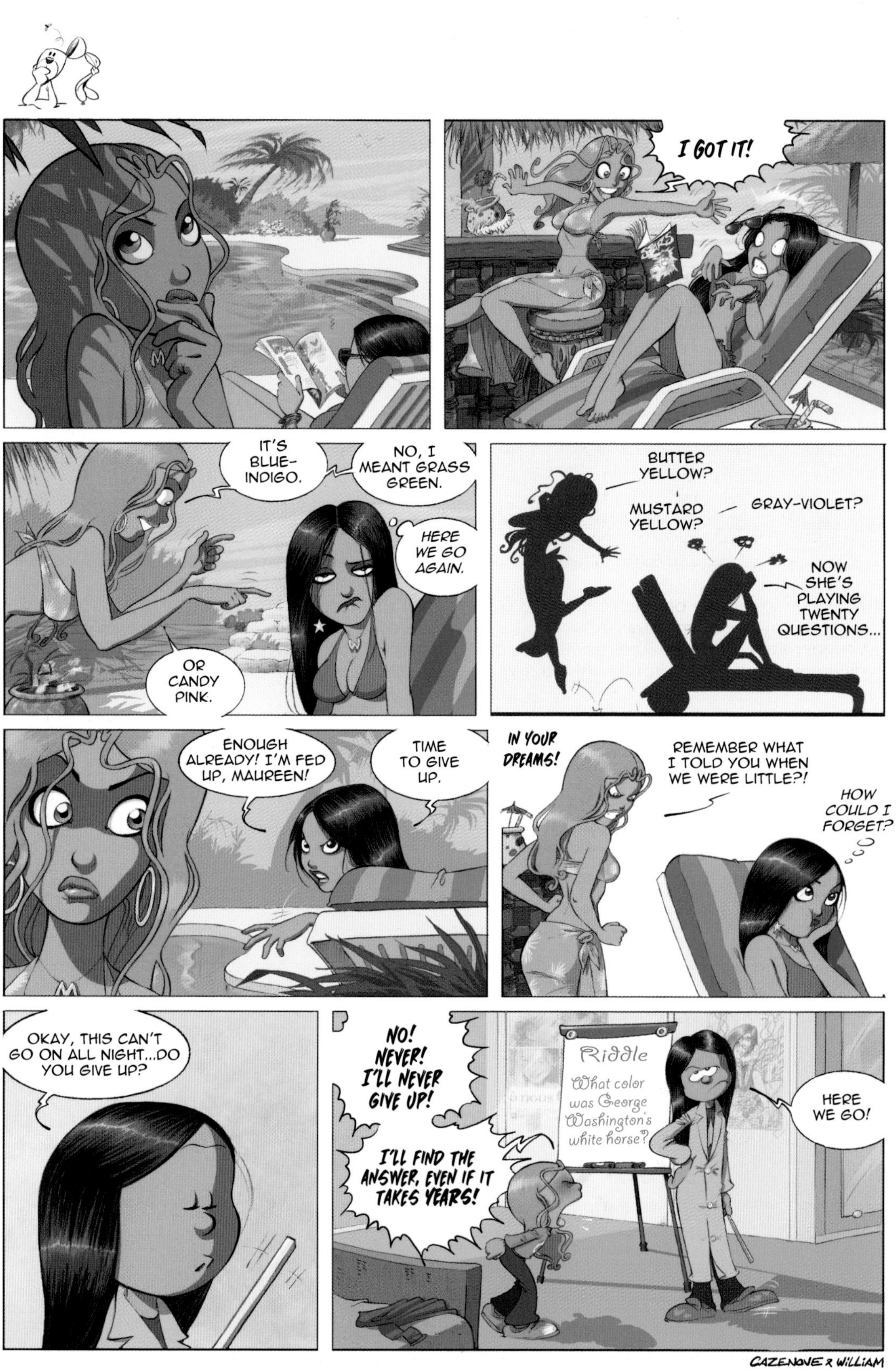
I GOT IT!
IT'S BLUE-INDIGO.
NO, I MEANT GRASS GREEN.
HERE WE GO AGAIN.
OR CANDY PINK.
BUTTER YELLOW?
MUSTARD YELLOW?
GRAY-VIOLET?
NOW SHE'S PLAYING TWENTY QUESTIONS...
ENOUGH ALREADY! I'M FED UP, MAUREEN!
TIME TO GIVE UP.
IN YOUR DREAMS!
REMEMBER WHAT I TOLD YOU WHEN WE WERE LITTLE?!
HOW COULD I FORGET?
OKAY, THIS CAN'T GO ON ALL NIGHT...DO YOU GIVE UP?
NO! NEVER! I'LL NEVER GIVE UP!
I'LL FIND THE ANSWER, EVEN IF IT TAKES YEARS!
Riddle
What color was George Washington's white horse?
HERE WE GO!
CAZENOVE & WILLIAM

WATCH OUT FOR PAPERCUTZ

Welcome to the second-in-a-series of squabbling sibling stories—THE SISTERS graphic novel, by Christophe Cazenove and William Maury, from Papercutz—those family-friendly folks dedicated to publishing great graphic novels for all ages. I'm Jim Salicrup, the Editor-in-Chief and big brother, and I'm here to take you behind-the-scenes at Papercutz...

While the majority of the fans for THE SISTERS may in fact be female, I'm also a fan of THE SISTERS and I'm a guy. And it's not just because the artwork by William Maury is so awesome or the clever writing by Christophe Cazenove is so funny, although I certainly enjoy well-written and beautifully drawn graphic novels. No, it's because I simply like Wendy and Maureen, the stars of this super-fun series, and their relationship to each other. As I mentioned, I'm an older brother. I still remember that day when I was just three years old and my parents came home with my baby brother—William Salicrup (He's so tired of hearing this story!). Months earlier my parents had asked if I wanted a little brother, and I happily agreed. But I didn't realize he'd be a baby! I thought they'd get me a brother who was already old enough for me to play with. But what did I know? I was only three years old at the time and didn't fully understand how these kinds of things worked.

I also remember my mom teasing me, saying that I was like a little old man because when we'd go to the playground, rather than run around and play, I preferred to sit with her. Well, after my brother came along, her hands were full chasing him around. He was like a Tasmanian Devil—like the one in the Warner Bros. cartoons. He was a bundle of energy, while I tended to just sit there. Fortunately, as Editor-in-Chief of Papercutz, all I have to do is sit at my desk and work. Who knew I was training to be graphic novel editor at such an early age?

Not only did my little brother keep my mom busy, he kept me busy as well. He simply demanded attention all of the time. And that's why I can relate to Wendy and how she has to deal with her younger sister Maureen. Sure they're girls, but aside from their specific interests they weren't all that different from how my brother and I acted toward each other when we were young.

But no matter how crazy I might think my childhood was, it's nothing compared to that of Lincoln Loud's! Lincoln doesn't have a little brother, or even a bigger brother—he has ten sisters: Lori (the oldest), Leni (the beauty), Luna (the rock star), Luan (the jokester), Lynn (the sport), Lucy (the emo), Lisa (the genius), Lily (the poop machine), and Lola and Lana (the twins). If they sound familiar, that's because they're the stars of the hit new Nickelodeon series *The Loud House*, created by Chris Savino. And they're also starring in an all-new graphic novel series from Papercutz! Not only will you find them in THE LOUD HOUSE graphic novels, but they'll be popping up, along with other super-stars such as *Sanjay and Craig*, *Breadwinners*, *Harvey Beaks*, and *Pig Goat Banana Cricket*, in the pages of NICKELODEON PANDEMONIUM yet another super-cool series from Papercutz.

And speaking of cool graphic novel series from Papercutz, check out the preview pages from DANCE CLASS #8 "Snow White and the Seven Dwarves." Friends and fellow dance students Julie, Alia, and Lucie are the stars of DANCE CLASS, but we do sometimes get a peek at the relationship between Julie and her younger sister Capucine. If you look real closely at parts of this graphic novel, you'll discover that Wendy and Maureen are obviously DANCE CLASS fans too!

And if THE LOUD HOUSE, NICKELODEON PANDEMONIUM, and DANCE CLASS series aren't enough to satisfy your need for great graphic novels until THE SISTERS #3 "Honestly, I Love My Sister" comes along, then look at what else we have to offer at papercutz.com. You'll be glad you did!

Thanks,

Jim

STAY IN TOUCH!

EMAIL: salicrup@papercutz.com
WEB: www.papercutz.com
TWITTER: @papercutzgn
FACEBOOK: PAPERCUTZGRAPHICNOVELS
REGULAR MAIL: Papercutz, 160 Broadway, Suite 700, East Wing, New York, NY 10038

Special Preview of DANCE CLASS #8 "Snow White and the Seven Dwarves"!

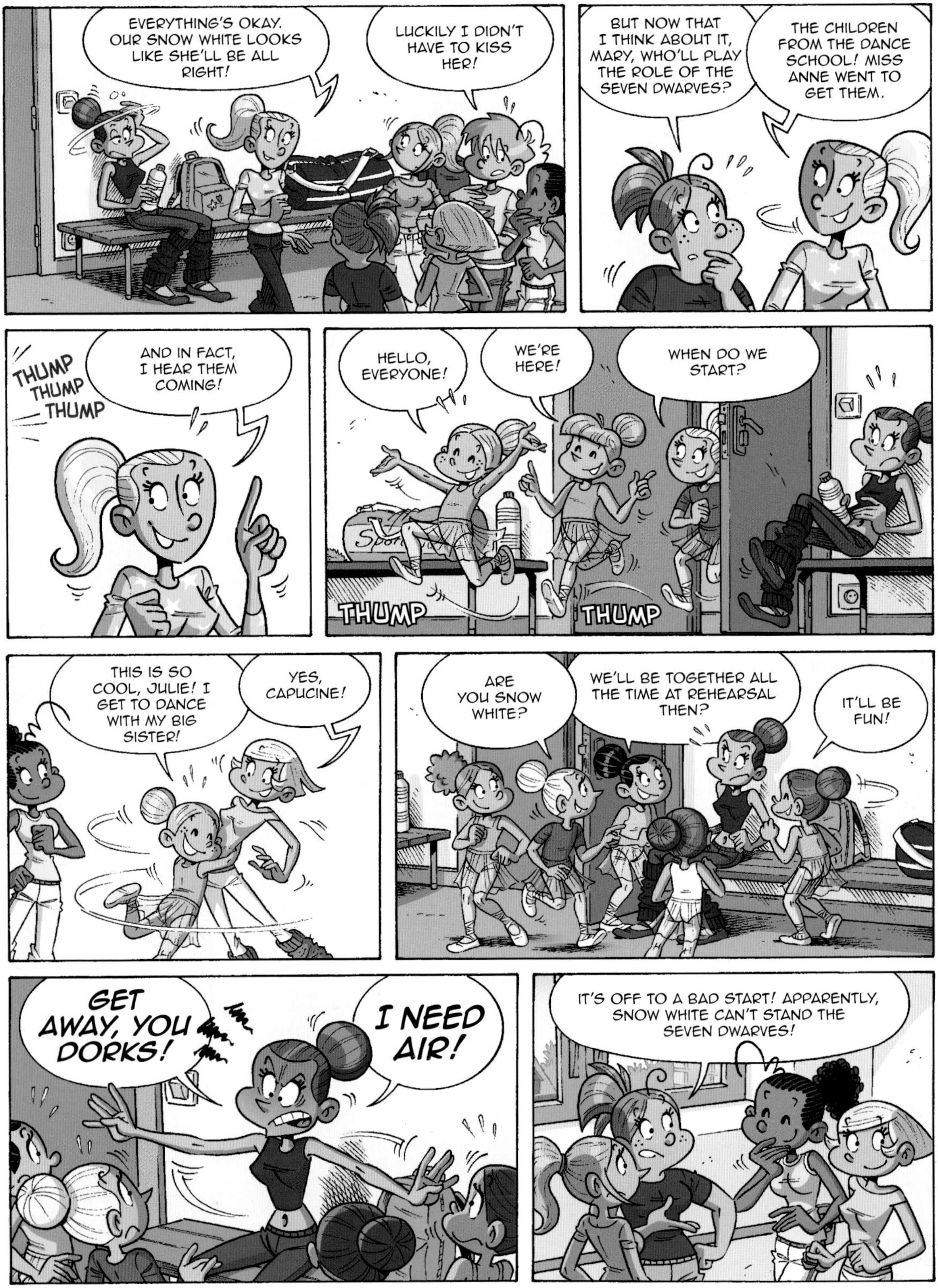

EVERYTHING'S OKAY. OUR SNOW WHITE LOOKS LIKE SHE'LL BE ALL RIGHT!
LUCKILY I DIDN'T HAVE TO KISS HER!
BUT NOW THAT I THINK ABOUT IT, MARY, WHO'LL PLAY THE ROLE OF THE SEVEN DWARVES?
THE CHILDREN FROM THE DANCE SCHOOL! MISS ANNE WENT TO GET THEM.
THUMP THUMP THUMP
AND IN FACT, I HEAR THEM COMING!
HELLO, EVERYONE!
WE'RE HERE!
WHEN DO WE START?
THUMP
THUMP
THIS IS SO COOL, JULIE! I GET TO DANCE WITH MY BIG SISTER!
YES, CAPUCINE!
ARE YOU SNOW WHITE?
WE'LL BE TOGETHER ALL THE TIME AT REHEARSAL THEN?
IT'LL BE FUN!
GET AWAY, YOU DORKS!
I NEED AIR!
IT'S OFF TO A BAD START! APPARENTLY, SNOW WHITE CAN'T STAND THE SEVEN DWARVES!

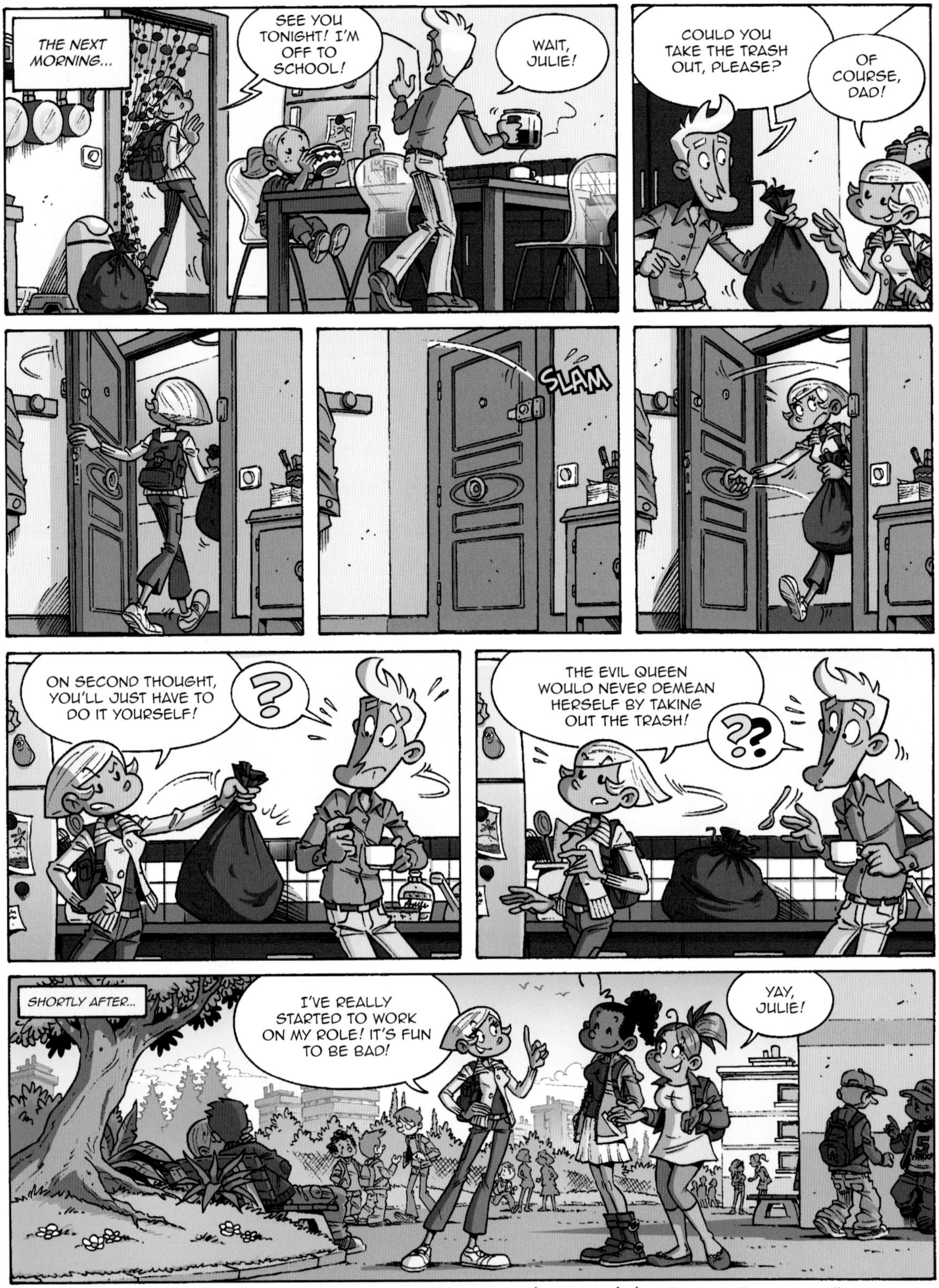
THE NEXT MORNING...
SEE YOU TONIGHT! I'M OFF TO SCHOOL!
WAIT, JULIE!
COULD YOU TAKE THE TRASH OUT, PLEASE?
OF COURSE, DAD!
SLAM
ON SECOND THOUGHT, YOU'LL JUST HAVE TO DO IT YOURSELF!
?
THE EVIL QUEEN WOULD NEVER DEMEAN HERSELF BY TAKING OUT THE TRASH!
??
SHORTLY AFTER...
I'VE REALLY STARTED TO WORK ON MY ROLE! IT'S FUN TO BE BAD!
YAY, JULIE!

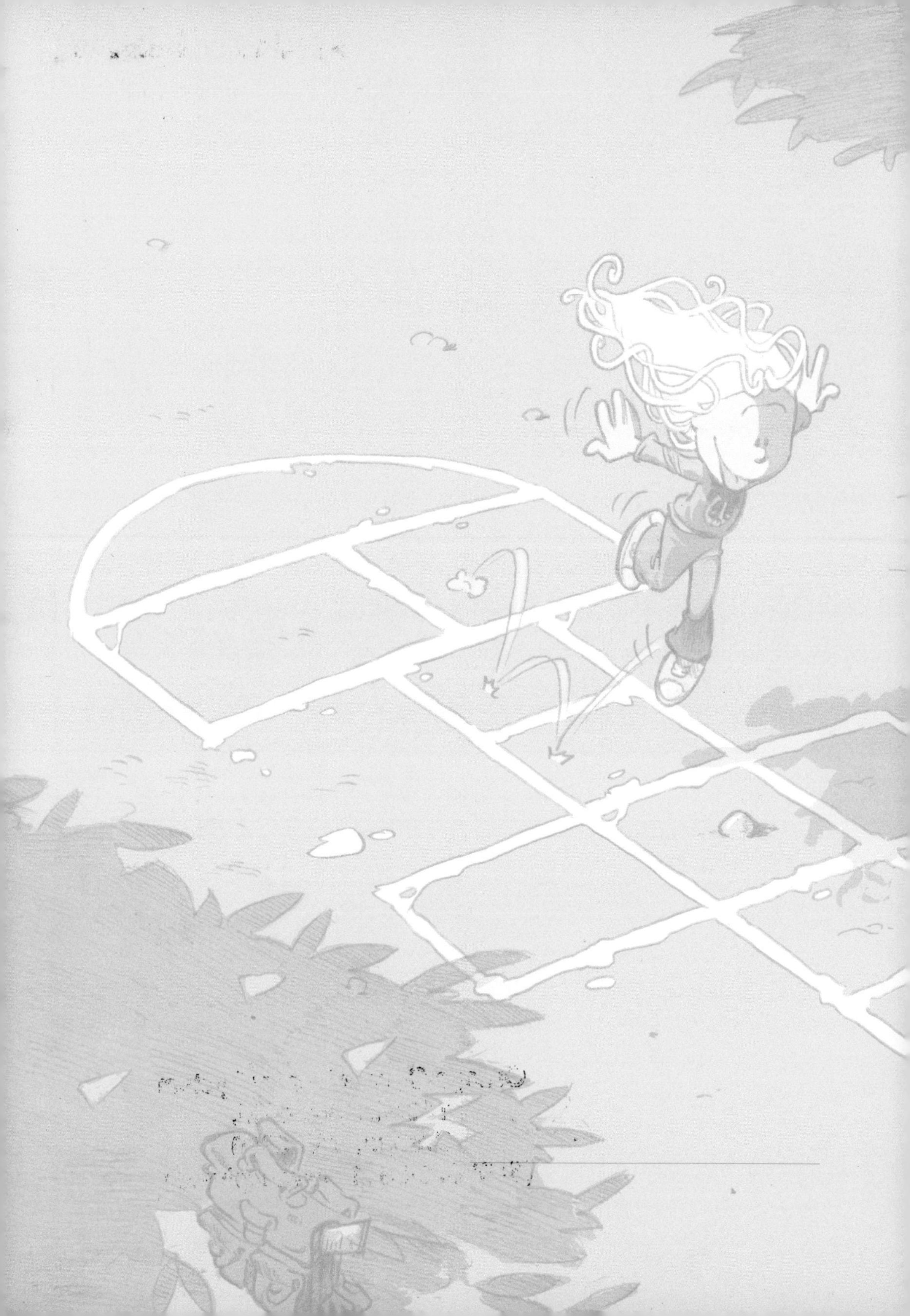